The Talleyrand Maxim

By J. S. Fletcher

Originally published in 1920

The Talleyrand Maxim

© 2012 Resurrected Press
www.ResurrectedPress.com

Published by Intrepid Ink, LLC

Intrepid Ink, LLC provides full publishing services to authors of fiction and non-fiction books, eBooks and websites. From editing to formatting, to publishing, to marketing, Intrepid Ink gets your creative works into the hands of the people who want to read them.
Find out more at www.IntrepidInk.com.

ISBN 13: 978-1-937022-38-9

Printed in the United States of America

OTHER RESURRECTED PRESS MYSTERIES

By J. S. Fletcher
The Orange-Yellow Diamond
The Middle Temple Murder
Scarhaven Keep
Ravensdene Court

By Louis Tracy
The Strange Case of Mortimer Fenley
The Albert Gate Mystery
The Stowmarket Mystery

By A. A. Milne
The Red House Mystery

By Agatha Christie
The Mysterious Affair at Styles

By Arthur Griffiths
The Passenger from Calais
The Rome Express

From the Dr. John Thorndyke Series
By R. Austin Freeman
The Red Thumb Mark
The Eye of Osiris
The Mystery of 31 New Inn
John Thorndyke's Cases
A Silent Witness
The Cat's Eye

By Arthur J. Rees
The Hampstead Mystery
The Mystery of the Downs
The Shrieking Pit
The Hand in The Dark
The Moon Rock

Visit RessurectedPress.com to see our entire catalog.

FOREWORD

J. S. Fletcher never forgot his Yorkshire roots. While most of his contemporaries centered their mysteries around London, and a number of Fletcher's books use that city as a setting, he seemed always more comfortable writing about the small towns and beloved dales of his native Yorkshire.

The Talleyrand Maxim takes place in the West Yorkshire industrial city of Barford. As far as I've been able to discover, there is no such place, but it does seem to be a thinly disguised version of Bradford, not too far from Halifax where Fletcher was born and Wakefield where he was educated. In any case, it is the sort of place that Fletcher would have been well familiar with both growing up and during his adult life. He wrote a great deal about Yorkshire both as a historian and a journalist, but it was with his many detective stories set in the region that he made his mark.

He was a master of the somewhat impenetrable north country dialect, some of which he displays in *The Talleyrand Maxim*. Indeed several of his early books were written in the Yorkshire dialect and was at one time declared the "Yorkshire Thomas Hardy". It was always done with affection and his Yorkshire-men, and women, too, might be rustic, but they are never simple, honest but shrewd when it's called for.

A number of his works involve the legal profession, often featuring small town solicitors and barristers rather than their more showy London counterparts. These portrayals ring particularly true as Fletcher studied the law before turning first to journalism and then to writing as a profession. Again, his north country lawyers tend towards the honest but shrewd.

Fletcher wrote well over two hundred books during his career, about half of them mysteries. They give the modern reader a look into the lives and crimes of a region which most other authors of the period neglected, the rural north of England. He was enormously popular in his day, though sadly somewhat forgotten now. His books are entertaining, his central characters appealing, his settings detailed and believable. His formula was a dependable mix of a bit of a mystery, a touch of danger, and a little romance that succeeds at the end. In short, they are thoroughly entertaining.

It is with great pleasure that Resurrected Press brings you this edition of *The Talleyrand Maxim.*

About the Author

Joseph Smith Fletcher (1863-1935) was a journalist and the author of over 200 books. Born in Halifax, West Yorkshire, he studied law before turning to journalism. His earlier works were either histories or historical fiction, and he was made a fellow of the Royal Historical Society. He didn't start writing mysteries until 1914, though before he died he had written over 100 in the genre.

Greg Fowlkes
Editor-In-Chief
Resurrected Press
www.ResurrectedPress.com

TABLE OF CONTENTS

1. DEATH BRINGS OPPORTUNITY

Linford Pratt, senior clerk to Eldrick & Pascoe, solicitors, of Barford, a young man who earnestly desired to get on in life, by hook or by crook, with no objection whatever to crookedness, so long as it could be performed in safety and secrecy, had once during one of his periodical visits to the town Reference Library, lighted on a maxim of that other unscrupulous person, Prince Talleyrand, which had pleased him greatly. "With time and patience," said Talleyrand, "the mulberry leaf is turned into satin." This seemed to Linford Pratt one of the finest and soundest pieces of wisdom which he had ever known put into words.

A mulberry leaf is a very insignificant thing, but a piece of satin is a highly marketable commodity, with money in it. Henceforth, he regarded himself as a mulberry leaf which his own wit and skill must transform into satin: at the same time he knew that there is another thing, in addition to time and patience, which is valuable to young men of his peculiar qualities, a thing also much beloved by Talleyrand—opportunity. He could find the patience, and he had the time—but it would give him great happiness if opportunity came along to help in the work. In everyday language, Linford Pratt wanted a chance—he waited the arrival of the tide in his affairs which would lead him on to fortune.

Leave him alone—he said to himself—to be sure to take it at the flood. If Pratt had only known it, as he stood in the outer office of Eldrick & Pascoe at the end of a certain winter afternoon, opportunity was slowly climbing the staircase outside—not only opportunity, but temptation, both assisted by the Devil. They came at the right moment, for Pratt was alone; the partners had gone:

the other clerks had gone: the office-boy had gone: in another minute Pratt would have gone, too: he was only looking round before locking up for the night. Then these things came—combined in the person of an old man, Antony Bartle, who opened the door, pushed in a queer, wrinkled face, and asked in a quavering voice if anybody was in.

"I'm in, Mr. Bartle," answered Pratt, turning up a gas jet which he had just lowered. "Come in, sir. What can I do for you?"

Antony Bartle came in, wheezing and coughing. He was a very, very old man, feeble and bent, with little that looked alive about him but his light, alert eyes. Everybody knew him—he was one of the institutions of Barford—as well known as the Town Hall or the Parish Church. For fifty years he had kept a second-hand bookshop in Quagg Alley, the narrow passage-way which connected Market Street with Beck Street. It was not by any means a common or ordinary second-hand bookshop: its proprietor styled himself an "antiquarian bookseller"; and he had a reputation in two Continents, and dealt with millionaire buyers and virtuosos in both.

Barford people sometimes marvelled at the news that Mr. Antony Bartle had given two thousand guineas for a Book of Hours, and had sold a Missal for twice that amount to some American collector; and they got a hazy notion that the old man must be well-to-do—despite his snuffiness and shabbiness, and that his queer old shop, in the window of which there was rarely anything to be seen but a few ancient tomes, and two or three rare engravings, contained much that he could turn at an hour's notice into gold. All that was surmise—but Eldrick & Pascoe—which term included Linford Pratt—knew all about Antony Bartle, being his solicitors: his will was safely deposited in their keeping, and Pratt had been one of the attesting witnesses.

The old man, having slowly walked into the outer office, leaned against a table, panting a little. Pratt hastened to open an inner door.

"Come into Mr. Eldrick's room, Mr. Bartle," he said. "There's a nice easy chair there—come and sit down in it. Those stairs are a bit trying, aren't they? I often wish we were on the ground floor."

He lighted the gas in the senior partner's room, and turning back, took hold of the visitor's arm, and helped him to the easy chair. Then, having closed the doors, he sat down at Eldrick's desk, put his fingers together and waited. Pratt knew from experience that old Antony Bartle would not have come there except on business: he knew also, having been at Eldrick & Pascoe's for many years, that the old man would confide in him as readily as in either of his principals.

"There's a nasty fog coming on outside," said Bartle, after a fit of coughing. "It gets on my lungs, and then it makes my heart bad. Mr. Eldrick in?"

"Gone," replied Pratt. "All gone, Mr. Bartle—only me here."

"You'll do," answered the old bookseller. "You're as good as they are." He leaned forward from the easy chair, and tapped the clerk's arm with a long, claw-like finger. "I say," he continued, with a smile that was something between a wink and a leer, and suggestive of a pleased satisfaction. "I've had a find!"

"Oh!" responded Pratt. "One of your rare books, Mr. Bartle? Got something for twopence that you'll sell for ten guineas? You're one of the lucky ones, you know, you are!"

"Nothing of the sort!" chuckled Bartle. "And I had to pay for my knowledge, young man, before I got it—we all have. No—but I've found something: not half an hour ago. Came straight here with it. Matters for lawyers, of course."

"Yes?" said Pratt inquiringly. "And—what may it be?" He was expecting the visitor to produce something, but the old man again leaned forward, and dug his finger once more into the clerk's sleeve.

"I say!" he whispered. "You remember John Mallathorpe and the affair of—how long is it since?"

"Two years," answered Pratt promptly. "Of course I do. Couldn't very well forget it, or him."

He let his mind go back for the moment to an affair which had provided Barford and the neighbourhood with a nine days' sensation. One winter morning, just two years previously, Mr. John Mallathorpe, one of the best-known manufacturers and richest men of the town, had been killed by the falling of his own mill-chimney. The condition of the chimney had been doubtful for some little time; experts had been examining it for several days: at the moment of the catastrophe, Mallathorpe himself, some of his principal managers, and a couple of professional steeple-jacks, were gathered at its base, consulting on a report. The great hundred-foot structure above them had collapsed without the slightest warning: Mallathorpe, his principal manager, and his cashier, had been killed on the spot: two other bystanders had subsequently died from injuries received. No such accident had occurred in Barford, nor in the surrounding manufacturing district, for many years, and there had been much interest in it, for according to the expert's conclusions the chimney was in no immediate danger.

Other mill-owners then began to examine their chimneys, and for many weeks Barford folk had talked of little else than the danger of living in the shadows of these great masses of masonry.

But there had soon been something else to talk of. It sprang out of the accident—and it was of particular interest to persons who, like Linford Pratt, were of the legal profession. John Mallathorpe, so far as anybody knew or could ascertain, had died intestate. No solicitor in the town had ever made a will for him. No solicitor elsewhere had ever made a will for him. No one had ever heard that he had made a will for himself. There was no will. Drastic search of his safes, his desks, his drawers revealed nothing—not even a memorandum. No friend of his had ever heard him mention a will. He had always been something of a queer man. He was a confirmed bachelor. The only relation he had in the world was his sister-in-law, the widow of his deceased younger brother, and her two children—a son and a daughter. And as soon as he was dead, and it was plain that he had died intestate, they put in their claim to his property.

John Mallathorpe had left a handsome property. He had been making money all his life. His business was a considerable one—he employed two thousand workpeople. His average annual profit from his mills was reckoned in thousands—four or five thousands at least. And some years before his death, he had bought one of the finest estates in the neighbourhood, Normandale Grange, a beautiful old house, set amidst charming and romantic scenery in a valley, which, though within twelve miles of Barford, might have been in the heart of the Highlands. Therefore, it was no small thing that Mrs. Richard Mallathorpe and her two children laid claim to. Up to the time of John Mallathorpe's death, they had lived in very humble fashion—lived, indeed, on an allowance from their well-to-do kinsman—for Richard Mallathorpe had been as much of a waster as his brother had been of a money-getter. And there was no withstanding their claim when it was finally decided that John Mallathorpe had died intestate—no withstanding that, at any rate, of the nephew and niece. The nephew had taken all the real estate: he and his sister had shared the personal property. And for some months they and their mother had been safely installed at Normandale Grange, and in full possession of the dead man's wealth and business.

All this flashed through Linford Pratt's mind in a few seconds—he knew all the story: he had often thought of the extraordinary good fortune of those young people. To be living on charity one week—and the next to be legal possessors of thousands a year!—oh, if only such luck would come his way!

"Of course!" he repeated, looking thoughtfully at the old bookseller. "Not the sort of thing one does forget in a hurry, Mr. Bartle. What of it?"

Antony Bartle leaned back in his easy chair and chuckled—something, some idea, seemed to be affording him amusement.

"I'm eighty years old," he remarked. "No, I'm more, to be exact. I shall be eighty-two come February. When you've lived as long as that, young Mr. Pratt, you'll know that this life is a game of topsy-turvy—to some folks, at any rate. Just so!"

"You didn't come here to tell me that, Mr. Bartle," said Pratt. He was an essentially practical young man who dined at half-past six every evening, having lunched on no more than bread-and-cheese and a glass of ale, and he also had his evenings well mapped out. "I know that already, sir."

"Aye, aye, but you'll know more of it later on," replied Bartle. "Well—you know, too, no doubt, that the late John Mallathorpe was a bit—only a bit—of a book-collector; collected books and pamphlets relating to this district?"

"I've heard of it," answered the clerk.

"He had that collection in his private room at the mill," continued the old bookseller, "and when the new folks took hold, I persuaded them to sell it to me. There wasn't such a lot—maybe a hundred volumes altogether—but I wanted what there was. And as they were of no interest to them, they sold 'em. That's some months ago. I put all the books in a corner—and I never really examined them until this very afternoon. Then—by this afternoon's post—I got a letter from a Barford man who's now out in America. He wanted to know if I could supply him with a nice copy of Hopkinson's *History of Barford*. I knew there was one in that Mallathorpe collection, so I got it out, and examined it. And in the pocket inside, in which there's a map, I found—what d'ye think?"

"Couldn't say," replied Pratt. He was still thinking of his dinner, and of an important engagement to follow it, and he had not the least idea that old Antony Bartle was going to tell him anything very important. "Letters? Bank-notes? Something of that sort?"

The old bookseller leaned nearer, across the corner of the desk, until his queer, wrinkled face was almost close to Pratt's sharp, youthful one. Again he lifted the claw-like finger: again he tapped the clerk's arm.

"I found John Mallathorpe's will!" he whispered. "His—will!"

Linford Pratt jumped out of his chair. For a second he stared in speechless amazement at the old man; then he plunged his hands deep into his trousers' pockets, opened his mouth, and let out a sudden exclamation.

"No!" he said. "No! John Mallathorpe's—will? His—will!"

"Made the very day on which he died," answered Bartle, nodding emphatically.

"Queer, wasn't it? He might have had some—premonition, eh?"

Pratt sat down again.

"Where is it?" he asked.

"Here in my pocket," replied the old bookseller, tapping his rusty coat. "Oh, it's all right, I assure you. All duly made out, signed, and witnessed. Everything in order, I know!—because a long, a very long time ago, I was like you, an attorney's clerk. I've drafted many a will, and witnessed many a will, in my time. I've read this, every word of it—it's all right. Nothing can upset it."

"Let's see it," said Pratt, eagerly.

"Well—I've no objection—I know you, of course," answered Bartle, "but I'd rather show it first to Mr. Eldrick. Couldn't you telephone up to his house and ask him to run back here?"

"Certainly," replied Pratt. "He mayn't be there, though. But I can try. You haven't shown it to anybody else?"

"Neither shown it to anybody, nor mentioned it to a soul," said Bartle. "I tell you it's not much more than half an hour since I found it. It's not a long document. Do you know how it is that it's never come out?" he went on, turning eagerly to Pratt, who had risen again. "It's easily explained. The will's witnessed by those two men who were killed at the same time as John Mallathorpe! So, of course, there was nobody to say that it was in evidence. My notion is that he and those two men—Gaukrodger and Marshall, his manager and cashier—had signed it not long before the accident, and that Mallathorpe had popped it into the pocket of that book before going out into the yard. Eh? But see if you can get Mr. Eldrick down here, and we'll read it together. And I say—this office seems uncommonly stuffy—can you open the window a bit or something?—I feel oppressed, like."

Pratt opened a window which looked out on the street. He glanced at the old man for a moment and saw that his face, always pallid, was even paler than usual.

"You've been talking too much," he said. "Rest yourself, Mr. Bartle, while I ring up Mr. Eldrick's house. If he isn't there, I'll try his club—he often turns in there for an hour before going home."

He went out by a private door to the telephone box, which stood in a lobby used by various occupants of the building. And when he had rung up Eldrick's private house and was waiting for the answer, he asked himself what this discovery would mean to the present holders of the Mallathorpe property, and his curiosity—a strongly developed quality in him—became more and more excited. If Eldrick was not at home, if he could not get in touch with him, he would persuade old Bartle to let him see his find—he would cheerfully go late to his dinner if he could only get a peep at this strangely discovered document. Romance! Why, this indeed was romance; and it might be—what else? Old Bartle had already chuckled about topsy-turvydom: did that mean that—

The telephone bell rang: Eldrick had not yet reached his house. Pratt got on to the club: Eldrick had not been there. He rang off, and went back to the private room.

"Can't get hold of him, Mr. Bartle," he began, as he closed the door. "He's not at home, and he's not at the club. I say!—you might as well let me have a look at——"

Pratt suddenly stopped. There was a strange silence in the room: the old man's wheezy breathing was no longer heard. And the clerk moved forward quickly and looked round the high back of the easy chair....

He knew at once what had happened—knew that old Bartle was dead before he laid a finger on the wasted hand which had dropped helplessly at his side. He had evidently died without a sound or a movement—died as quietly as he would have gone to sleep. Indeed, he looked as if he had just laid his old head against the padding of the chair and dropped asleep, and Pratt, who had seen death before, knew that he would never wake again. He waited a moment, listening in the silence. Once he touched the old man's hand; once, he bent nearer, still listening. And then, without hesitation, and with fingers that remained as steady as if nothing had happened, he unbuttoned Antony Bartle's coat, and drew a folded paper from the inner pocket.

2. IN TRUST

As quietly and composedly as if he were discharging the most ordinary of his daily duties, Pratt unfolded the document, and went close to the solitary gas jet above Eldrick's desk. What he held in his hand was a half-sheet of ruled foolscap paper, closely covered with writing, which he at once recognized as that of the late John Mallathorpe. He was familiar with that writing—he had often seen it. It was an old-fashioned writing—clear, distinct, with every letter well and fully formed.

"Made it himself!" muttered Pratt. "Um!—looks as if he wanted to keep the terms secret. Well——"

He read the will through—rapidly, but with care, murmuring the phraseology half aloud.

"This is the last will of me, John Mallathorpe, of Normandale Grange, in the parish of Normandale, in the West Riding of the County of York. I appoint Martin William Charlesworth, manufacturer, of Holly Lodge, Barford, and Arthur James Wyatt, chartered accountant, of 65, Beck Street, Barford, executors and trustees of this my will. I give and devise all my estate and effects real and personal of which I may die possessed or entitled to unto the said Martin William Charlesworth and Arthur James Wyatt upon trust for the following purposes to be carried out by them under the following instructions, namely:—As soon after my death as is conveniently possible they will sell all my real estate, either by private treaty or by public auction; they shall sell all my personal property of any nature whatsoever; they shall sell my business at Mallathorpe's mill in Barford as a going concern to any private purchaser or to any company already in existence or formed for the purpose of acquiring it; and they shall collect all debts and moneys due to me. And having sold and disposed of all my property, real and personal, and brought all the proceeds of such sales and of such collection of debts and moneys into one common fund they shall first pay all debts owing by me and all legal duties and expenses arising out of my death and this disposition of my property and shall then distribute my estate as follows, namely: to each of themselves, Martin William Charlesworth and Arthur James Wyatt, they shall pay the sum of five thousand pounds; to my sister-in-law, Ann Mallathorpe, they shall pay the sum of ten thousand pounds; to my nephew, Harper John Mallathorpe, they shall pay the sum of ten thousand pounds; to my niece, Nesta Mallathorpe, they shall pay the sum of ten thousand pounds. And as to the whole of the remaining residue they shall pay it in one sum to the Mayor and Corporation of the borough of Barford in the County of York to be applied by the said Mayor and Corporation at their own absolute discretion and in any manner which seems good to them to the establishment, furtherance and development of technical and commercial education in the said borough of Barford. Dated this sixteenth day of November, 1906.

Signed by the testator in   the presence of us both present at the same   time who in his presence   } JOHN MALLATHORPE   and in the presence   of each other   have hereunto set our   names as witnesses.

HENRY   GAUKRODGER,   16,   Florence   Street, Barford, Mill Manager.

CHARLES WATSON MARSHALL, 56, Laburnum Terrace,   Barford, Cashier."

As the last word left his lips Pratt carefully folded up the will, slipped it into an inner pocket of his coat, and firmly buttoned the coat across his chest. Then, without as much as a glance at the dead man, he left the room, and again visited the telephone box. He was engaged in it for a few minutes. When he came out he heard steps coming up the staircase, and looking over the banisters he saw the senior partner, Eldrick, a middle-aged man. Eldrick looked up, and saw Pratt.

"I hear you've been ringing me up at the club, Pratt," he said. "What is it?"

Pratt waited until Eldrick had come up to the landing. Then he pointed to the door of the private room, and shook his head.

"It's old Mr. Bartle, sir," he whispered. "He's in your room there—dead!"

"Dead?" exclaimed Eldrick. "Dead!"

Pratt shook his head again.

"He came up not so long after you'd gone, sir," he said. "Everybody had gone but me—I was just going. Wanted to see you about something I don't know what. He was very tottery when he came in—complained of the stairs and the fog. I took him into your room, to sit down in the easy chair. And—he died straight off. Just," concluded Pratt, "just as if he was going quietly to sleep!"

"You're sure he is dead?—not fainting?" asked Eldrick.

"He's dead, sir—quite dead," replied Pratt. "I've rung up Dr. Melrose—he'll be here in a minute or two—and the Town Hall—the police—as well. Will you look at him, sir?"

Eldrick silently motioned his clerk to open the door; together they walked into the room. And Eldrick looked at his quiet figure and wan face, and knew that Pratt was right.

"Poor old chap!" he murmured, touching one of the thin hands. "He was a fine man in his time, Pratt; clever man! And he was very, very old—one of the oldest men in Barford. Well, we must wire to his grandson, Mr. Bartle Collingwood. You'll find his address in the book. He's the only relation the old fellow had."

"Come in for everything, doesn't he, sir?" asked Pratt, as he took an address book from the desk, and picked up a sheaf of telegram forms.

"Every penny!" murmured Eldrick. "Nice little fortune, too—a fine thing for a young fellow who's just been called to the Bar. As a matter of fact, he'll be fairly well independent, even if he never sees a brief in his life."

"He has been called, has he, sir?" asked Pratt, laying a telegram form on Eldrick's writing pad and handing him a pen. "I wasn't aware of that."

"Called this term—quite recently—at Gray's Inn," replied Eldrick, as he sat down. "Very promising, clever young man. Look here!—we'd better send two wires, one to his private address, and one to his chambers. They're both in that book. It's six o'clock, isn't it?—he might be at his chambers yet, but he may have gone home. I'll write both messages—you put the addresses on, and get the wire off—we must have him down here as soon as possible."

"One address is 53x, Pump Court; the other's 96, Cloburn Square," remarked Pratt consulting the book. "There's an express from King's Cross at 8.15 which gets here midnight."

"Oh, it would do if he came down first thing in the morning—leave it to him," said Eldrick. "I say, Pratt, do you think an inquest will be necessary?"

Pratt had not thought of that—he began to think. And while he was thinking, the doctor whom he had summoned came in. He looked at the dead man, asked the clerk a few questions, and was apparently satisfied. "I don't think there's any need for an inquest," he said in reply to Eldrick. "I knew the old man very well—he was much feebler than he would admit. The exertion of coming up these stairs of yours, and the coughing brought on by the fog outside—that was quite enough. Of course, the death will have to be reported in the usual way, but I have no hesitation in giving a certificate. You've let the Town Hall people know? Well, the body had better be removed to his rooms—we must send over and tell his housekeeper. He'd no relations in the town, had he?"

"Only one in the world that he ever mentioned—his grandson—a young barrister in London," answered Eldrick. "We've just been wiring to him. Here, Pratt, you take these messages now, and get them off. Then we'll see about making all arrangements. By-the-by," he added, as Pratt moved towards the door, "you don't know what— what he came to see me about?"

"Haven't the remotest idea, sir," answered Pratt, readily and glibly. "He died—just as I've told you—before he could tell me anything."

He went downstairs, and out into the street, and away to the General Post Office, only conscious of one thing, only concerned about one thing—that he was now the sole possessor of a great secret. The opportunity which he had so often longed for had come. And as he hurried along through the gathering fog he repeated and repeated a fragment of the recent conversation between the man who was now dead, and himself—who remained very much alive.

"You haven't shown it to anybody else?" Pratt had asked.

"Neither shown it to anybody, nor mentioned it to a soul," Antony Bartle had answered. So, in all that great town of Barford, he, Linford Pratt, he, alone out of a quarter of a million people, knew—what? The magnitude of what he knew not only amazed but exhilarated him. There were such possibilities for himself in that knowledge. He wanted to be alone, to think out those possibilities; to reckon up what they came to. Of one thing he was already certain—they should be, must be, turned to his own advantage.

It was past eight o'clock before Pratt was able to go home to his lodgings. His landlady, meeting him in the hall, hoped that his dinner would not be spoiled: Pratt, who relied greatly on his dinner as his one great meal of the day, replied that he fervently hoped it wasn't, but that if it was it couldn't be helped, this time. For once he was thinking of something else than his dinner—as for his engagement for that evening, he had already thrown it over: he wanted to give all his energies and thoughts and time to his secret. Nevertheless, it was characteristic of him that he washed, changed his clothes, ate his dinner, and even glanced over the evening newspaper before he turned to the real business which was already deep in his brain. But at last, when the maid had cleared away the dinner things, and he was alone in his sitting-room, and had lighted his pipe, and mixed himself a drop of whisky-and-water—the only indulgence in such things that he allowed himself within the twenty-four hours—he drew John Mallathorpe's will from his pocket, and read it carefully three times. And then he began to think, closely and steadily.

First of all, the will was a good will. Nothing could upset it. It was absolutely valid. It was not couched in the terms which a solicitor would have employed, but it clearly and plainly expressed John Mallathorpe's intentions and meanings in respect to the disposal of his property. Nothing could be clearer. The properly appointed trustees were to realize his estate. They were to distribute it according to his specified instructions. It was all as plain as a pikestaff. Pratt, who was a good lawyer, knew what the Probate Court would say to that will if it were ever brought up before it, as he did, a quite satisfactory will. And it was validly executed. Hundreds of people, competent to do so, could swear to John Mallathorpe's signature; hundreds to Gaukrodger's; thousands to Marshall's—who as cashier was always sending his signature broadcast. No, there was nothing to do but to put that into the hands of the trustees named in it, and then....

Pratt thought next of the two trustees. They were well-known men in the town. They were comparatively young men—about forty. They were men of great energy. Their chief interests were in educational matters—that, no doubt, was why John Mallathorpe had appointed them trustees. Wyatt had been plaguing the town for two years suggested to her that her visitor had called on any matter actually relating to herself or her family.

The room into which Pratt had been taken was a small apartment opening out of the library—John Mallathorpe, when he bought Normandale Grange, had it altered and fitted to suit his own tastes, and Pratt, as soon as he entered it, saw that it was a place in which privacy and silence could be ensured. He noticed that it had double doors, and that there were heavy curtains before the window. And during the few minutes which elapsed between his entrance and Mrs. Mallathorpe's, he took the precaution to look behind those curtains, and to survey his surroundings—what he had to say was not to be overheard, if he could help it.

Mrs. Mallathorpe looked her curiosity as soon as she came in. She did not remember that she had ever seen this young man before, but she recognized at once that he was a shrewd and sharp person, and she knew from his manner that he had news of importance to give her. She quietly acknowledged Pratt's somewhat elaborate bow, and motioned him to take a chair at the side of the big desk which stood before the fireplace—she herself sat down at the desk itself, in John Mallathorpe's old elbow-chair. And Pratt thought to himself that however much young Harper John Mallathorpe might be nominal master of Normandale Grange, the real master was there, in the self-evident, quiet-looking woman who turned to him in business-like fashion.

"You want to see me?" said Mrs. Mallathorpe. "What is it?"

"Business, Mrs. Mallathorpe," replied Pratt. "As I said on my card—of a private and important sort."

"To do with me?" she asked.

"With you—and with your family," said Pratt. "And before we go any further, not a soul knows of it but—me."

Mrs. Mallathorpe took another searching look at her visitor. Pratt was leaning over the corner of the desk, to start commercial schools: Charlesworth was a devoted champion of technical schools. Pratt knew how the hearts of both would leap, if he suddenly told them that enormous funds were at their disposal for the furtherance of their schemes. And he also knew something else—that neither Charlesworth nor Wyatt had the faintest, remotest notion or suspicion that John Mallathorpe had ever made such a will, or they would have moved heaven and earth, pulled down Normandale Grange and Mallathorpe's Mill, in their efforts to find it.

But the effect—the effect of producing the will—now? Pratt, like everybody else, had been deeply interested in the Mallathorpe affair. There was so little doubt that John Mallathorpe had died intestate, such absolute certainty that his only living relations were his deceased brother's two children and their mother, that the necessary proceedings for putting Harper Mallathorpe and his sister Nesta in possession of the property, real and personal, had been comparatively simple and speedy. But—what was it worth? What would the two trustees have been able to hand over to the Mayor and Corporation of Barford, if the will had been found as soon as John Mallathorpe died? Pratt, from what he remembered of the bulk and calculations at the time, made a rapid estimate. As near as he could reckon, the Mayor and Corporation would have got about £300,000.

That, then—and this was what he wanted to get at— was what these young people would lose if he produced the will. Nay!—on second thoughts, it would be much more, very much more in some time; for the manufacturing business was being carried on by them, and was apparently doing as well as ever. It was really an enormous amount which they would lose—and they would get—what? Ten thousand apiece and their mother a like sum. Thirty thousand pounds in all—in comparison with hundreds of thousands. But they would have no choice in the matter. Nothing could upset that will.

He began to think of the three people whom the production of this will would dispossess. He knew little of them beyond what common gossip had related at the time of John Mallathorpe's sudden death. They had lived in very quiet fashion, somewhere on the outskirts of the town, until this change in their fortunes. Once or twice Pratt had seen Mrs. Mallathorpe in her carriage in the Barford streets—somebody had pointed her out to him, and had observed sneeringly that folk can soon adapt themselves to circumstances, and that Mrs. Mallathorpe now gave herself all the airs of a duchess, though she had been no more than a hospital nurse before she married Richard Mallathorpe. And Pratt had also seen young Harper Mallathorpe now and then in the town—since the good fortune arrived—and had envied him: he had also thought what a strange thing it was that money went to young fellows who seemed to have no particular endowments of brain or energy. Harper was a very ordinary young man, not over intelligent in appearance, who, Pratt had heard, was often seen lounging about the one or two fashionable hotels of the place. As for the daughter, Pratt did not remember having ever set eyes on her—but he had heard that up to the time of John Mallathorpe's death she had earned her own living as a governess, or a nurse, or something of that sort.

He turned from thinking of these three people to thoughts about himself. Pratt often thought about himself, and always in one direction—the direction of self-advancement. He was always wanting to get on. He had nobody to help him. He had kept himself since he was seventeen. His father and mother were dead; he had no brothers or sisters—the only relations he had, uncles and aunts, lived—some in London, some in Canada. He was now twenty-eight, and earning four pounds a week. He had immense confidence in himself, but he had never seen much chance of escaping from drudgery. He had often thought of asking Eldrick & Pascoe to give him his articles—but he had a shrewd idea that his request would be refused. No—it was difficult to get out of a rut. And yet—he was a clever fellow, a good-looking fellow, a sharp, shrewd, able—and here was a chance, such a chance as scarcely ever comes to a man. He would be a fool if he did not take it, and use it to his own best and lasting advantage.

And so he locked up the will in a safe place, and went to bed, resolved to take a bold step towards fortune on the morrow.

3. THE SHOP-BOY

When Pratt arrived at Eldrick & Pascoe's office at his usual hour of nine next morning, he found the senior partner already there. And with him was a young man whom the clerk at once set down as Mr. Bartle Collingwood, and looked at with considerable interest and curiosity. He had often heard of Mr. Bartle Collingwood, but had never seen him. He knew that he was the only son of old Antony Bartle's only child—a daughter who had married a London man; he knew, too, that Collingwood's parents were both dead, and that the old bookseller had left their son everything he possessed—a very nice little fortune, as Eldrick had observed last night. And since last night he had known that Collingwood had just been called to the Bar, and was on the threshold of what Eldrick, who evidently knew all about it, believed to be a promising career. Well, there he was in the flesh; and Pratt, who was a born observer of men and events, took a good look at him as he stood just within the private room, talking to Eldrick.

A good-looking fellow; what most folk would call handsome; dark, clean-shaven, tall, with a certain air of reserve about his well-cut features, firm lips, and steady eyes that suggested strength and determination. He would look very well in wig and gown, decided Pratt, viewing matters from a professional standpoint; he was just the sort that clients would feel a natural confidence in, and that juries would listen to. Another of the lucky ones, too; for Pratt knew the contents of Antony Bartle's will, and that the young man at whom he was looking had succeeded to a cool five-and-twenty thousand pounds, at least, through his grandfather's death.

"Here is Pratt," said Eldrick, glancing into the outer office as the clerk entered it. "Pratt, come in here—here is Mr. Bartle Collingwood, He would like you to tell him the facts about Mr. Bartle's death."

Pratt walked in—armed and prepared. He was a clever hand at foreseeing things, and he had known all along that he would have to answer questions about the event of the previous night.

"There's very little to tell, sir," he said, with a polite acknowledgment of Collingwood's greeting. "Mr. Bartle came up here just as I was leaving—everybody else had left. He wanted to see Mr. Eldrick. Why, he didn't say. He was coughing a good deal when he came in, and he complained of the fog outside, and of the stairs. He said something—just a mere mention—about his heart being bad. I lighted the gas in here, and helped him into the chair. He just sat down, laid his head back, and died."

"Without saying anything further?" asked Collingwood.

"Not a word more, Mr. Collingwood," answered Pratt. "He—well, it was just as if he had dropped off to sleep. Of course, at first I thought he'd fainted, but I soon saw what it was—it so happens that I've seen a death just as sudden as that, once before—my landlady's husband died in a very similar fashion, in my presence. There was nothing I could do, Mr. Collingwood—except ring up Mr. Eldrick, and the doctor, and the police."

"Mr. Pratt made himself very useful last night in making arrangements," remarked Eldrick, looking at Collingwood. "As it is, there is very little to do. There will be no need for any inquest; Melrose has given his certificate. So—there are only the funeral arrangements. We can help you with that matter, of course. But first you'd no doubt like to go to your grandfather's place and look through his papers? We have his will here, you know—and I've already told you its effect."

"I'm much obliged to you, Mr. Pratt," said Collingwood, turning to the clerk. He turned again to

Eldrick. "All right," he went on. "I'll go over to Quagg Alley. Bye-the-bye, Mr. Pratt—my grandfather didn't tell you anything of the reason of his call here?"

"Not a word, sir," replied Pratt. "Merely said he wanted Mr. Eldrick."

"Had he any legal business in process?" asked Collingwood.

Eldrick and his clerk both shook their heads. No, Mr. Bartle had no business of that sort that they knew of. Nothing—but there again Pratt was prepared.

"It might have been about the lease of that property in Horsebridge Land, sir," he said, glancing at his principal. "He did mention that, you know, when he was in here a few weeks ago."

"Just so," agreed Eldrick. "Well, you'll let me know if we can be of use," he went on, as Collingwood turned away. "Pratt can be at your disposal, any time."

Collingwood thanked him and went off. He had travelled down from London by the earliest morning train, and leaving his portmanteau at the hotel of the Barford terminus, had gone straight to Eldrick & Pascoe's office; accordingly this was his first visit to the shop in Quagg Alley. But he knew the shop and its surroundings well enough, though he had not been in Barford for some time; he also knew Antony Bartle's old housekeeper, Mrs. Clough, a rough and ready Yorkshirewoman, who had looked after the old man as long as he, Collingwood, could remember. She received him as calmly as if he had merely stepped across the street to inquire after his grandfather's health.

"I thowt ye'd be down here first thing, Mestur Collingwood," she said, as he walked into the parlor at the back of the shop. "Of course, there's naught to be done except to see after yer grandfather's burying. I don't know if ye were surprised or no when t' lawyers tellygraphed to yer last night? I weren't surprised to hear what had happened. I'd been expecting summat o' that sort this last month or two."

"You mean—he was failing?" asked Collingwood.

"He were gettin' feebler and feebler every day," said the housekeeper. "But nobody dare say so to him, and he wouldn't admit it his-self. He were that theer high-spirited 'at he did things same as if he were a young man. But I knew how it 'ud be in the end—and so it has been— I knew he'd go off all of a sudden. And of course I had all in readiness—when they brought him back last night there was naught to do but lay him out. Me and Mrs. Thompson next door, did it, i' no time. Wheer will you be for buryin' him, Mestur Collingwood?"

"We must think that over," answered Collingwood.

"Well, an' theer's all ready for that, too," responded Mrs. Clough. "He's had his grave all ready i' the cemetery this three year—I remember when he bowt it—it's under a yew-tree, and he told me 'at he'd ordered his monnyment an' all. So yer an' t' lawyers'll have no great trouble about them matters. Mestur Eldrick, he gev' orders for t' coffin last night."

Collingwood left these gruesome details—highly pleasing to their narrator—and went up to look at his dead grandfather. He had never seen much of him, but they had kept up a regular correspondence, and always been on terms of affection, and he was sorry that he had not been with the old man at the last. He remained looking at the queer, quiet, old face for a while; when he went down again, Mrs. Clough was talking to a sharp-looking lad, of apparently sixteen or seventeen years, who stood at the door leading into the shop, and who glanced at Collingwood with keen interest and speculation.

"Here's Jabey Naylor wants to know if he's to do aught, Mestur," said the housekeeper. "Of course, I've told him 'at we can't have the shop open till the burying's over—so I don't know what theer is that he can do."

"Oh, well, let him come into the shop with me," answered Collingwood. He motioned the lad to follow him out of the parlour. "So you were Mr. Bartle's assistant, eh?" he asked. "Had he anybody else?"

"Nobody but me, sir," replied the lad. "I've been with him a year."

"And your name's what?" inquired Collingwood.

"Jabez Naylor, sir, but everybody call me Jabey."

"I see—Jabey for short, eh?" said Collingwood good-humouredly. He walked into the shop, followed by the boy, and closed the door. The outer door into Quagg Alley was locked: a light blind was drawn over the one window; the books and engravings on the shelves and in the presses were veiled in a half-gloom. "Well, as Mrs. Clough says, we can't do any business for a few days, Jabey—after that we must see what can be done. You shall have your wages just the same, of course, and you may look in every day to see if there's anything you can do. You were here yesterday, of course? Were you in the shop when Mr. Bartle went out?"

"Yes, sir," replied the lad. "I'd been in with him all the afternoon. I was here when he went out—and here when they came to say he'd died at Mr. Eldrick's."

Collingwood sat down in his grandfather's chair, at a big table, piled high with books and papers, which stood in the middle of the floor.

"Did my grandfather seem at all unwell when he went out?" he asked.

"No, sir. He had been coughing a bit more than usual—that was all. There was a fog came on about five o'clock, and he said it bothered him."

"What had he been doing during the afternoon? Anything particular?"

"Nothing at all particular before half-past four or so, sir."

Collingwood took a closer look at Jabez Naylor. He saw that he was an observant lad, evidently of superior intelligence—a good specimen of the sharp town lad, well trained in a modern elementary school.

"Oh?" he said. "Nothing particular before half-past four, eh? Did he do something particular after half-past four?"

"There was a post came in just about then, sir," answered Jabey. "There was an American letter—that's it, sir—just in front of you. Mr. Bartle read it, and asked me if we'd got a good clear copy of Hopkinson's *History of Barford*. I reminded him that there was a copy amongst the books that had been bought from Mallathorpe's Mill some time ago."

"Books that had belonged to Mr. John Mallathorpe, who was killed?" asked Collingwood, who was fully acquainted with the chimney accident.

"Yes, sir, Mr. Bartle bought a lot of books that Mr. Mallathorpe had at the Mill—local books. They're there in that corner: they were put there when I fetched them, and he'd never looked over them since, particularly."

"Well—and this *History of Barford*? You reminded him of it?"

"I got it out for him, sir. He sat down—where you're sitting—and began to examine it. He said something about it being a nice copy, and he'd get it off that night— that's it, sir: I didn't read it, of course. And then he took some papers out of a pocket that's inside it, and I heard him say 'Bless my soul—who'd have thought it!'"

Collingwood picked up the book which the boy indicated—a thick, substantially bound volume, inside one cover of which was a linen pocket, wherein were some loose maps and plans of Barford.

"These what he took out?" he asked, holding them up.

"Yes, sir, but there was another paper, with writing on it—a biggish sheet of paper—written all over."

"Did you see what the writing was? Did you see any of it?"

"No, sir—only that it was writing, I was dusting those shelves out, over there; when I heard Mr. Bartle say what he did. I just looked round, over my shoulder—that was all."

"Was he reading this paper that you speak of?"

"Yes, sir—he was holding it up to the gas, reading it."

"Do you know what he did with it?"

"Yes, sir—he folded it up and put it in his pocket."

"Did he say any more—make any remark?"

"No, sir. He wrote a letter then."

"At once?"

"Yes, sir—straight off. But he wasn't more than a minute writing it. Then he sent me to post it at the pillar-box, at the end of the Alley."

"Did you read the address?"

The lad turned to a book which stood with others in a rack over the chimney-piece, and tapped it with his finger.

"Yes, sir—because Mr. Bartle gave orders when I first came here that a register of every letter sent out was to be kept—I've always entered them in this book."

"And this letter you're talking about—to whom was it addressed?"

"Miss Mallathorpe, Normandale Grange, sir."

"You went and posted it at once?"

"That very minute, sir."

"Was it soon afterwards that Mr. Bartle went out?"

"He went out as soon as I came back, sir."

"And you never saw him again?"

Jabey shook his head.

"Not alive, sir," he answered. "I saw him when they brought him back."

"How long had he been out when you heard he was dead?"

"About an hour, sir—just after six it was when they told Mrs. Clough and me. He went out at ten minutes past five."

Collingwood got up. He gave the lad's shoulder a friendly squeeze.

"All right!" he said. "Now you seem a smart, intelligent lad—don't mention a word to any one of what we've been talking about. You have not mentioned it before, I suppose? Not a word? That's right—don't. Come in again tomorrow morning to see if I want you to be here as usual. I'm going to put a manager into this shop."

When the boy had gone Collingwood locked up the shop from the house side, put the key in his pocket, and went into the kitchen.

"Mrs. Clough," he said. "I want to see the clothes which my grandfather was wearing when he was brought home last night. Where are they?"

"They're in that little room aside of his bed-chamber, Mestur Collingwood," replied the housekeeper. "I laid 'em all there, on the clothes-press, just as they were taken off of him, by Lawyer Eldrick's orders—he said they hadn't been examined, and wasn't to be, till you came. Nobody whatever's touched 'em since."

Collingwood went upstairs and into the little room—a sort of box-room opening out of that in which the old man lay. There were the clothes; he went through the pockets of every garment. He found such things as keys, a purse, loose money, a memorandum book, a bookseller's catalogue or two, two or three letters of a business sort—but there was no big folded paper, covered with writing, such as Jabey Naylor had described.

The mention of that paper had excited Collingwood's curiosity. He rapidly summed up what he had learned. His grandfather had found a paper, closely written upon, in a book which had been the property of John Mallathorpe, deceased. The discovery had surprised him, for he had given voice to an exclamation of what was evidently astonishment. He had put the paper in his pocket. Then he had written a letter—to Mrs. Mallathorpe of Normandale Grange. When his shop-boy had posted that letter, he himself had gone out—to his solicitor. What, asked Collingwood, was the reasonable presumption? The old man had gone to Eldrick to show him the paper which he had found.

He lingered in the little room for a few minutes, thinking. No one but Pratt had been with Antony Bartle at the time of his seizure and sudden death. What sort of a fellow was Pratt? Was he honest? Was his word to be trusted? Had he told the precise truth about the old man's death? He was evidently a suave, polite, obliging sort of fellow, this clerk, but it was a curious thing that if Antony Bartle had that paper, whatever it was—in his pocket when he went to Eldrick's office it should not be in his pocket still—if his clothing had really remained untouched. Already suspicion was in Collingwood's mind—vague and indefinable, but there.

He was half inclined to go straight back to Eldrick & Pascoe's and tell Eldrick what Jabey Naylor had just told him. But he reflected that while Naylor went out to post the letter, the old bookseller might have put the paper elsewhere; locked it up in his safe, perhaps. One thing, however, he, Collingwood, could do at once—he could ask Mrs. Mallathorpe if the letter referred to the paper. He was fully acquainted with all the facts of the Mallathorpe history; old Bartle, knowing they would interest his grandson, had sent him the local newspaper accounts of its various episodes. It was only twelve miles to Normandale Grange—a motor-car would carry him there within the hour. He glanced at his watch—just ten o 'clock.

An hour later, Collingwood found himself standing in a fine oak-panelled room, the windows of which looked out on a romantic valley whose thickly wooded sides were still bright with the red and yellow tints of autumn. A door opened—he turned, expecting to see Mrs. Mallathorpe. Instead, he found himself looking at a girl, who glanced inquiringly at him, and from him to the card which he had sent in on his arrival.

4. THE FORTUNATE POSSESSORS

Collingwood at once realized that he was in the presence of one of the two fortunate young people who had succeeded so suddenly—and, according to popular opinion, so unexpectedly—to John Mallathorpe's wealth. This was evidently Miss Nesta Mallathorpe, of whom he had heard, but whom he had never seen. She, however, was looking at him as if she knew him, and she smiled a little as she acknowledged his bow.

"My mother is out in the grounds, with my brother," she said, motioning Collingwood towards a chair. "Won't you sit down, please?—I've sent for her; she will be here in a few minutes."

Collingwood sat down; Nesta Mallathorpe sat down, too, and as they looked at each other she smiled again.

"I have seen you before, Mr. Collingwood," she said. "I knew it must be you when they brought up your card."

Collingwood used his glance of polite inquiry to make a closer inspection of his hostess. He decided that Nesta Mallathorpe was not so much pretty as eminently attractive—a tall, well-developed, warm-coloured young woman, whose clear grey eyes and red lips and general bearing indicated the possession of good health and spirits. And he was quite certain that if he had ever seen her before he would not have forgotten it.

"Where have you seen me?" he asked, smiling back at her.

"Have you forgotten the mock-trial—year before last?" she asked.

Collingwood remembered what she was alluding to. He had taken part, in company with various other law students, in a mock-trial, a breach of promise case, for the benefit of a certain London hospital, to him had fallen one of the principal parts, that of counsel for the plaintiff. "When I saw your name, I remembered it at once," she went on. "I was there—I was a probationer at St. Chad's Hospital at that time."

"Dear me!" said Collingwood, "I should have thought our histrionic efforts would have been forgotten. I'm afraid I don't remember much about them, except that we had a lot of fun out of the affair. So you were at St. Chad's?" he continued, with a reminiscence of the surroundings of the institution they were talking of. "Very different to Normandale!"

"Yes," she replied. "Very—very different to Normandale. But when I was at St. Chad's, I didn't know that I—that we should ever come to Normandale."

"And now that you are here?" he asked.

The girl looked out through the big window on the valley which lay in front of the old house, and she shook her head a little.

"It's very beautiful," she answered, "but I sometimes wish I was back at St. Chad's—with something to do. Here—there's nothing to do but to do nothing." Collingwood realized that this was not the complaint of the well-to-do young woman who finds time hang heavy— it was rather indicative of a desire for action.

"I understand!" he said. "I think I should feel like that. One wants—I suppose—is it action, movement, what is it?"

"Better call it occupation—that's a plain term," she answered. "We're both suffering from lack of occupation here, my brother and I. And it's bad for us—especially for him."

Before Collingwood could think of any suitable reply to this remarkably fresh and candid statement, the door opened, and Mrs. Mallathorpe came in, followed by her son. And the visitor suddenly and immediately noticed the force and meaning of Nesta Mallathorpe's last remark. Harper Mallathorpe, a good-looking, but not remarkably intelligent appearing young man, of about

Collingwood's own age, gave him the instant impression of being bored to death; the lack-lustre eye, the aimless lounge, the hands thrust into the pockets of his Norfolk jacket as if they took refuge there from sheer idleness—all these things told their tale. Here, thought Collingwood, was a fine example of how riches can be a curse—relieved of the necessity of having to earn his daily bread by labour, Harper Mallathorpe was finding life itself laborious.

But there was nothing of aimlessness, idleness, or lack of vigour in Mrs. Mallathorpe. She was a woman of character, energy, of brains—Collingwood saw all that at one glance. A little, neat-figured, compact sort of woman, still very good-looking, still on the right side of fifty, with quick movements and sharp glances out of a pair of shrewd eyes: this, he thought, was one of those women who will readily undertake the control and management of big affairs. He felt, as Mrs. Mallathorpe turned inquiring looks on him, that as long as she was in charge of them the Mallathorpe family fortunes would be safe.

"Mother," said Nesta, handing Collingwood's card to Mrs. Mallathorpe, "this gentleman is Mr. Bartle Collingwood. He's—aren't you?—yes, a barrister. He wants to see you. Why, I don't know. I have seen Mr. Collingwood before—but he didn't remember me. Now he'll tell you what he wants to see you about."

"If you'll allow me to explain why I called on you, Mrs. Mallathorpe," said Collingwood, "I don't suppose you ever heard of me—but you know, at any rate, the name of my grandfather, Mr. Antony Bartle, the bookseller, of Barford? My grandfather is dead—he died very suddenly last night."

Mrs. Mallathorpe and Nesta murmured words of polite sympathy. Harper suddenly spoke—as if mere words were some relief to his obvious boredom.

"I heard that, this morning," he said, turning to his mother. "Hopkins told me—he was in town last night. I meant to tell you."

"Dear me!" exclaimed Mrs. Mallathorpe, glancing at some letters which stood on a rack above the mantelpiece. "Why—I had a letter from Mr. Bartle this very morning!"

"It is that letter that I have come to see you about," said Collingwood. "I only got down here from London at half-past eight this morning, and of course, I have made some inquiries about the circumstances of my grandfather's sudden death. He died very suddenly indeed at Mr. Eldrick's office. He had gone there on some business about which nobody knows nothing—he died before he could mention it. And according to his shop-boy, Jabey Naylor, the last thing he did was to write a letter to you. Now—I have reason for asking—would you mind telling me, Mrs. Mallathorpe, what that letter was about?" Mrs. Mallathorpe moved over to the hearth, and took an envelope from the rack. She handed it to Collingwood, indicating that he could open it. And Collingwood drew out one of old Bartle's memorandum forms, and saw a couple of lines in the familiar crabbed handwriting:

"MRS. MALLATHORPE, Normandale Grange.

"Madam,—If you should drive into town tomorrow, will you kindly   give me a call? I want to see you particularly.

"Respectfully, A. BARTLE."

Collingwood handed back the letter.

"Have you any idea to what that refers?" he asked.

"Well, I think I have—perhaps," answered Mrs. Mallathorpe. "Mr. Bartle persuaded us to sell him some books—local books—which my late brother-in-law had at his office in the mill. And since then he has been very anxious to buy more local books and pamphlets about this neighbourhood, and he had some which Mr. Bartle was very anxious indeed to get hold of. I suppose he wanted to see me about that." Collingwood made no remarks for the moment. He was wondering whether or not to tell what Jabey Naylor had told him about this paper taken from the linen pocket inside the *History of Barford*. But Mrs.

Mallathorpe's ready explanation had given him a new idea, and he rose from his chair.

"Thank you," he said. "I suppose that's it. You may think it odd that I wanted to know what he'd written about, but as it was certainly the last letter he wrote——"

"Oh, I'm quite sure it must have been that!" exclaimed Mrs. Mallathorpe. "And as I am going into Barford this afternoon, in any case, I meant to call at Mr. Bartle's. I'm sorry to hear of his death, poor old gentleman! But he was very old indeed, wasn't he?"

"He was well over eighty," replied Collingwood. "Well, thank you again—and good-bye—I have a motorcar waiting outside there, and I have much to do in Barford when I get back."

The two young people accompanied Collingwood into the hall. And Harper suddenly brightened.

"I say!" he said. "Have a drink before you go. It's a long way in and out. Come into the dining-room."

But Collingwood caught Nesta's eye, and he was quick to read a signal in it.

"No, thanks awfully!" he answered. "I won't really—I must get back—I've such a lot of things to attend to. This is a very beautiful place of yours," he went on, as Harper, whose face had fallen at the visitor's refusal, followed with his sister to where the motor-car waited. "It might be a hundred miles from anywhere."

"It's a thousand miles from anywhere!" muttered Harper. "Nothing to do here!"

"No hunting, shooting, fishing?" asked Collingwood. "Get tired of 'em? Well, why not make a private golf-links in your park? You'd get a fine sporting course round there."

"That's a good notion, Harper," observed Nesta, with some eagerness. "You could have it laid out this winter."

Harper suddenly looked at Collingwood.

"Going to stop in Barford?" he asked.

"Till I settle my grandfather's affairs—yes," answered Collingwood.

"Come and see us again," said Harper. "Come for the night—we've got a jolly good billiard table."

"Do!" added Nesta heartily.

"Since you're so kind, I will, then," replied Collingwood. "But not for a few days."

He drove off—to wonder why he had visited Normandale Grange at all. For Mrs. Mallathorpe's explanation of the letter was doubtless the right one: Collingwood, little as he had seen of Antony Bartle, knew what a veritable sleuth-hound the old man was where rare books or engravings were concerned. Yet—why the sudden exclamation on finding that paper? Why the immediate writing of the letter to Mrs. Mallathorpe? Why the setting off to Eldrick & Pascoe's office as soon as the letter was written? It all looked as if the old man had found some document, the contents of which related to the Mallathorpe family, and was anxious to communicate its nature to Mrs. Mallathorpe, and to his own solicitor, as soon as possible.

"But that's probably only my fancy," he mused, as he sped back to Barford; "the real explanation is doubtless that suggested by Mrs. Mallathorpe. Something made the old man think of the collection of local books at Normandale Grange—and he immediately wrote off to ask her to see him, with the idea of persuading her to let him have them. That's all there is in it—what a suspicious sort of party I must be getting! And suspicious of whom—and of what? Anyhow, I'm glad I went out there—and I'll certainly go again."

On his way back to Barford he thought a good deal of the two young people he had just left. There was something of the irony of fate about their situation. There they were, in possession of money and luxury and youth—and already bored because they had nothing to do. He felt what closely approached a contemptuous pity for Harper—why didn't he turn to some occupation? There was their own business—why didn't he put in so many hours a day there, instead of leaving it to managers? Why didn't he interest himself in local affairs?—work at something? Already he had all the appearance of a man who is inclined to slackness—and in that case, mused Collingwood, his money would do him positive harm. But he had no thoughts of that sort about Nesta Mallathorpe: he had seen that she was of a different temperament.

"She'll not stick there—idling," he said. "She'll break out and do something or other. What did she say? 'Suffering from lack of occupation'? A bad thing to suffer from, too—glad I'm not similarly afflicted!"

There was immediate occupation for Collingwood himself when he reached the town. He had already made up his mind as to his future plans. He would sell his grandfather's business as soon as he could find a buyer— the old man had left a provision in his will, the gist of which Eldrick had already communicated to Collingwood, to the effect that his grandson could either carry on the business with the help of a competent manager until the stock was sold out, or could dispose of it as a going concern—Collingwood decided to sell it outright, and at once. But first it was necessary for him to look round the collection of valuable books and prints, and get an idea of what it was that he was about to sell. And when he had reached Barford again, and had lunched at his hotel, he went to Quagg Alley, and shut himself in the shop, and made a careful inspection of the treasures which old Bartle had raked up from many quarters.

Within ten minutes of beginning his task Collingwood knew that he had gone out to Normandale Grange about a mere nothing. Picking up the *History of Barford* which Jabey Naylor had spoken of, and turning over its leaves, two papers dropped out; one a half sheet of foolscap, folded; the other, a letter from some correspondent in the United States. Collingwood read the letter first—it was evidently that which Naylor had referred to as having been delivered the previous afternoon. It asked for a good, clear copy of Hopkinson's *History of Barford*—and then it went on, "If you should come across a copy of what is, I believe, a very rare tract or pamphlet, *Customs of the Court Leet of the Manor of Barford*, published, I think, about 1720, I should be glad to pay you any price you like to ask for it—in reason." So much for the letter— Collingwood turned from it to the folded paper. It was headed "List of Barford Tracts and Pamphlets in my box marked B.P. in the library at N Grange," and it was initialled at the foot J.M. Then followed the titles of some twenty-five or thirty works—amongst them was the very tract for which the American correspondent had inquired. And now Collingwood had what he believed to be a clear vision of what had puzzled him—his grandfather having just read the American buyer's request had found the list of these pamphlets inside the *History of Barford*, and in it the entry of the particular one he wanted, and at once he had written to Mrs. Mallathorpe in the hope of persuading her to sell what his American correspondent desired to buy. It was all quite plain—and the old man's visit to Eldrick & Pascoe's had nothing to do with the letter to Mrs. Mallathorpe. Nor had he carried the folded paper in his pocket to Eldrick's—when Jabey Naylor went out to post the letter, Antony had placed the folded paper and the American letter together in the book and left them there. Quite, quite simple!—he had had his run to Normandale Grange and back all about nothing, and for nothing—except that he had met Nesta Mallathorpe, whom he was already sufficiently interested in to desire to see again. But having arrived at an explanation of what had puzzled him and made him suspicious, he dismissed that matter from his mind and thought no more of it.

But across the street, all unknown to Collingwood, Linford Pratt was thinking a good deal. Collingwood had taken his car from a rank immediately opposite Eldrick & Pascoe's windows; Pratt, whose desk looked on to the street, had seen him drive away soon after ten o'clock and return about half-past twelve. Pratt, who knew everybody in the business centre of the town, knew the man who had driven Collingwood, and when he went out to his lunch he asked him where he had been that morning. The man, who knew no reason for secrecy, told him—and Pratt went off to eat his bread and cheese and drink his one glass of ale and to wonder why young Collingwood had been to Normandale Grange. He became slightly anxious and uneasy. He knew that Collingwood must have made some slight examination of old Bartle's papers. Was it—could it be possible that the old man, before going to Eldrick's, had left some memorandum of his discovery in his desk—or in a diary? He had said that he had not shown the will, nor mentioned the will, to a soul—but he might;—old men were so fussy about things—he might have set down in his diary that he had found it on such a day, and under such-and-such circumstances.

However, there was one person who could definitely inform him of the reason of Collingwood's visit to Normandale Grange—Mrs. Mallathorpe. He would see her at once, and learn if he had any grounds for fear. And so it came about that at nine o'clock that evening, Mrs. Mallathorpe, for the second time that day, found herself asked to see a limb of the law.

5. POINT-BLANK

Mrs. Mallathorpe was alone when Pratt's card was taken to her. Harper and Nesta were playing billiards in a distant part of the big house. Dinner had been over for an hour; Mrs. Mallathorpe, who had known what hard work and plenty of it was, in her time, was trifling over the newspapers—rest, comfort, and luxury were by no means boring to her. She looked at the card doubtfully— Pratt had pencilled a word or two on it: "Private and important business." Then she glanced at the butler—an elderly man who had been with John Mallathorpe many years before the catastrophe occurred.

"Who is he, Dickenson?" she asked. "Do you know him?"

"Clerk at Eldrick & Pascoe's, in the town, ma'am," replied the butler. "I know the young man by sight."

"Where is he?" inquired Mrs. Mallathorpe.

"In the little morning room, at present, ma'am," said Dickenson.

"Take him into the study," commanded Mrs. Mallathorpe. "I'll come to him presently." She was utterly at a loss to understand Pratt's presence there. Eldrick & Pascoe were not her solicitors, and she had no business of a legal nature in which they could be in any way concerned. But it suddenly struck her that that was the second time she had heard Eldrick's name mentioned that day—young Mr. Collingwood had said that his grandfather's death had taken place at Eldrick & Pascoe's office. Had this clerk come to see her about that?—and if so, what had she to do with it? Before she reached the room in which Pratt was waiting for her, Mrs. Mallathorpe was filled with curiosity. But in that curiosity there was not a trace of apprehension; nothing towards her; already he had lowered his tones to the mysterious and confidential note.

"I don't know what you're talking about," she said. "Go on."

Pratt bent a little nearer.

"A question or two first, if you please, Mrs. Mallathorpe. And—answer them! They're for your own good. Young Mr. Collingwood called on you today."

"Well—and what of it?"

"What did he want?"

Mrs. Mallathorpe hesitated and frowned a little. And Pratt hastened to reassure her. "I'm using no idle words, Mrs. Mallathorpe, when I say it's for your own good. It is! What did he come for?"

"He came to ask what there was in a letter which his grandfather wrote to me yesterday afternoon."

"Antony Bartle had written to you, had he? And what did he say, Mrs. Mallathorpe? For that is important!"

"No more than that he wanted me to call on him today, if I happened to be in Barford."

"Nothing more?"

"Nothing more—not a word."

"Nothing as to—why he wanted to see you?"

"No! I thought that he probably wanted to see me about buying some books of the late Mr. Mallathorpe's."

"Did you tell Collingwood that?" asked Pratt, eagerly.

"Yes—of course."

"Did it satisfy him?"

Mrs. Mallathorpe frowned again.

"Why shouldn't I?" she demanded. "It was the only explanation I could possibly give him. How do I know what the old man really wanted?"

Pratt drew his chair still nearer to the desk. His voice dropped to a whisper and his eyes were full of meaning.

"I'll tell you what he wanted!" he said speaking very slowly. "It's what I've come for. Listen! Antony Bartle came to our office soon after five yesterday afternoon. I was alone—everybody else had gone. I took him into

Eldrick's room. He told me that in turning over one of the books which he had bought from Mallathorpe Mill, some short time ago, he had found—what do you think?"

Mrs. Mallathorpe's cheek had flushed at the mention of the books from the Mill. Now, at Pratt's question, and under his searching eye, she turned very pale, and the clerk saw her fingers tighten on the arms of her chair.

"What?" she asked. "What?"

"John Mallathorpe's will!" he answered. "Do you understand? His—will!"

The woman glanced quickly about her—at the doors, the uncurtained window.

"Safe enough here," whispered Pratt. "I made sure of that. Don't be afraid—no one knows—but me."

But Mrs. Mallathorpe seemed to find some difficulty in speaking, and when she at last got out a word her voice sounded hoarse.

"Impossible!"

"It's a fact!" said Pratt. "Nothing was ever more a fact as you'll see. But let me finish my story. The old man told me how he'd found the will—only half an hour before—and he asked me to ring up Eldrick, so that we might all read it together. I went to the telephone—when I came back, Bartle was dead—just dead. And—I took the will out of his pocket."

Mrs. Mallathorpe made an involuntary gesture with her right hand. And Pratt smiled, craftily, and shook his head.

"Much too valuable to carry about, Mrs. Mallathorpe," he said. "I've got it—all safe—under lock and key. But as I've said—nobody knows of it but myself. Not a living soul. No one has any idea! No one can have any idea. I was a bit alarmed when I heard that young Collingwood had been to you, for I thought that the old man, though he didn't tell me of any such thing, might have dropped you a line saying what he'd found. But as he didn't—well, not one living soul knows that the will's in existence, except me—and you!"

Mrs. Mallathorpe was regaining her self-possession. She had had a great shock, but the worst of it was over. Already she knew, from Pratt's manner, insidious and suggesting, that the will was of a nature that would dispossess her and hers of this recently acquired wealth—the clerk had made that evident by look and tone. So—there was nothing but to face things.

"What—what does it—say?" she asked, with an effort.

Pratt unbuttoned his overcoat, plunged a hand into the inner pocket, drew out a sheet of paper, unfolded it and laid it on the desk.

"An exact copy," he said tersely. "Read it for yourself."

In spite of the determined effort which she made to be calm, Mrs. Mallathorpe's fingers still trembled as she took up the sheet on which Pratt had made a fair copy of the will. The clerk watched her narrowly as she read. He knew that presently there would be a tussle between them: he knew, too, that she was a woman who would fight hard in defence of her own interest, and for the interests of her children.

Always keeping his ears open to local gossip, especially where money was concerned, Pratt had long since heard that Mrs. Mallathorpe was a keen and sharp business woman. And now he was not surprised when, having slowly and carefully read the copy of the will from beginning to end, she laid it down, and turned to him with a business-like question.

"The effect of that?" she asked. "What would it be—curtly?"

"Precisely what it says," answered Pratt. "Couldn't be clearer!"

"We—should lose all?" she demanded, almost angrily. "All?"

"All—except what he says—there," agreed Pratt.

"And that," she went on, drumming her fingers on the paper, "that—would stand?"

"What it's a copy of would stand," said Pratt. "Oh, yes, don't you make any mistake about it, Mrs. Mallathorpe!

Nothing can upset that will. It is plain as a pikestaff how it came to be made. Your late brother-in-law evidently wrote his will out—it's all in his own handwriting—and took it down to the Mill with him the very day of the chimney accident. Just as evidently he signed it in the presence of his manager, Gaukrodger, and his cashier, Marshall—they signed at the same time, as it says, there. Now I take it that very soon after that, Mr. Mallathorpe went out into his mill yard to have a look at the chimney—Gaukrodger and Marshall went with him. Before he went, he popped the will into the book, where old Bartle found it yesterday—such things are easily done. Perhaps he was reading the book—perhaps it lay handy—he slipped the will inside, anyway. And then—he was killed—and, what's more the two witnesses were killed with him. So there wasn't a man left who could tell of that will! But—there's half Barford could testify to these three signatures! Mrs. Mallathorpe, there's not a chance for you if I put that will into the hands of the two trustees!"

He leaned back in his chair after that—nodding confidently, watching keenly. And now he saw that the trembling fingers were interlacing each other, twisting the rings on each other, and that Mrs. Mallathorpe was thinking as she had most likely never thought in her life. After a moment's pause Pratt went on. "Perhaps you didn't understand," he said. "I mean, you don't know the effect. Those two trustees—Charlesworth & Wyatt—could turn you all clean out of this—tomorrow, in a way of speaking. Everything's theirs! They can demand an account of every penny that you've all had out of the estate and the business—from the time you all took hold. If anything's been saved, put aside, they can demand that. You're entitled to nothing but the three amounts of ten thousand each. Of course, thirty thousand is thirty thousand—it means, at five per cent., fifteen hundred a year—if you could get five per cent. safely. But—I should say your son and daughter are getting a few thousand a year each, aren't they, Mrs. Mallathorpe? It would be a nice come-down! Five hundred a year apiece—at the outside. A small house instead of Normandale Grange. Genteel poverty—comparatively speaking—instead of riches. That is—if I hand over the will to Charlesworth & Wyatt."

Mrs. Mallathorpe slowly turned her eyes on Pratt. And Pratt suddenly felt a little afraid—there was anger in those eyes; anger of a curious sort. It might be against fate—against circumstance: it might not—why should it?—be against him personally, but it was there, and it was malign and almost evil, and it made him uncomfortable.

"Where is the will!" she asked.

"Safe! In my keeping," answered Pratt.

She looked him all over—surmisingly.

"You'll sell it to me?" she suggested. "You'll hand it over—and let me burn it—destroy it?"

"No!" answered Pratt. "I shall not!"

He saw that his answer produced personal anger at last. Mrs. Mallathorpe gave him a look which would have warned a much less observant man than Pratt. But he gave her back a look that was just as resolute.

"I say no—and I mean no!" he continued. "I won't sell—but I'll bargain. Let's be plain with each other. You don't want that will to be handed over to the trustees named in it, Charlesworth & Wyatt?"

"Do you think I'm a fool—man!" she flashed out.

"I should be a fool myself if I did," replied Pratt calmly. "And I'm not a fool. Very well—then you'll square me. You'll buy me. Come to terms with me, and nobody shall ever know. I repeat to you what I've said before— not a soul knows now, no nor suspects! It's utterly impossible for anybody to find out. The testator's dead. The attesting witnesses are dead. The man who found this will is dead. No one but you and myself ever need know a word about all this. If—you make terms with me, Mrs. Mallathorpe."

"What do you want?" she asked sullenly. "You forget—
I've nothing of my own. I didn't come into anything."

"I've a pretty good notion who's real master here—and
at Mallathorpe Mill, too," retorted Pratt. "I should say
you're still in full control of your children, Mrs.
Mallathorpe, and that you can do pretty well what you
like with them."

"With one of them perhaps," she said, still angry and
sullen. "But—I tell you, for you may as well know—if my
daughter knew of what you've told me, she'd go straight
to these trustees and tell! That's a fact that you'd better
realize. I can't control her."

"Oh!" remarked Pratt. "Um!—then we must take care
that she doesn't know. But we don't intend that anybody
should know but you and me, Mrs. Mallathorpe. You
needn't tell a soul—not even your son. You mustn't tell!
Listen, now—I've thought out a good scheme which'll
profit me, and make you safe. Do you know what you
want on this estate?"

She stared at him as if wondering what this question
had to do with the matter which was of such infinite
importance. And Pratt smiled, and hastened to enlighten
her.

"You want—a steward," he said. "A steward and
estate agent. John Mallathorpe managed everything for
himself, but your son can't, and pardon me if I say that
you can't—properly. You need a man—you need me. You
can persuade your son to that effect. Give me the job of
steward here. I'll suggest to you how to do it in such a
fashion that it'll arouse no suspicion, and look just like an
ordinary—very ordinary—business job—at a salary and
on conditions to be arranged, and—you're safe! Safe, Mrs.
Mallathorpe—you know what that means!"

Mrs. Mallathorpe suddenly rose from her chair.

"I know this!" she said. "I'll discuss nothing, and do
nothing, till I've seen that will!"

Pratt rose, too, nodding his head as if quite satisfied. He took up the copy, tore it in two pieces, and carefully dropped them into the glowing fire.

"I shall be at my lodgings at any time after five-thirty tomorrow evening," he answered quietly. "Call there. You have the address. And you can then read the will with your own eyes. I shan't bring it here. The game's in my hands, Mrs. Mallathorpe."

Within a few minutes he was out in the park again, and making his way to the little railway station in the valley below. He felt triumphant—he knew that the woman he had just left was at his mercy and would accede to his terms. And all the way back to town, and through the town to his lodgings, he considered and perfected the scheme he was going to suggest to Mrs. Mallathorpe on the morrow.

Pratt lived in a little hamlet of old houses on the very outskirts of Barford—on the edge of a stretch of Country honeycombed by stone-quarries, some in use, some already worked out. It was a lonely neighbourhood, approached from the nearest tramway route by a narrow, high-walled lane. He was half-way along that lane when a stealthy foot stole to his side, and a hand was laid on his arm—just as stealthily came the voice of one of his fellow-clerks at Eldrick & Pascoe's.

"A moment, Pratt! I've been waiting for you. I want—a word or two—in private!"

6. THE UNEXPECTED

Pratt started when he heard that voice and felt the arresting hand. He knew well enough to whom they belonged—they were those of one James Parrawhite, a little, weedy, dissolute chap who had been in Eldrick & Pascoe's employ for about a year. It had always been a mystery to him and the other clerks that Parrawhite had been there at all, and that being there he was allowed to stop. He was not a Barford man. Nobody knew anything whatever about him, though his occasional references to it seemed to indicate that he knew London pretty thoroughly. Pratt shrewdly suspected that he was a man whom Eldrick had known in other days, possibly a solicitor who had been struck off the rolls, and to whom Eldrick, for old times' sake, was disposed to extend a helping hand.

All that any of them knew was that one morning some fifteen months previously, Parrawhite, a complete stranger, had walked into the office, asked to see Eldrick, had remained closeted with him half an hour, and had been given a job at two pounds a week, there and then. That he was a clever and useful clerk no one denied, but no one liked him.

He was always borrowing half-crowns. He smelt of rum. He was altogether undesirable. It was plain to the clerks that Pascoe disliked him. But he was evidently under Eldrick's protection, and he did his work and did it well, and there was no doubt that he knew more law than either of the partners, and was better up in practice than Pratt himself. But—he was not desirable ... and Pratt never desired him less than on this occasion.

"What are you after—coming on a man like that!" growled Pratt.

"You," replied Parrawhite. "I knew you'd got to come up this lane, so I waited for you. I've something to say."

"Get it said, then!" retorted Pratt.

"Not here," answered Parrawhite. "Come down by the quarry—nobody about there."

"And suppose I don't?" asked Pratt.

"Then you'll be very sorry for yourself—tomorrow," replied Parrawhite. "That's all!"

Pratt had already realized that this fellow knew something. Parrawhite's manner was not only threatening but confident. He spoke as a man speaks who has got the whip hand. And so, still growling, and inwardly raging and anxious, he turned off with his companion into a track which lay amongst the stone quarries. It was a desolate, lonely place; no house was near; they were as much alone as if they had been in the middle of one of the great moors outside the town, the lights of which they could see in the valley below them. In the grey sky above, a waning moon gave them just sufficient light to see their immediate surroundings—a grass-covered track, no longer used, and the yawning mouths of the old quarries, no longer worked, the edges of which were thick with gorse and bramble. It was the very place for secret work, and Pratt was certain that secret work was at hand.

"Now then!" he said, when they had walked well into the wilderness. "What is it? And no nonsense!"

"You'll get no nonsense from me," sneered Parrawhite. "I'm not that sort. This is what I want to say. I was in Eldrick's office last night all the time you were there with old Bartle."

This swift answer went straight through Pratt's defences. He was prepared to hear something unpleasant and disconcerting, but not that. And he voiced the first thought that occurred to him.

"That's a lie!" he exclaimed. "There was nobody there!"

"No lie," replied Parrawhite. "I was there. I was behind the curtain of that recess—you know. And since I know what you did, I don't mind telling you—we're in the same boat, my lad!—what I was going to do. You thought I'd gone—with the others. But I hadn't. I'd merely done what I've done several times without being found out— slipped in there—to wait until you'd gone. Why? Because friend Eldrick, as you know, is culpably careless about leaving loose cash in the unlocked drawer of his desk, culpably careless, too, about never counting it. And—a stray sovereign or half-sovereign is useful to a man who only gets two quid a week. Understand?"

"So you're a thief?" said Pratt bitterly.

"I'm precisely what you are—a thief!" retorted Parrawhite. "You stole John Mallathorpe's will last night. I heard everything, I tell you!—and saw everything. I heard the whole business—what the old man said—what you, later, said to Eldrick. I saw old Bartle die—I saw you take the will from his pocket, read it, and put it in your pocket. I know all!—except the terms of the will. But— I've a pretty good idea of what those terms are. Do you know why? Because I watched you set off to Normandale by the eight-twenty train tonight!"

"Hang you for a dirty sneak!" growled Pratt.

Parrawhite laughed, and flourished a heavy stick which he carried.

"Not a bit of it!" he said, almost pleasantly. "I thought you were more of a philosopher—I fancied I'd seen gleams—mere gleams—of philosophy in you at times. Fortunes of war, my boy! Come now—you've seen enough of me to know I'm an adventurer. This is an adventure of the sort I love. Go into it heart and soul, man! Own up!— you've found out that the will leaves the property away from the present holders, and you've been to Normandale to—bargain? Come, now!"

"What then!" demanded Pratt.

"Then, of course, I come in at the bargaining," answered Parrawhite. "I'm going to have my share. That's a certainty. You'd better take my advice. Because you're absolutely in my power. I've nothing to do but to tell Eldrick tomorrow morning."

"Suppose I tell Eldrick tomorrow morning of what you've told me?" interjected Pratt.

"Eldrick will believe me before you," retorted Parrawhite, imperturbably. "I'm a much cleverer, more plausible man than you are, my friend—I've had an experience of the world which you haven't, I can easily invent a fine excuse for being in that room. For two pins I'll incriminate you! See? Be reasonable—for if it comes to a contest of brains, you haven't a rabbit's chance against a fox. Tell me all about the will—and what you've done. You've got to—for, by the Lord Harry!—I'm going to have my share. Come, now!"

Pratt stood, in a little hollow wherein they had paused, and thought, rapidly and angrily. There was no doubt about it—he was trapped. This fearful scoundrel at his side, who boasted of his cleverness, would stick to him like a leach—he would have to share. All his own smart schemes for exploiting Mrs. Mallathorpe, for ensuring himself a competence for life, were knocked on the head. There was no helping it—he would have to tell—and to share. And so, sullenly, resentfully, he told.

Parrawhite listened in silence, taking in every point. Pratt, knowing that concealment was useless, told the truth about everything, concisely, but omitting nothing.

"All right!" remarked Parrawhite at the end, "Now, then, what terms do you mean to insist on?"

"What's the good of going into that?" growled Pratt. "Now that you've stuck your foot in it, what do my terms matter?"

"Quite right," agreed Parrawhite, "They don't. What matter is—our terms. Now let me suggest—no, insist on—what they must be. Cash! Do you know why I insist on that? No? Then I'll tell you. Because this young barrister chap, Collingwood, has evidently got some suspicion of—something."

"I can't see it," said Pratt uneasily. "He was only curious to know what that letter was about."

"Never mind," continued Parrawhite. "He had some suspicion—or he wouldn't have gone out there almost as soon as he reached Barford after his grandfather's death. And even if suspicion is put to sleep for awhile, it can easily be reawakened, so—cash! We must profit at once— before any future risk arises. But—what terms were you thinking of?"

"Stewardship of this estate for life," muttered Pratt gloomily.

"With the risk of some discovery being made, some time, any time!" sneered Parrawhite. "Where are your brains, man? The old fellow, John Mallathorpe, probably made a draft or two of that will before he did his fair copy—he may have left those drafts among his papers."

"If he did, Mrs. Mallathorpe 'ud find 'em," said Pratt slowly. "I don't believe there's the slightest risk. I've figured everything out. I don't believe there's any danger from Collingwood or from anybody—it's impossible! And if we take cash now—we're selling for a penny what we ought to get pounds for."

"The present is much more important than the future, my friend," answered Parrawhite. "To me, at any rate. Now, then, this is my proposal. I'll be with you when this lady calls at your place tomorrow evening. We'll offer her the will, to do what she likes with, for ten thousand pounds. She can find that—quickly. When she pays—as she will!—we share, equally, and then—well, you can go to the devil! I shall go—somewhere else. So that's settled."

"No!" said Pratt.

Parrawhite turned sharply, and Pratt saw a sinister gleam in his eyes.

"Did you say no?" he asked.

"I said—no!" replied Pratt. "I'm not going to take five thousand pounds for a chance that's worth fifty thousand. Hang you!—if you hadn't been a black sneak-thief, as you are, I'd have had the whole thing to myself! And I don't know that I will give way to you. If it comes to it, my word's as good as yours—and I don't believe Eldrick would believe you before me. Pascoe wouldn't anyway. You've got a past!—in quod, I should think—my past's all right. I've a jolly good mind to let you do your worst—after all, I've got the will. And by george! now I come to think of it, you can do your worst! Tell what you like tomorrow morning. I shall tell 'em what you are—a scoundrel."

He turned away at that—and as he turned, Parrawhite, with a queer cry of rage that might have come from some animal which saw its prey escaping, struck out at him with the heavy stick. The blow missed Pratt's head, but it grazed the tip of his ear, and fell slantingly on his left shoulder. And then the anger that had been boiling in Pratt ever since the touch on his arm in the dark lane, burst out in activity, and he turned on his assailant, gripped him by the throat before Parrawhite could move, and after choking and shaking him until his teeth rattled and his breath came in jerking sobs, flung him violently against the masses of stone by which they had been standing.

Pratt was of considerable physical strength. He played cricket and football; he visited a gymnasium thrice a week. His hands had the grip of a blacksmith; his muscles were those of a prize-fighter. He had put more strength than he was aware of into his fierce grip on Parrawhite's throat; he had exerted far more force than he knew he was exerting, when he flung him away. He heard a queer cracking sound as the man struck something, and for the moment he took no notice of it—the pain of that glancing blow on his shoulder was growing acute, and he began to rub it with his free hand and to curse its giver.

"Get up, you fool, and I'll give you some more!" he growled. "I'll teach you to——"

He suddenly noticed the curiously still fashion in which Parrawhite was lying where he had flung him—noticed, too, as a cloud passed the moon and left it unveiled, how strangely white the man's face was. And just as suddenly Pratt forgot his own injury, and dropped on his knees beside his assailant. An instant later, and he knew that he was once more confronting death. For Parrawhite was as dead as Antony Bartle—violent contact of his head with a rock had finished what Pratt had nearly completed with that vicious grip. There was no questioning it, no denying it—Pratt was there in that lonely place, staring half consciously, half in terror, at a dead man.

He stood up at last, cursing Parrawhite with the anger of despair. He had not one scrap of pity for him. All his pity was for himself. That he should have been brought into this!—that this vile little beast, perfect scum that he was, should have led him to what might be the utter ruin of his career!—it was shameful, it was abominable, it was cruel! He felt as if he could cheerfully tear Parrawhite's dead body to pieces. But even as these thoughts came, others of a more important nature crowded on them. For—there lay a dead man, who was not to be put in one's pocket, like a will. It was necessary to hide that thing from the light—ever that light. Within a few hours, morning would break, and lonely and deserted as that place was nowadays, some one might pass that way. Out of sight with him, then!—and quickly.

Pratt was very well acquainted with the spot at which he stood. Those old quarries had a certain picturesqueness. They had become grass-grown; ivy, shrubs, trees had clustered about them—the people who lived in the few houses half a mile away, sometimes walked around them; the children made a playground of the place: Pratt himself had often gone into some quiet corner to read and smoke. And now his quick mind immediately suggested a safe hiding place for this thing that he could not carry away with him, and dare not leave to the morning sun—close by was a pit, formerly used for some quarrying purpose, which was filled, always filled, with water. It was evidently of considerable depth; the water was black in it; the mouth was partly obscured by a maze of shrub and bramble. It had been like that ever since Pratt came to lodge in that part of the district—ten or twelve years before; it would probably remain like that for many a long year to come. That bit of land was absolutely useless and therefore neglected, and as long as rain fell and water drained, that pit would always be filled to its brim.

He remembered something else: also close by where he stood—a heap of old iron things—broken and disused picks, smashed rails, fragments thrown aside when the last of the limestone had been torn out of the quarries. Once more luck was playing into his hands—those odds and ends might have been put there for the very purpose to which he now meant to turn them. And being certain that he was alone, and secure, Pratt proceeded to go about his unpleasant task skilfully and methodically. He fetched a quantity of the iron, fastened it to the dead man's clothing, drew the body, thus weighted, to the edge of the pit, and prepared to slide it into the black water. But there an idea struck him. While he made these preparations he had had hosts of ideas as to his operations next morning—this idea was supplementary to them. Quickly and methodically he removed the contents of Parrawhite's pockets to his own—everything: money, watch and chain, even a ring which the dead man had been evidently vain of. Then he let Parrawhite glide into the water—and after him he sent the heavy stick, carefully fastened to a bar of iron.

Five minutes later, the surface of the water in that pit was as calm and unruffled as ever—not a ripple showed that it had been disturbed. And Pratt made his way out of

the wilderness, swearing that he would never enter it
again.

7. THE SUPREME INDUCEMENT

Pratt was in Eldrick & Pascoe's office soon after half-past eight next morning, and for nearly forty minutes he had the place entirely to himself. But it took only a few of those minutes for him to do what he had carefully planned before he went to bed the previous night. Shutting himself into Eldrick's private room, and making sure that he was alone that time, he immediately opened the drawer in the senior partner's desk, wherein Eldrick, culpably enough, as Parrawhite had sneeringly remarked, was accustomed to put loose money. Eldrick was strangely careless in that way: he would throw money into that drawer in presence of his clerks—notes, gold, silver. If it happened to occur to him, he would take the money out at the end of the afternoon and hand it to Pratt to lock up in the safe; but as often as not, it did not occur. Pratt had more than once ventured on a hint which was almost a remonstrance, and Eldrick had paid no attention to him. He was a careless, easy-going man in many respects, Eldrick, and liked to do things in his own way. And after all, as Pratt had decided, when he found that his hints were not listened to, it was Eldrick's own affair if he liked to leave the money lying about.

There was money lying about in that drawer when Pratt drew it open; it was never locked, day or night, or, if it was, the key was left in it. As soon as he opened it, he saw gold—two or three sovereigns—and silver—a little pile of it. And, under a letter weight, four banknotes of ten pounds each. But this was precisely what Pratt had expected to see; he himself had handed banknotes, gold, and silver to Eldrick the previous evening, just after receiving them from a client who had called to pay his bill. And he had seen Eldrick place them in the drawer, as usual, and soon afterwards Eldrick had walked out, saying he was going to the club, and he had never returned.

What Pratt now did was done as the result of careful thought and deliberation. There was a cheque-book lying on top of some papers in the drawer; he took it up and tore three cheques out of it. Then he picked up the bank-notes, tore them and the abstracted blank cheques into pieces, and dropped the pieces in the fire recently lighted by the caretaker. He watched these fragments burn, and then he put the gold and silver in his hip-pocket, where he already carried a good deal of his own, and walked out.

Nine o'clock brought the office-boy; a quarter-past nine brought the clerks; at ten o'clock Eldrick walked in. According to custom, Pratt went into Eldrick's room with the letters, and went through them with him. One of them contained a legal document over which the solicitor frowned a little.

"Ask Parrawhite's opinion about that," he said presently, indicating a marked paragraph.

"Parrawhite has not come in this morning, sir," observed Pratt, gathering up letters and papers. "I'll draw his attention to it when he arrives."

He went into the outer office, only to be summoned back to Eldrick a few minutes later. The senior partner was standing by his desk, looking a little concerned, and, thought Pratt, decidedly uncomfortable. He motioned the clerk to close the door.

"Has Parrawhite come?" he asked.

"No," replied Pratt, "Not yet, Mr. Eldrick."

"Is—is he usually late?" inquired Eldrick.

"Usually quite punctual—half-past nine," said Pratt.

Eldrick glanced at his watch; then at his clerk.

"Didn't you give me some cash last night?" he asked.

"Forty-three pounds nine," answered Pratt. "Thompson's bill of costs—he paid it yesterday afternoon."

Eldrick looked more uncomfortable than ever.

"Well—the fact is," he said, "I—I meant to hand it to you to put in the safe, Pratt, but I didn't come back from the club. And—it's gone!"

Pratt simulated concern—but not astonishment. And Eldrick pulled open the drawer, and waved a hand over it.

"I put it down there," he said. "Very careless of me, no doubt—but nothing of this sort has ever happened before, and—however, there's the unpleasant fact, Pratt. The money's gone!"

Pratt, who had hastily turned over the papers and other contents of the drawer, shook his head and used his privilege as an old and confidential servant. "I've always said, sir, that it was a great mistake to leave loose money lying about," he remarked mournfully. "If there'd only been a practice of letting me lock anything of that sort up in the safe every night—and this chequebook, too, sir— then——"

"I know—I know!" said Eldrick. "Very reprehensible on my part—I'm afraid I am careless—no doubt of it. But——"

He in his turn was interrupted by Pratt, who was turning over the cheque-book.

"Some cheque forms have been taken out of this," he said. "Three! at the end. Look there, sir!"

Eldrick uttered an exclamation of intense annoyance and disgust. He looked at the despoiled cheque-book, and flung it into the drawer.

"Pratt!" he said, turning half appealingly, half confidentially to the clerk. "Don't say a word of this— above all, don't mention it to Mr. Pascoe. It's my fault and I must make the forty-three pounds good. Pratt, I'm afraid this is Parrawhite's work. I—well, I may as well tell you—he'd been in trouble before he came here. I gave him another chance—I'd known him, years ago. I thought he'd go straight. But—I fear he's been tempted. He may have seen me leave money about. Was he in here last night?"

Pratt pointed to a document which lay on Eldrick's desk.

"He came in here to leave that for your perusal," he answered. "He was in here—alone—a minute or two before he left."

All these lies came readily and naturally—and Eldrick swallowed each. He shook his head.

"My fault—all my fault!" he said. "Look here—keep it quiet. But—do you know where Parrawhite has lived—lodged?"

"No!" replied Pratt. "Some of the others may, though!"

"Try to find out—quickly," continued Eldrick; "Then, make some excuse to go out—take papers somewhere, or something—and find if he's left his lodgings! I—I don't want to set the police on him. He was a decent fellow, once. See what you can make out, Pratt. In strict secrecy, you know—-I do not want this to go further."

Pratt could have danced for joy when he presently went out into the town. There would be no hue-and-cry after Parrawhite—none! Eldrick would accept the fact that Parrawhite had robbed him and flown—and Parrawhite would never be heard of—never mentioned again. It was the height of good luck for him. Already he had got rid of any small scraps of regret or remorse about the killing of his fellow-clerk. Why should he be sorry? The scoundrel had tried to murder him, thinking no doubt that he had the will on him. And he had not meant to kill him—what he had done, he had done in self-defence. No—everything was working most admirably—Parrawhite's previous bad record, Eldrick's carelessness and his desire to shut things up: it was all good. From that day forward, Parrawhite would be as if he had never been. Pratt was not even afraid of the body being discovered—though he believed that it would remain where it was for ever—for the probability was that the authorities would fill up that pit with earth and stones.

But if it was brought to light? Why, the explanation was simple.

Parrawhite, having robbed his employer, had been robbed himself, possibly by men with whom he had been drinking, and had been murdered in the bargain. No suspicion could attach to him, Pratt—he had nothing to fear—nothing!

For the form of the thing, he called at the place whereat Parrawhite had lodged—they had seen nothing of him since the previous morning. They were poor, cheap lodgings in a mean street. The woman of the house said that Parrawhite had gone out as usual the morning before, and had never been in again. In order to find out all he could, Pratt asked if he had left much behind him in the way of belongings, and—just as he had expected—he learned that Parrawhite's personal property was remarkably limited: he possessed only one suit of clothes and not over much besides, said the landlady.

"Is there aught wrong?" she asked, when Pratt had finished his questions. "Are you from where he worked?"

"That's it," answered Pratt, "And he hasn't turned up this morning, and we think he's left the town. Owe you anything, missis?"

"Nay, nothing much," she replied. "Ten shillings 'ud cover it, mister."

Pratt gave her half a sovereign. It was not out of consideration for her, nor as a concession to Parrawhite's memory: it was simply to stop her from coming down to Eldrick & Pascoe's.

"Well, I don't think you'll see him again," he remarked. "And I dare say you won't care if you don't."

He turned away then, but before he had gone far, the woman called him back.

"What am I to do with his bits of things, mister, if he doesn't come back?" she asked.

"Aught you please," answered Pratt, indifferently. "Throw 'em on the dust-heap."

As he went back to the centre of the town, he occupied himself in considering his attitude to Mrs. Mallathorpe when she called on him that evening. In spite of his own previous notion, and of his carefully-worked-out scheme about the stewardship, he had been impressed by what Parrawhite has said as to the wisdom of selling the will for cash. Pratt did not believe that there was anything in the Collingwood suggestion—no doubt whatever, he had decided, that old Bartle had meant to tell Mrs. Mallathorpe of his discovery when she called in answer to his note, but as he had died before she could call, and as he had told nobody but him, Pratt, what possible danger could there be from Collingwood? And a stewardship for life appealed to him. He knew, from observation of the world, what a fine thing it is to have a certainty.

Once he became steward and agent of the Normandale Grange estate, he would stick there, until he had saved a tidy heap of money. Then he would retire—with a pension and a handsome present—and enjoy himself. To be provided for, for life!—what more could a wise man want? And yet—there was something in what that devil Parrawhite had urged.

For there was a risk—however small—of discovery, and if discovery were made, there would be a nice penalty to pay. It might, after all, be better to sell the will outright—for as much ready money as ever he could get, and to take his gains far away, and start out on a career elsewhere. After all, there was much to be said for the old proverb. The only question was—was the bird in hand worth the two; or the money, which he believed he would net in the bush?

Pratt's doubts on this point were settled in a curious fashion. He had reached the centre of the town in his return to Eldrick's, and there, in the fashionable shopping street, he ran up against an acquaintance. He and the acquaintance stopped and chatted—about nothing. And as they lounged on the curb, a smart victoria drew up close by, and out of it, alone, stepped a girl who immediately attracted Pratt's eyes. He watched her across the pavement; he watched her into the shop. And his companion laughed.

"That's the sort!" he remarked flippantly. "If you and I had one each, old man—what?"

"Who is she?" demanded Pratt.

The acquaintance stared at him in surprise.

"What!" he exclaimed. "You don't know. That's Miss Mallathorpe."

"I didn't know," said Pratt. "Fact!"

He waited until Nesta Mallathorpe came out and drove away—so that he could get another and a closer look at her. And when she was gone, he went slowly back to the office, his mind made up. Risk or no risk, he would carry out his original notion. Whatever Mrs. Mallathorpe might offer, he would stick to his idea of close and intimate connection with Normandale Grange.

8. TERMS

Mrs. Mallathorpe, left to face the situation which Pratt had revealed to her in such sudden and startling fashion, had been quick to realize its seriousness. It had not taken much to convince her that the clerk knew what he was talking about. She had no doubt whatever that he was right when he said that the production of John Mallathorpe's will would mean dispossession to her children, and through them to herself. Nor had she any doubt, either, of Pratt's intention to profit by his discovery. She saw that he was a young man of determination, not at all scrupulous, eager to seize on anything likely to turn to his own advantage. She was, in short, at his mercy. And she had no one to turn to. Her son was weak, purposeless, almost devoid of character; he cared for nothing beyond ease and comfort, and left everything to her so long as he was allowed to do what he liked. She dared not confide in him—he was not fit to be entrusted with such a secret, nor endowed with the courage to carry it boldly and unflinchingly. Nor dare she confide it to her daughter—Nesta was as strong as her brother was weak: Mrs. Mallathorpe had only told the plain truth when she said to Pratt that if her daughter knew of the will she would go straight to the two trustees. No—she would have to do everything herself. And she could do nothing save under Pratt's dictation. So long as he had that will in his possession, he could make her agree to whatever terms he liked to insist upon.

She spent a sleepless night, resolving all sorts of plans; she resolved more plans and schemes during the day which followed. But they all ended at the same point—Pratt. All the future depended upon—Pratt. And by the end of the day it had come to this—she must make a determined effort to buy Pratt clean out, so that she could get the will into her own possession and destroy it. She knew that she could easily find the necessary money—Harper Mallathorpe had such a natural dislike of all business matters and was so little fitted to attend to them that he was only too well content to leave everything relating to the estate and the mill at Barford to his mother. Up to that time Mrs. Mallathorpe had managed the affairs of both, and she had large sums at her disposal, out of which she could pay Pratt without even Harper being aware that she was paying him anything. And surely no young man in Pratt's position—a mere clerk, earning a few pounds a week—would refuse a big sum of ready money! It seemed incredible to her—and she went into Barford towards evening hoping that by the time she returned the will would have been burned to grey ashes.

Mrs. Mallathorpe used some ingenuity in making her visit to Pratt. Giving out that she was going to see a friend in Barford, of whose illness she had just heard, she drove into the town, and on arriving near the Town Hall dismissed her carriage, with orders to the coachman to put up his horses at a certain livery stable, and to meet her at the same place at a specified time. Then she went away on foot, and drew a thick veil over her face before hiring a cab in which she drove up to the outskirt on which Pratt had his lodging. She was still veiled when Pratt's landlady showed her into the clerk's sitting-room.

"Is it safe here?" she asked at once. "Is there no fear of anybody hearing what we may say?"

"None!" answered Pratt reassuringly. "I know these folks—I've lived here several years. And nobody could hear however much they put their ears to the keyhole. Good thick old walls, these, Mrs. Mallathorpe, and a solid door. We're as safe here as we were in your study last night."

Mrs. Mallathorpe sat down in the chair which Pratt politely drew near his fire. She raised her veil and looked at him, and the clerk saw at once how curious and eager she was.

"That—will!" she said, in a low voice. "Let me see it—first."

"One moment," answered Pratt. "First—you understand that I'm not going to let you handle it. I'll hold it before you, so you can read it. Second—you give me your promise—I'm trusting you—that you'll make no attempt to seize it. It's not going out of my hands."

"I'm only a woman—and you're a strong man," she retorted sullenly.

"Quite so," said Pratt. "But women have a trick of snatching at things. And—if you please—you'll do exactly what I tell you to do. Put your hands behind you! If I see you make the least movement with them—back goes the will into my pocket!"

If Pratt had looked more closely at her just then, he would have taken warning from the sudden flash of hatred and resentment which swept across Mrs. Mallathorpe's face—it would have told him that he was dealing with a dangerous woman who would use her wits to circumvent and beat him—if not now, then later. But he was moving the gas bracket over the mantelpiece, and he did not see.

"Very well—but I had no intention of touching it," said Mrs. Mallathorpe. "All I want is to see it—and read it."

She obediently followed out Pratt's instructions, and standing in front of her he produced the will, unfolded it, and held it at a convenient distance before her eyes. He watched her closely, as she read it, and he saw her grow very pale.

"Take your time—read it over two or three times," he said quietly. "Get it well into your mind, Mrs. Mallathorpe."

She nodded her head at last, and Pratt stepped back, folded up the will, and turning to a heavy box which lay open on the table, placed it within, under lock and key.

And that done, he turned back and took a chair, close to his visitor.

"Safe there, Mrs. Mallathorpe," he said with a glance that was both reassuring and cunning. "But only for the night. I keep a few securities of my own at one of the banks in the town—never mind which—and that will shall be deposited with them tomorrow morning."

Mrs. Mallathorpe shook her head.

"No!" she said. "Because—you'll come to terms with me."

Pratt shook his head, too, and he laughed.

"Of course I shall come to terms with you," he answered. "But they'll be my terms—and they don't include any giving up of that document. That's flat, Mrs. Mallathorpe!"

"Not if I make it worth your while?" she asked. "Listen!—you don't know what ready money I can command. Ready money, I tell you—cash down, on the spot!"

"I've a pretty good notion," responded Pratt. "It's generally understood in the town that your son's a mere figure-head, and that you're the real boss of the whole show. I know that you're at the mill four times a week, and that the managers are under your thumb. I know that you manage everything connected with the estate. So, of course, I know you've lots of ready money at your disposal."

"And I know that you don't earn more than four or five pounds a week, at the outside," said Mrs. Mallathorpe quietly. "Come, now—just think what a nice, convenient thing it would be to a young man of your age to have—a capital. Capital! It would be the making of you. You could go right away—to London, say, and start out on whatever you liked. Be sensible—sell me that paper—and be done with the whole thing."

"No!" replied Pratt.

Mrs. Mallathorpe looked at him for a full moment. She was a shrewd judge of character, and she felt that

Pratt was one of those men who are hard to stir from a position once adopted. But she had to make her effort—and she made it in what she thought the most effective way.

"I'll give you five thousand pounds—cash—for it," she said. "Meet me with it tomorrow—anywhere you like in the town—any time you like—and I'll hand you the money—in notes."

"No!" said Pratt. "No!"

Once more she looked at him. And Pratt looked back—and smiled.

"When I say no, I mean no," he went on. "And I never meant 'No' more firmly than I do now."

"I don't believe you," she answered, affecting a doubt which she certainly did not feel. "You're only holding out for more money."

"If I were holding out for more money, Mrs. Mallathorpe," replied Pratt, "if I meant to sell you that will for cash payment, I should have stated my terms to you last night. I should have said precisely how much I wanted—and I shouldn't have budged from the amount. Mrs. Mallathorpe!—it's no good. I've got my own schemes, and my own ideas—and I'm going to carry 'em out. I want you to appoint me steward to your property, your affairs, for life."

"Life!" she exclaimed. "Life!"

"My life," answered Pratt. "And let me tell you—you'll find me a first-class man—a good, faithful, honest servant. I'll do well by you and yours. You'll never regret it as long as you live. It'll be the best day's work you've ever done. I'll look after your son's interests—everybody's interests—as if they were my own. As indeed," he added, with a sly glance, "they will be."

Mrs. Mallathorpe realized the finality, the resolve, in all this—but she made one more attempt.

"Ten thousand!" she said. "Come, now!—think what ten thousand pounds in cash would mean to you!"

"No—nor twenty thousand," replied Pratt. "I've made up my mind. I'll have my own terms. It's no use—not one bit of use—haggling or discussing matters further. I'm in possession of the will—and therefore of the situation, Mrs. Mallathorpe, you've just got to do what I tell you!"

He got up from his chair, and going over to a side-table took from it a blotting-pad, some writing paper and a pencil. For the moment his back was turned—and again he did not see the look of almost murderous hatred which came into his visitor's eyes; had he seen and understood it, he might even then have reconsidered matters and taken Mrs. Mallathorpe's last offer. But the look had gone when he turned again, and he noticed nothing as he handed over the writing materials.

"What are these for?" she asked.

"You'll see in a moment," replied Pratt, reseating himself, and drawing his chair a little nearer her own. "Now listen—because it's no good arguing any more. You're going to give me that stewardship and agency. You'll simply tell your son that it's absolutely necessary to have a steward. He'll agree. If he doesn't, no matter— you'll convince him. Now, then, we must do it in a fashion that won't excite any suspicion. Thus—in a few days—say next week—you'll insert in the Barford papers—all three of them—the advertisement I'm going to dictate to you. We'll put it in the usual, formal phraseology. Write this down, if you please, Mrs. Mallathorpe."

He dictated an advertisement, setting forth the requirements of which he had spoken, and Mrs. Mallathorpe obeyed him and wrote. She hated Pratt more than ever at that moment—there was a quiet, steadfast implacability about him that made her feel helpless. But she restrained all sign of it, and when she had done his bidding she looked at him as calmly as he looked at her.

"I am to insert this in the Barford papers next week," she said. "And—what then?"

"Then you'll get a lot of applications for the job," chuckled Pratt. "There'll be mine amongst them. You can throw most of 'em in the fire. Keep a few for form's sake. Profess to discuss them with Mr. Harper—but let the discussion be all on your side. I'll send two or three good testimonials—you'll incline to me from the first. You'll send for me. Your interview with me will be highly satisfactory. And you'll give me the appointment."

"And—your terms?" asked Mrs. Mallathorpe. Now that her own scheme had failed, she seemed quite placable to all Pratt's proposals—a sure sign of danger to him if he had only known it. "Better let me know them now—and have done with it."

"Quite so," agreed Pratt. "But first of all—can you keep this secret to yourself and me? The money part, any way?"

"I can—and shall," she answered.

"Good!" said Pratt. "Very well. I want a thousand a year. Also I want two rooms—and a business room—at the Grange. I shall not interfere with you or your family, or your domestic arrangements, but I shall expect to have all my meals served to me from your kitchen, and to have one of your servants at my disposal. I know the Grange— I've been over it more than once. There's much more room there than you can make use of. Give me the rooms I want in one of the wings. I shan't disturb any of you. You'll never see me except on business—and if you want to."

Again the calm acquiescence which would have surprised some men. Why Pratt failed to be surprised by it was because he was just then feeling exceedingly triumphant—he believed that Mrs. Mallathorpe was, metaphorically, at his feet. He had more than a little vanity in him, and it pleased him greatly, that dictating of terms: he saw himself a conqueror, with his foot on the neck of his victim.

"Is that all, then?" asked the visitor.

"All!" answered Pratt.

Mrs. Mallathorpe calmly folded up the draft advertisement and placed it in her purse. Then she rose and adjusted her veil.

"Then—there is nothing to be done until I get your answer to this—your application?" she asked. "Very well."

Pratt showed her out, and walked to the cab with her. He went back to his rooms highly satisfied—and utterly ignorant of what Mrs. Mallathorpe was thinking as she drove away.

9. UNTIL NEXT SPRING

Within a week of his sudden death in Eldrick's private office, old Antony Bartle was safely laid in the tomb under the yew-tree of which Mrs. Clough had spoken with such appreciation, and his grandson had entered into virtual possession of all that he had left. Collingwood found little difficulty in settling his grandfather's affairs. Everything had been left to him: he was sole executor as well as sole residuary legatee. He found his various tasks made uncommonly easy. Another bookseller in the town hurried to buy the entire stock and business, goodwill, book debts, everything—Collingwood was free of all responsibility of the shop in Quagg Alley within a few days of the old man's funeral. And when he had made a handsome present to the housekeeper, a suitable one to the shop-boy, and paid his grandfather's last debts, he was free to depart—a richer man by some five-and-twenty thousand pounds than when he hurried down to Barford in response to Eldrick's telegram.

He sat in Eldrick's office one afternoon, winding up his affairs with him. There were certain things that Eldrick & Pascoe would have to do; as for himself it was necessary for him to get back to London.

"There's something I want to propose to you," said Eldrick, when they had finished the immediate business. "You're going to practise, of course?"

"Of course!" replied Collingwood, with a laugh. "If I get the chance!"

"You'll get the chance," said Eldrick. "What were you going in for?"

"Commercial law—company law—as a special thing," answered Collingwood.

"Why?"

"I'll tell you what it is," continued Eldrick eagerly. "There's a career for you if you'll take my advice. Leave London—come down here and take chambers in the town, and go the North-Eastern Circuit. I'll promise you—for our firm alone—plenty of work. You'll get more—there's lots of work waiting here for a good, smart young barrister. Ah!—you smile, but I know what I'm talking about. You don't know Barford men. They believe in the old adage that one should look at home before going abroad. They're terribly litigious, too, and if you were here, on the spot, they'd give you work. What do you say, Collingwood?"

"That sounds very tempting. But I was thinking of sticking to London."

"Not one hundredth part of the chance in London that there is here!" affirmed Eldrick. "We badly want two or three barristers in this place. A man who's really well up in commercial and company law would soon have his hands full. There's work, I tell you. Take my advice, and come!"

"I couldn't come—in any case—for a few months," said Collingwood, musingly. "Of course, if you really think there's an opening——"

"I know there is!" asserted Eldrick. "I'll guarantee you lots of work—our work. I'm sick of fetching men down all the way from town, or getting them from Leeds. Come!—and you'll see."

"I might come in a few months' time, and try things for a year or two," replied Collingwood. "But I'm off to India, you know, next week, and I shall be away until the end of spring—four months or so."

"To India!" exclaimed Eldrick. "What are you going to do there?"

"Sir John Standridge," said Collingwood, mentioning a famous legal luminary of the day, "is going out to Hyderabad to take certain evidence, and hold a sort of inquiry, in a big case, and I'm going with him as his secretary and assistant—I was in his chambers for two years, you know. We leave next week, and we shall not be back until the end of April."

"Lucky man!" remarked the solicitor. "Well, when you return, don't forget what I've said. Come back!—you'll not regret it. Come and settle down. Bye-the-bye, you're not engaged, are you?"

"Engaged?" said Collingwood. "To what—to whom—what do you mean?"

"Engaged to be married," answered Eldrick coolly. "You're not? Good! If you want a wife, there's Miss Mallathorpe. Nice, clever girl, my boy—and no end of what Barford folk call brass. The very woman for you."

"Do you Barford people ever think of anything else but what you call brass?" asked Collingwood, laughing.

"Sometimes," replied Eldrick. "But it's generally of something that nothing but brass can bring or produce. After all, a rich wife isn't a despicable thing, nowadays. You've seen this young lady?"

"I've been there once," asserted Collingwood.

"Go again—before you leave," counselled Eldrick. "You're just the right man. Listen to the counsels of the wise! And while you're in India, think well over my other advice. I tell you there's a career for you, here in the North, that you'd never get in town."

Collingwood left him and went out—to find a motorcar and drive off to Normandale Grange, not because Eldrick had advised him to go, but because of his promise to Harper and Nesta Mallathorpe. And once more he found Nesta alone, and though he had no spice of vanity in his composition it seemed to him that she was glad when he walked into the room in which they had first met.

"My mother is out—gone to town—to the mill," she said. "And Harper is knocking around the park with a gun—killing rabbits—and time. He'll be in presently to tea—and he'll be delighted to see you. Are you going to stay in Barford much longer?"

"I'm going up to town this evening—seven o'clock train," answered Collingwood, watching her keenly. "All my business is finished now—for the present."

"But—you'll be coming back?" she asked.

"Perhaps," he said. "I may come back—after a while."

"When you do come back," she went on, a little hurriedly, "will you come and see us again? I—it's difficult to explain—but I do wish Harper knew more men—the right sort of men. Do you understand?"

"You mean—he needs more company?"

"More company of the right kind. He doesn't know many nice men. And he has so little to occupy him. He's no head for business—my mother attends to all that—and he doesn't care much about sport—and when he goes into Barford he only hangs about the club, and, I'm afraid, at two or three of the hotels there, and—it's not good for him."

"Can't you get him interested in anything?" suggested Collingwood. "Is there nothing that he cares about?"

"He never did care about anything," replied Nesta with a sigh. "He's apathetic! He just moves along. Sometimes I think he was born half asleep, and he's never been really awakened. Pity, isn't it?"

"Considering everything—a great pity," agreed Collingwood. "But—he's provided for."

Nesta gave him a swift glance.

"It might have been a good deal better for him if he hadn't been provided for!" she said. "He'd have just had to do something, then. But—if you come back, you'll come here sometimes?"

"Of course!" answered Collingwood. "And if I come back, it will probably be to stop here. Mr. Eldrick says there's a lot of work going begging in Barford—for a smart young barrister well up in commercial law. Perhaps I may try to come up to his standard—I'm certainly young, but I don't know whether I'm smart."

"Better come and try," she said, smiling. "Don't forget that I've seen you look the part, anyway—your wig and gown suited you very well."

"Theatrical properties," he replied, laughing. "The wig was too small, and the gown too long. Well—we'll see. But in the meantime, I'm going away for four months—to India."

"To India—four months!" she exclaimed. "That sounds nice."

"Legal business," said Collingwood. "I shall be back about the end of April—and then I shall probably come down here again, and seriously consider Eldrick's suggestion. I'm very much inclined to take it."

"Then—you'd leave London?" she asked.

"I've little to leave there," replied Collingwood. "My father and mother are dead, and I've no brothers, no sisters—no very near relations. Sounds lonely, doesn't it?"

"One can feel lonely when one has relations," said Nesta.

"Are you saying that from—experience?" he asked.

"I often wish I had more to do," she answered frankly. "What's the use of denying it? I've next to nothing to do, here. I liked my work at the hospital—I was busy all day. Here——"

"If I were you," interrupted Collingwood, "I'd set to work nursing in another fashion. Look after your brother! Get him going at something—even if it's playing golf. Play with him! It would do him—and you—all the good in the world if you got thoroughly infatuated with even a game. Don't you see?"

"You mean—anything is better than nothing," she replied. "All right—I'll try that, anyway. For—I'm anxious about Harper. All this money!—and no occupation!"

Collingwood, who was sitting near the windows, looked out across the park and into the valley beyond.

"I should have thought that a man who had come into an estate like this would have found plenty of occupation," he remarked. "What is there, beside the house and this park?"

Nesta, who had busied herself with some fancy-work since Collingwood's entrance, laid it down and came to the windows. She pointed to certain roofs and gables in the valley.

"There's the whole village of Normandale," she said. "A busy place, no doubt, but it's all Harper's—he's lord of the manor. He's patron of the living, too. It's all his— farms, cottages, everything. And the woods, and the park, and this house, and a stretch of the moors, as well. Of course, he ought to find a lot to do—but he doesn't. Perhaps because my mother does everything. She really is a business woman."

Collingwood looked out over the area which Nesta had indicated. Harper Mallathorpe, he calculated, must be possessed of some three or four thousand acres.

"A fine property!" he said. "He's a very fortunate fellow!"

Just then this very fortunate fellow came in. His face, dull enough as he entered, lighted up at sight of a visitor, and fell again when Collingwood explained that his visit was a mere flying one, and that he was returning to London that night. Collingwood led him on to the project which he had mentioned at his previous visit—the making of golf links in the park, and pointed out, as a devotee of the sport, what a fine course could be made. Before he left he had succeeded in arousing like interest in Harper—he promised to go into the matter, and to employ a man whom Collingwood recommended as an expert in laying out golf courses.

"You'll have got your greens in something like order by this time next year, if you start operations soon," said Collingwood. "And then, if I settle down at Barford, I'll come out now and then, if you'll let me."

"Let you!" exclaimed Harper. "By Jove!—we're only too glad to have anybody out here—aren't we, Nesta?"

"We shall always be glad to see Mr. Collingwood," said Nesta.

Collingwood went away with that last intimation warm in his memory. He had an idea that the girl meant what she said—and for a moment he was sorry that he was going to India. He might have settled down at Barford there and then, and—but at that he laughed at himself.

"A young woman with several thousands a year of her own!" he said. "Of course, she'll marry some big pot in the county. They feel a little lonely, those two, just now, because everything's new to them, and they're new to their changed circumstances. But when I get back—ah!— I guess they'll have got plenty of people around them."

And he determined, being a young man of sense, not to think any more—for already he had thought a good deal of Nesta Mallathorpe, until he returned from his Indian travels. Let him attend to his business, and leave possibilities until they came nearer.

"All the same." he mused, as he drew near the town again, "I'm pretty sure I shall come back here next spring—I feel like it."

He called in at Eldrick's office on his way to the hotel, to take some documents which had been preparing for him. It was then late in the afternoon, and no one but Pratt was there—Pratt, indeed, had been waiting until Collingwood called.

"Going back to town, Mr. Collingwood?" asked Pratt as he handed over a big envelope. "When shall we have the pleasure of seeing you again, sir?"

Something in the clerk's tone made Collingwood think—he could not tell why—that Pratt was fishing for information. And—also for reasons which he could not explain—Collingwood had taken a curious dislike to Pratt, and was not inclined to give him any confidence.

"I don't know," he answered, a little icily. "I am leaving for India next week."

He bade the clerk a formal farewell and went off, and Pratt locked the office door and slowly followed him downstairs.

"To India!" he said to himself, watching the young barrister's retreating figure. "To India, eh? For a time—or for—what?"

Anyway, that was good news, Pratt had seen in Collingwood a possible rival.

10. THE FOOT-BRIDGE

Collingwood's return to London was made on a Friday evening: next day he began the final preparations for his departure to India on the following Thursday. He was looking forward to his journey and his stay in India with keen expectation. He would have the society of a particularly clever and brilliant man; they were to break their journey in Italy and in Egypt; he would enjoy exceptional facilities for seeing the native life of India; he would gain valuable experience. It was a chance at which any young man would have jumped, and Collingwood had been greatly envied when it was known that Sir John Standridge had offered it to him. And yet he was conscious that if he could have done precisely what he desired, he would have stayed longer at Barford, in order to see more of Nesta Mallathorpe. Already it seemed a long time to the coming spring, when he would be back—and free to go North again.

But Collingwood was fated to go North once more much sooner than he had dreamed of. As he sat at breakfast in his rooms on the Monday morning after his departure from Barford, turning over his newspaper with no particular aim or interest, his attention was suddenly and sharply arrested by a headline. Even that headline might not have led him to read what lay beneath. But in the same instant in which he saw it he also saw a name— Mallathorpe. In the next he knew that heavy trouble had fallen on Normandale Grange, the very day after he had left it.

This is what Collingwood read as he sat, coffee-cup in one hand, newspaper in the other—staring at the lines of unleaded type:

TRAGIC FATE OF YOUNG YORKSHIRE SQUIRE

"A fatal accident, of a particularly sad and disturbing nature, occurred near Barford, Yorkshire, on Saturday. About four o'clock on Saturday afternoon, Mr. Linford Pratt, managing clerk to Messrs. Eldrick & Pascoe, Solicitors, of Barford, who was crossing the grounds of Normandale Grange on his way to a business appointment, discovered the dead body of Mr. H. J. Mallathorpe, the owner of the Normandale Estate, lying in a roadway which at that point is spanned, forty feet above, by a narrow foot-bridge. The latter is an ancient construction of wood, and there is no doubt that it was in extremely bad repair, and had given way when the unfortunate young gentleman, who was out shooting in his park, stepped upon it. Mr. Mallathorpe, who was only twenty-four years of age, succeeded to the Normandale estates, one of the finest properties in the neighbourhood of Barford, about two years ago, under somewhat romantic—and also tragic— circumstances, their previous owner, his uncle, Mr. John Mallathorpe, a well-known Barford manufacturer, meeting a sudden death by the falling of his mill chimney—a catastrophe which also caused the deaths of several of his employees. Mr. John Mallathorpe died intestate, and the estate at Normandale passed to the young gentleman who met such a sad fate on Saturday afternoon. Mr. H.J. Mallathorpe was unmarried, and it is understood that Normandale (which includes the village of that name, the advowson of the living, and about four thousand acres of land) now becomes the property of his sister, Miss Nesta Mallathorpe."

Collingwood set down his cup, and dropped the newspaper. He was but half way through his breakfast, but all his appetite had vanished. All that he was conscious of was that here was trouble and grief for a girl in whom—it was useless to deny it—he had already begun to take a warm interest. And suddenly he started from his chair and snatched up a railway guide. As he turned over its pages, he thought rapidly. The preparations for his journey to India were almost finished—what was not done he could do in a few hours. He had no further appointment with Sir John Standridge until nine o'clock on Thursday morning, when he was to meet him at the train for Dover and Paris. Monday— Tuesday—Wednesday—he had three days—ample time to hurry down to Normandale, to do what he could to help there, and to get back in time to make his own last arrangements. He glanced at his watch—he had forty minutes in which to catch an express from King's Cross to Barford. Without further delay he picked up a suit-case which was already packed and set out for the station.

He was in Barford soon after two o'clock—in Eldrick's office by half-past two. Eldrick shook his head at sight of him.

"I can guess what's brought you down, Collingwood," he said. "Good of you, of course—I don't think they've many friends out there."

"I can scarcely call myself that—yet," answered Collingwood. "But—I thought I might be of some use. I'll drive out there presently. But first—how was it?"

Eldrick shook his head.

"Don't know much more than what the papers say," he answered. "There's an old foot-bridge there that spans a road in the park—road cut through a ravine. They say it was absolutely rotten, and the poor chap's weight was evidently too much for it. And there was a drop of forty feet into a hard road. Extraordinary thing that nobody on the estate seems to have known of the dangerous condition of that bridge!—but they say it was little used— simply a link between one plantation and another. However;—it's done, now. Our clerk—Pratt, you know— found the body. Hadn't been dead five minutes, Pratt says."

"What was Pratt doing there?" asked Collingwood.

"Oh, business of his own," replied Eldrick. "Not ours. There was an advertisement in Saturday's papers which set out that a steward was wanted for the Normandale

estate, and Pratt mentioned it to me in the morning that
he thought of applying for the job if we'd give him a good
testimonial. I suppose he'd gone out there to see about the
preliminaries. Anyway, he was walking through the park
when he found young Mallathorpe's body. I understand
he made himself very useful, too, and I've sent him out
there again today, to do anything he can—smart chap,
Pratt!"

"Possibly, then, there is nothing I can do," remarked
Collingwood.

"I should say you'll do a lot by merely going there,"
answered Eldrick. "As I said just now, they've few friends,
and no relations, and I hear that Mrs. Mallathorpe is
absolutely knocked over. Go, by all means—a bit of
sympathy goes a long way on these occasions. I say!—
what a regular transformation an affair of this sort
produces. Do you know, that young fellow, just like his
uncle, had not made any will! Fact!—I had it from
Robson, their solicitor, this very morning. The whole of
the estate comes to the sister, of course—she and the
mother will share the personal property. By that lad's
death, Nesta Mallathorpe becomes one of the wealthiest
young women in Yorkshire!"

Collingwood made no reply to this communication.
But as he drove off to Normandale Grange, it was fresh in
his mind. And it was not very pleasant to him. One of the
wealthiest young women in Yorkshire!—and he was
already realizing that he would like to make Nesta
Mallathorpe his wife: it was because he felt what he did
for her that he had rushed down to do anything he could
that would be of help. Supposing—only supposing—that
people—anybody—said that he was fortune-hunting!
Somewhat unduly sensitive, proud, almost to a fault, he
felt his cheek redden at the thought, and for a moment he
wished that old John Mallathorpe's wealth had never
passed to his niece. But then he sneered at himself for his
presumption.

"Ass!" he said. "She's never even thought of me—in that way, most likely! Anyway, I'm a stupid fool for thinking of these things at present."

But he knew, within a few minutes of entering the big, desolate-looking house, that Nesta had been thinking of him. She came to him in the room where they had first met, and quietly gave him her hand.

"I was not surprised when they told me you were here," she said. "I was thinking about you—or, rather, expecting to hear from you."

"I came at once," answered Collingwood, who had kept her hand in his. "I—well, I couldn't stop away. I thought, perhaps, I could do something—be of some use."

"It's a great deal of use to have just—come," she said. "Thank you! But—I suppose you'll have to go?"

"Not for two days, anyway," he replied. "What can I do?"

"I don't know that you can actually do anything," she answered. "Everything is being done. Mr. Eldrick sent his clerk, Mr. Pratt—who found Harper—he's been most kind and useful. He—and our own solicitor—are making all arrangements. There's got to be an inquest. No—I don't know that you can do actual things. But—while you're here—you can look in when you like. My mother is very ill—she has scarcely spoken since Saturday."

"I'll tell you what I will do," said Collingwood determinedly. "I noticed in coming through the village just now that there's quite a decent inn there. I'll go down and arrange to stay there until Wednesday evening— then I shall be close by—if you should need me."

He saw by her look of quick appreciation and relief that this suggestion pleased her. She pressed his hand and withdrew her own. "Thank you again!" she said. "Do you know—I can't quite explain—I should be glad if you were close at hand? Everybody has been very kind—but I do feel that there is nobody I can talk to. If you arrange this, will you come in again this evening?"

"I shall arrange it," answered Collingwood. "I'll see to it now. Tell your people I am to be brought in whenever I call. And—I'll be close by whenever you want me."

It seemed little to say, little to do, but he left her feeling that he was being of some use. And as he went off to make his arrangements at the inn he encountered Pratt, who was talking to the butler in the outer hall.

The clerk looked at Collingwood with an unconcern and a composure which he was able to assume because he had already heard of his presence in the house. Inwardly, he was malignantly angry that the young barrister was there, but his voice was suave, and polite enough when he spoke.

"Good afternoon, Mr. Collingwood," he said quietly. "Very sad occasion on which we meet again, sir. Come to offer your sympathy, Mr. Collingwood, of course—very kind of you."

"I came," answered Collingwood, who was not inclined to bandy phrases with Pratt, "to see if I could be of any practical use."

"Just so, sir," said Pratt. "Mr. Eldrick sent me here for the same purpose. There's really not much to do—beyond the necessary arrangements, which are already pretty forward. Going back to town, sir?" he went on, following Collingwood out to his motor-car, which stood waiting in the drive.

"No!" replied Collingwood. "I'm going to send this man to Barford to fetch my bag to the inn down there in the village, where I'm going to stay for a few days. Did you hear that?" he continued, turning to the driver. "Go back to Barford—get my bag from the *Station Hotel* there—bring it to the *Normandale Arms*—I'll meet you there on your return."

The car went off, and Collingwood, with a nod to Pratt, was about to turn down a side path towards the village. But Pratt stopped him.

"Would you care to see the place where the accident happened, Mr. Collingwood?" he said. "It's close by—won't take five minutes."

Collingwood hesitated a moment; then he turned back. It might be well, he reflected, if he made himself acquainted with all the circumstances of this case, simple as they seemed.

"Thank you," he said. "If it's so near."

"This way, sir," responded Pratt. He led his companion along the front of the house, through the shrubberies at the end of a wing, and into a plantation by a path thickly covered with pine needles. Presently they emerged upon a similar track, at right angles to that by which they had come, and leading into a denser part of the woods. And at the end of a hundred yards of it they came to a barricade, evidently of recent construction, over which Pratt stretched a hand. "There!" he said. "That's the bridge, sir." Collingwood looked over the barricade. He saw that he and Pratt were standing at the edge of one thick plantation of fir and pine; the edge of a similar plantation stretched before them some ten yards away. But between the two lay a deep, dark ravine, which, immediately in front of the temporary barricade, was spanned by a narrow rustic bridge—a fragile-looking thing of planks, railed in by boughs of trees. And in the middle was a jagged gap in both floor and side-rails, showing where the rotten wood had given way.

"I'll explain, Mr. Collingwood," said the clerk presently. "I knew this park, sir—I knew it well, before the late Mr. John Mallathorpe bought the property. That path at the other end of the bridge makes a short cut down to the station in the valley—through the woods and the lower part of the park. I came up that path, from the station, on Saturday afternoon, intending to cross this bridge and go on to the house, where I had private business. When I got to the other end of the bridge, there, I saw the gap in the middle. And then I looked down into the cut—there's a road—a paved road—down there, and I saw—him! And so I made shift to scramble down—stiff job it was!—to get to him. But he was dead, Mr. Collingwood—stone dead, sir!—though I'm certain he hadn't been dead five minutes. And——"

"Aye, an' he'd never ha' been dead at all, wouldn't young Squire, if only his ma had listened to what I telled her!" interrupted a voice behind them. "He'd ha' been alive at this minute, he would, if his ma had done what I said owt to be done—now then!"

Collingwood turned sharply—to confront an old man, evidently one of the woodmen on the estate who had come up behind them unheard on the thick carpeting of pine needles. And Pratt turned, too—with a keen look and a direct question.

"What do you mean?" he asked. "What are you talking about?"

"I know what I'm talking about, young gentleman," said the man doggedly. "I ain't worked, lad and man, on this one estate nine-and-forty years—and happen more— wi'out knowin' all about it. I tell'd Mrs. Mallathorpe on Friday noon 'at that there owd brig 'ud fall in afore long if it worn't mended. I met her here, at this very place where we're standin', and I showed her 'at it worn't safe to cross it. I tell'd her 't she owt to have it fastened up theer an' then. It's been rottin' for many a year, has this owd brig— why, I mind when it wor last repaired, and that wor years afore owd Mestur Mallathorpe bowt this estate!"

"When do you say you told Mrs. Mallathorpe all that?" asked Pratt.

"Friday noon it were, sir," answered the woodman. "When I were on my way home—dinner time. 'Cause I met the missis here, and I made bold to tell her what I'd noticed. That there owd brig!—lor' bless yer, gentlemen! it were black rotten i' the middle, theer where poor young maister he fell through it. 'Ye mun hev' that seen to at once, missis,' I says. 'Sartin sure, 'tain't often as it's used,' I says, 'but surely sartin 'at if it ain't mended, or closed altogether,' I says, 'summun 'll be going through and brekkin' their necks,' I says. An' reight, too, gentlemen—forty feet it is down to that road. An' a mortal hard road, an' all, paved wi' granite stone all t' way to t' stable-yard."

"You're sure it was Friday noon?" repeated Pratt.

"As sure as that I see you," answered the woodman. "An' Mrs. Mallathorpe she said she'd hev it seen to. Dear-a-me!—it should ha' been closed!"

The old man shook his head and went off amongst the trees, and Pratt, giving his vanishing figure a queer look, turned silently back along the path, followed by Collingwood. At the point where the other path led to the house, he glanced over his shoulder at the young barrister.

"If you keep straight on, Mr. Collingwood," he said, "you'll get straight down to the village and the inn. I must go this way."

He went off rapidly, and Collingwood walked on through the plantation towards the *Normandale Arms*—wondering, all the way, why Pratt was so anxious to know exactly when it was that Mrs. Mallathorpe had been warned about the old bridge.

11. THE PREVALENT ATMOSPHERE

Until that afternoon Collingwood had never been in the village to which he was now bending his steps; on that and his previous visits to the Grange he had only passed the end of its one street. Now, descending into it from the slopes of the park, he found it to be little more than a hamlet—a church, a farmstead or two, a few cottages in their gardens, all clustering about a narrow stream spanned by a high-arched bridge of stone. The *Normandale Arms*, a roomy, old-fashioned place, stood at one end of the bridge, and from the windows of the room into which Collingwood was presently shown he could look out on the stream itself and on the meadows beyond it. A peaceful, pretty, quiet place—but the gloom which was heavy at the big house or the hill seemed to have spread to everybody that he encountered.

"Bad job, this, sir!" said the landlord, an elderly, serious-faced man, to whom Collingwood had made known his wants, and who had quickly formed the opinion that his guest was of the legal profession. "And a queer one, too! Odd thing, sir, that our old squire, and now the young one, should both have met their deaths in what you might term violent fashion."

"Accident—in both cases," remarked Collingwood.

The landlord nodded his head—and then shook it in a manner which seemed to indicate that while he agreed with this proposition in one respect he entertained some sort of doubt about it in others.

"Ay, well!" he answered. "Of course, a mill chimney falling, without notice, as it were, and a bridge giving way—them's accidents, to be sure. But it's a very strange thing about this foot-bridge, up yonder at the Grange— very strange indeed! There's queer talk about it, already."

"What sort of talk?" asked Collingwood. Ever since the old woodman had come up to him and Pratt, as they stood looking at the foot-bridge, he had been aware of a curious sense of mystery, and the landlord's remark tended to deepen it. "What are people talking about?"

"Nay—it's only one or two," replied the landlord. "There's been two men in here since the affair happened that crossed that bridge Friday afternoon—and both of 'em big, heavy men. According to what one can learn that there bridge wasn't used much by the Grange people—it led to nowhere in particular for them. But there is a right of way across that part of the park, and these two men as I'm speaking of—they made use of it on Friday—getting towards dark. I know 'em well—they'd both of 'em weigh four times as much—together—as young Squire Mallathorpe, and yet it didn't give way under them. And then—only a few hours later, as you might say, down it goes with him!"

"I don't think you can form any opinion from that!" said Collingwood. "These things, these old structures, often give way quite suddenly and unexpectedly."

"Ay, well, they did admit, these men too, that it seemed a bit tottery, like," remarked the landlord. "Talking it over, between themselves, in here, they agreed, to be sure, that it felt to give a bit. All the same, there's them as says that it's a queer thing it should ha' given altogether when young squire walked on it."

Collingwood clinched matters with a straight question.

"You don't mean to say that people are suggesting that the foot-bridge had been tampered with?" he asked.

"There is them about as wouldn't be slow to say as much," answered the landlord. "Folks will talk! You see, sir—nobody saw what happened. And when country folk doesn't see what takes place, with their own eyes, then they——"

"Make mysteries out of it," interrupted Collingwood, a little impatiently. "I don't think there's any mystery here, landlord—I understood that this foot-bridge was in a very unsafe condition. No! I'm afraid the whole affair was only too simple."

But he was conscious, as he said this, that he was not precisely voicing his own sentiments. He himself was mystified. He was still wondering why Pratt had been so pertinacious in asking the old woodman when, precisely, he had told Mrs. Mallathorpe about the unsafe condition of the bridge—still wondering about a certain expression which had come into Pratt's face when the old man told them what he did—still wondering at the queer look which Pratt had given the information as he went off into the plantation. Was there, then, something—some secret which was being kept back by—somebody?

He was still pondering over these things when he went back to the Grange, later in the evening—but he was resolved not to say anything about them to Nesta. And he saw Nesta only for a few minutes. Her mother, she said, was very ill indeed—the doctor was with her then, and she must go back to them. Since her son's death, Mrs. Mallathorpe had scarcely spoken, and the doctor, knowing that her heart was not strong, was somewhat afraid of a collapse.

"If there is anything that I can do,—or if you should want me, during the night," said Collingwood, earnestly, "promise me that you'll send at once to the inn!"

"Yes," answered Nesta. "I will. But—I don't think there will be any need. We have two nurses here, and the doctor will stop. There is something I should be glad if you would do tomorrow," she went on, looking at him a little wistfully, "You know about—the inquest?"

"Yes," said Collingwood.

"They say we—that is I, because, of course, my mother couldn't—that I need not be present," she continued. "Mr. Robson—our solicitor—says it will be a very short, formal affair. He will be there, of course,—but—would you mind being there, too!—so that you can—afterwards—tell me all about it?"

"Will you tell me something—straight out?" answered Collingwood, looking intently at her. "Have you any doubt of any description about the accepted story of your brother's death? Be plain with me!"

Nesta hesitated for awhile before answering.

"Not of the actual circumstances," she replied at last,—"none at all of what you call the accepted story. The fact is, I'm not a good hand at explaining anything, and perhaps I can't convey to you what I mean. But I've a feeling—an impression—that there is—or was some mystery on Saturday which might have—and might not have—oh, I can't make it clear, even to myself.

"If you would be at the inquest tomorrow, and listen carefully to everything—and then tell me afterwards—do you understand?"

"I understand," answered Collingwood. "Leave it to me."

Whether he expected to hear anything unusual at the inquest, whether he thought any stray word, hint, or suggestion would come up during the proceedings, Collingwood was no more aware than Nesta was certain of her vague ideas. But he was very soon assured that there was going to be nothing beyond brevity and formality. He had never previously been present at an inquest—his legal mind was somewhat astonished at the way in which things were done. It was quickly evident to him that the twelve good men and true of the jury—most of them cottagers and labourers living on the estate— were quite content to abide by the directions of the coroner, a Barford solicitor, whose one idea seemed to be to get through the proceedings as rapidly and smoothly as possible. And Collingwood felt bound to admit that, taking the evidence as it was brought forward, no simpler or more straightforward cause of investigation could be adduced. It was all very simple indeed—as it appeared there and then.

The butler, a solemn-faced, respectable type of the old family serving-man, spoke as to his identification of the dead master's body, and gave his evidence in a few sentences. Mr. Mallathorpe, he said, had gone out of the front door of the Grange at half-past two on Saturday afternoon, carrying a gun, and had turned into the road leading towards the South Shrubbery. At about three o'clock Mr. Pratt had come running up the drive to the house, and told him and Miss Mallathorpe that he had just found Mr. Mallathorpe lying dead in the sunken cut between the South and North Shrubbery. Nobody had any question to ask the butler. Nor were any questions asked of Pratt—the one really important witness.

Pratt gave his evidence tersely and admirably. On Saturday morning he had seen an advertisement in the Barford newspapers which stated that a steward and agent was wanted for the Normandale Estate, and all applications were to be made to Mrs. Mallathorpe. Desirous of applying for the post, he had written out a formal letter during Saturday morning, had obtained a testimonial from his present employers, Messrs. Eldrick & Pascoe, and, anxious to present his application as soon as possible, had decided to take it to Normandale Grange himself, that afternoon. He had left Barford by the two o'clock train, which arrived at Normandale at two-thirty-five. Knowing the district well, he had taken the path through the plantations. Arrived at the foot-bridge, he had at once noticed that part of it had fallen in. Looking into the cutting, he had seen a man lying in the roadway beneath—motionless. He had scrambled down the side of the cutting, discovered that the man was Mr. Harper Mallathorpe, and that he was dead, and had immediately hurried up the road to the house, where he had informed the last witness and Miss Mallathorpe.

A quite plain story, evidently thought everybody—no questions needed. Nor were there any questions needed in the case of the only other witnesses—the estate carpenter who said that the foot-bridge was very old, but that he had not been aware that it was in quite so bad a condition, and who gave it as his opinion that the recent heavy rains had had something to do with the matter; and the doctor who testified that the victim had suffered injuries which would produce absolutely instantaneous death. A clear case—nothing could be clearer, said the coroner to his obedient jury, who presently returned the only verdict—one of accidental death—which, on the evidence, was possible.

Collingwood heard no comments on the inquest from those who were present. But that evening, as he sat in his parlour at the *Normandale Arms*, the landlord, coming in on pretence of attending to the fire, approached him with an air of mystery and jerked his thumb in the direction of the regions which he had just quitted.

"You remember what we were talking of this afternoon when you come in, sir?" he whispered. "There's some of 'em—regular nightly customers, village folk, you understand—talking of the same thing now, and of this here inquest. And if you'd like to hear a bit of what you may call local opinion—and especially one man's—I'll put you where you can hear it, without being seen. It's worth hearing, anyway."

Collingwood, curious to know what the village wiseacres had to say, rose, and followed the landlord into a small room at the back of the bar-parlour.

An open hatchment in the wall, covered by a thin curtain, allowed him to hear every word which came from what appeared to be a full company. But it was quickly evident that in that company there was one man who either was, or wished to be dictator and artifex—a man of loud voice and domineering tone, who was laying down the law to the accompaniment of vigorous thumpings of the table at which he sat. "What I say is—and I say it agen—-I reckon nowt at all o' crowners' quests!" he was affirming, as Collingwood and his guide drew near the curtained opening. "What is a crowner's quest, anyway? It's nowt but formality—all form and show—it means nowt. All them 'at sits on t' jury does and says just what t' crowner tells 'em to say and do. They nivver ax no questions out o' their own mouths—they're as dumb as sheep—that's what yon jury wor this mornin'—now then!"

"That's James Stringer, the blacksmith," whispered the landlord, coming close to Collingwood's elbow. "He thinks he knows everything!"

"And pray, what would you ha' done, Mestur Stringer, if you'd been on yon jury?" inquired a milder voice. "I suppose ye'd ha' wanted to know a bit more, what?" "Mestur Stringer 'ud ha' wanted to know a deal more," observed another voice. "He would do!"

"There's a many things I want to know," continued the blacksmith, with a stout thump of the table. "They all tak' it for granted 'at young squire walked on to yon bridge, an' 'at it theer and then fell to pieces. Who see'd it fall to pieces? Who was theer to see what did happen?"

"What else did happen or could happen nor what were testified to?" asked a new voice. "Theer wor what they call circumstantial evidence to show how all t' affair happened!"

"Circumstantial evidence be blowed!" sneered the blacksmith heartily. "I reckon nowt o' circumstantial evidence! Look ye here! How do you know—how does anybody know 'at t' young squire worn't thrown off that bridge, and 'at t' bridge collapsed when he wor thrown? He might ha' met somebody on t' bridge, and quarrelled wi' 'em, and whoivver it wor might ha' been t' strongest man, and flung him into t' road beneath!"

"Aye, but i' that case t' other feller—t' assailant—'ud ha' fallen wi' him," objected somebody.

"Nowt o' t' sort!" retorted the blacksmith. "He'd be safe on t' sound part o' t' bridge—it's only a piece on 't that gave way. I say that theer idea wants in-quirin' into. An' theer's another thing—what wor that lawyer-clerk chap fro' Barford—Pratt—doin' about theer? What reight had he to be prowlin' round t' neighbourhood o' that bridge, and at that time? Come, now!—theer's a tickler for somebody."

"He telled that," exclaimed several voices. "He had business i' t' place. He had some papers to 'liver."

"Then why didn't he go t' nearest way to t' house t' 'liver 'em?" demanded Stringer. "T' shortest way to t' house fro' t' railway station is straight up t' carriage drive—not through them plantations. I ax agen—what wor that feller doin' theer? It's important."

"Why, ye don't suspect him of owt, do yer, Mestur Stringer?" asked somebody. "A respectable young feller like that theer—come!"

"I'm sayin' nowt about suspectin' nobody!" vociferated the blacksmith. "I'm doin' nowt but puttin' a case, as t' lawyers 'ud term it. I say 'at theer's a lot o' things 'at owt to ha' comed out. I'll tell ye one on 'em—how is it 'at nowt—not a single word—wor said at yon inquest about Mrs. Mallathorpe and t' affair? Not one word!"

A sudden silence fell on the company, and the landlord tapped Collingwood's arm and took the liberty of winking at him.

"Why," inquired somebody, at last, "what about Mrs. Mallathorpe and t' affair? What had she to do wi' t' affair?"

The blacksmith's voice became judicial in its solemnity.

"Ye listen to me!" he said with emphasis. "I know what I'm talking about. Ye know what came out at t' inquest. When this here Pratt ran to tell t' news at t' house he returned to what they term t' fatal spot i' company wi' t' butler, and a couple of footmen, and Dan Scholes, one o' t' grooms. Now theer worn't a word said at t' inquest about what that lot—five on em, mind yer—found when they reached t' dead corpse—not one word! But I know—Dan Scholes tell'd me!"

"What did they find, then, Mestur Stringer?" asked an eager member of the assemblage. "What wor it?"

The blacksmith's voice sank to a mysterious whisper.

"I'll tell yer!" he replied. "They found Mrs. Mallathorpe, lyin' i' a dead faint—close by! And they say 'at she's nivver done nowt but go out o' one faint into another, ivver since. So, of course, she's nivver been able to tell if she saw owt or knew owt! And what I say is," he concluded, with a heavy thump of the table, "that theer crowner's quest owt to ha' been what they term adjourned, until Mrs. Mallathorpe could tell if she did see owt, or if she knew owt, or heer'd owt! She mun ha' been close by—or else they wo'dn't ha' found her lyin' theer aside o' t' corpse. What did she see? What did she hear? Does she know owt? I tell ye 'at theer's questions 'at wants answerin'—and theer's trouble ahead for somebody if they aren't answered—now then!"

Collingwood went away from his retreat, beckoning the landlord to follow. In the parlour he turned to him.

"Have you heard anything of what Stringer said just now?" he asked. "I mean—about Mrs. Mallathorpe?"

"Heard just the same—and from the same chap, Scholes, the groom, sir," replied the landlord. "Oh, yes! Of course, people will wonder why they didn't get some evidence from Mrs. Mallathorpe—just as Stringer says."

Collingwood sat a long time that night, thinking over the things he had heard. He came to the conclusion that the domineering blacksmith was right in one of his dogmatic assertions—there was trouble ahead. And next morning, before going up to the Grange, he went to the nearest telegraph office, and sent Sir John Standridge a lengthy message in which he resigned the appointment that would have taken him to India.

12. THE POWER OF ATTORNEY

Collingwood had many things to think over as he walked across Normandale Park that morning. He had deliberately given up his Indian appointment for Nesta's sake, so that he might be near her in case the trouble which he feared arose suddenly. But it was too soon yet to let her know that she was the cause of his altered arrangements—in any case, that was not the time to tell her that it was on her account that he had altered them.

He must make some plausible excuse: then he must settle down in Barford, according to Eldrick's suggestion. He would then be near at hand—and if the trouble, whatever it might be, took tangible form, he would be able to help. But he was still utterly in the dark as to what that possible trouble might be—yet, of one thing he felt convinced—it would have some connection with Pratt.

He remembered, as he walked along, that he had formed some queer, uneasy suspicion about Pratt when he first hurried down to Barford on hearing of Antony Bartle's death: that feeling, subsequently allayed to some extent, had been revived. There might be nothing in it, he said to himself, over and over again; everything that seemed strange might be easily explained; the evidence of Pratt at the inquest had appeared absolutely truthful and straightforward, and yet the blunt, rough, downright question of the blacksmith, crudely voiced as it was, found a ready agreement in Collingwood's mind. As he drew near the house he found himself repeating Stringer's broad Yorkshire—"What wor that lawyer-clerk chap fro' Barford—Pratt—doin' about theer? What reight had he to be prowlin' round t' neighbourhood o' that bridge, and at that time? Come, now—theer's a tickler for somebody!" And even as he smiled at the remembrance of the whole rustic conversation of the previous evening, and thought that the blacksmith's question certainly might be a ticklish one—for somebody—he looked up from the frosted grass at his feet, and saw Pratt.

Pratt, a professional-looking bag in his hand, a morning newspaper under the other arm, was standing at the gate of one of the numerous shrubberies which flanked the Grange, talking to a woman who leaned over it. Collingwood recognized her as a person whom he had twice seen in the house during his visits on the day before—-a middle-aged, slightly built woman, neatly dressed in black, and wearing a sort of nurse's cap which seemed to denote some degree of domestic servitude. She was a woman who had once been pretty, and who still retained much of her good looks; she was also evidently of considerable shrewdness and intelligence and possessed a pair of remarkably quick eyes—the sort of eyes, thought Collingwood, that see everything that happens within their range of vision. And she had a firm chin and a mouth which expressed determination; he had seen all that as she exchanged some conversation with the old butler in Collingwood's presence—a noticeable woman altogether. She was evidently in close conference with Pratt at that moment—but as Collingwood drew near she turned and went slowly in the direction of the house, while Pratt, always outwardly polite, stepped towards the interrupter of this meeting, and lifted his hat.

"Good morning, Mr. Collingwood," he said. "A fine, sharp morning, sir! I was just asking Mrs. Mallathorpe's maid how her mistress is this morning—she was very ill when I left last night. Better, sir, I'm glad to say—Mrs. Mallathorpe has had a much better night."

"I'm very pleased to hear it," replied Collingwood. He was going towards the front of the Grange, and Pratt walked at his side, evidently in the same direction. "I am afraid she has had a great shock. You are still here, then?" he went on, feeling bound to make some remark, and saying the first obvious thing. "Still busy?"

"Mr. Eldrick has lent me—so to speak—until the funeral's over, tomorrow," answered Pratt. "There are a lot of little things in which I can be useful, you know, Mr. Collingwood. I suppose your arrangements—you said you were sailing for India—won't permit of your being present tomorrow, sir?"

Collingwood was not sure if the clerk was fishing for information. Pratt's manner was always polite, his questions so innocently put, that it was difficult to know what he was actually after. But he was not going to give him any information—either then, or at any time.

"I don't quite know what my arrangements may be," he answered. And just then they came to the front entrance, and Collingwood was taken off in one direction by a footman, while Pratt, who already seemed to be fully acquainted with the house and its arrangements, took himself and his bag away in another.

Nesta came to Collingwood looking less anxious than when he had left her at his last call the night before. He had already told her what his impressions of the inquest were, and he was now wondering whether to tell her of the things he had heard said at the village inn. But remembering that he was now going to stay in the neighbourhood, he decided to say nothing at that time—if there was anything in these vague feelings and suspicions it would come out, and could be dealt with when it arose. At present he had need of a little diplomacy.

"Oh!—I wanted to tell you," he said, after talking to her awhile about Mrs. Mallathorpe. "I—there's a change in my arrangements, I'm not going to India, after all."

He was not prepared for the sudden flush that came over the girl's face. It took him aback. It also told him a good deal that he was glad to know—and it was only by a strong effort of will that he kept himself from taking her hands and telling her the truth. But he affected not to see anything, and he went on talking rapidly. "Complete change in the arrangements at the last minute," he said. "I've just been writing about it. So—as that's off, I think I shall follow Eldrick's advice, and take chambers in Barford for a time, and see how things turn out. I'm going into Barford now, to see Eldrick about all that."

Nesta, who was conscious of her betrayal of more than she cared to show just then, tried to speak calmly.

"But—isn't it an awful disappointment?" she said. "You were looking forward so to going there, weren't you?"

"Can't be helped," replied Collingwood. "All these affairs are—provisional. I thought I'd tell you at once, however—so that you'll know—if you ever want me—that I shall be somewhere round about. In fact, as it's quite comfortable there, I shall stop at the inn until I've got rooms in the town."

Then, not trusting himself to remain longer, he went off to Barford, certain that he was now definitely pledged in his own mind to Nesta Mallathorpe, and not much less that when the right time came she would not be irresponsive to him. And on that, like a cold douche, came the remembrance of her actual circumstances—she was what Eldrick had said, one of the wealthiest young women in Yorkshire. The thought of her riches made Collingwood melancholy for a while—he possessed a curious sort of pride which made him hate and loathe the notion of being taken for a fortune-hunter. But suddenly, and with a laugh, he remembered that he had certain possessions of his own—ability, knowledge, and perseverance. Before he reached Eldrick's office, he had had a vision of the Woolsack.

Eldrick received Collingwood's news with evident gratification. He immediately suggested certain chambers in an adjacent building; he volunteered information as to where the best rooms in the town were to be had. And in proof of his practical interest in Collingwood's career, he there and then engaged his professional services for two cases which were to be heard at a local court within the following week.

"Pratt shall deliver the papers to you at once," he said. "That is, as soon as he's back from Normandale this afternoon. I sent him there again to make himself useful."

"I saw him this morning," remarked Collingwood. "He appears to be a very useful person."

"Clever chap," asserted Eldrick, carelessly. "I don't know what'll be done about that stewardship that he was going to apply for. Everything will be altered now that young Mallathorpe's dead. Of course, I, personally, shouldn't have thought that Pratt would have done for a job like that, but Pratt has enough self-assurance and self-confidence for a dozen men, and he thought he would do, and I couldn't refuse him a testimonial. And as he's made himself very useful out there, it may be that if this steward business goes forward, Pratt will get the appointment. As I say, he's a smart chap."

Collingwood offered no comment. But he was conscious that it would not be at all pleasing to him to know that Linford Pratt held any official position at Normandale. Foolish as it might be, mere inspiration though it probably was, he could not get over his impression that Eldrick's clerk was not precisely trustworthy. And yet, he reflected, he himself could do nothing—it would be utter presumption on his part to offer any gratuitous advice to Nesta Mallathorpe in business matters. He was very certain of what he eventually meant to say to her about his own personal hopes, some time hence, when all the present trouble was over, but in the meantime, as regarded anything else, he could only wait and watch, and be of service to her if she asked him to render any.

Some time went by before Collingwood was asked to render service of any sort. At Normandale Grange, events progressed in apparently ordinary and normal fashion. Harper Mallathorpe was buried; his mother began to make some recovery from the shock of his death; the legal folk were busied in putting Nesta in possession of the estate, and herself and her mother in proprietorship of the mill and the personal property. In Barford, things went on as usual, too. Pratt continued his round of duties at Eldrick & Pascoe's; no more was heard—by outsiders, at any rate—of the stewardship at Normandale. As for Collingwood, he settled down in chambers and lodgings and, as Eldrick had predicted, found plenty of work. And he constantly went out to Normandale Grange, and often met Nesta elsewhere, and their knowledge of each other increased, and as the winter passed away and spring began to show on the Normandale woods and moors, Collingwood felt that the time was coming when he might speak. He was professionally engaged in London for nearly three weeks in the early part of that spring—when he returned, he had made up his mind to tell Nesta the truth, at once. He had faced it for himself—he was by that time so much in love with her that he was not going to let monetary considerations prevent him from telling her so.

But Collingwood found something else than love to talk about when he presented himself at Normandale Grange on the morning after his arrival from his three weeks' absence in town. As soon as he met her, he saw that Nesta was not only upset and troubled, but angry.

"I am glad you have come," she said, when they were alone. "I want some advice. Something has happened—something that bothers—and puzzles—me very, very much! I'm dreadfully bothered."

"Tell me," suggested Collingwood.

Nesta frowned—at some recollection or thought.

"Yesterday afternoon," she answered, "I was obliged to go into Barford, on business. I left my mother fairly well—-she has been recovering fast lately, and she only has one nurse now. Unfortunately, she, too, was out for the afternoon. I came back to find my mother ill and much upset—-and there's no use denying it—she'd all the symptoms of having been—well, frightened. I can't think of any other term than that—frightened. And then I learned that, in my absence, Mr. Eldrick's clerk, Mr.

Pratt—you know him—had been here, and had been with her for quite an hour. I am furiously angry!"

Collingwood had expected this announcement as soon as she began to explain. So—the trouble was beginning!

"How came Pratt to be admitted to your mother?" he asked.

"That makes me angry, too," answered Nesta. "Though I confess I ought to be angry with myself for not giving stricter orders. I left the house about two—he came about three, and asked to see my mother's maid, Esther Mawson. He told her that it was absolutely necessary for him to see my mother on business, and she told my mother he was there. My mother consented to see him—and he was taken up. And as I say, I found her ill—and frightened—and that's not the worst of it!"

"What is the worst of it?" asked Collingwood, anxiously. "Better tell me!—I may be able to do something."

"The worst of it," she said, "is just this—my mother won't tell me what that man came about! She flatly refuses to tell me anything! She will only say that it was business of her own. She won't trust me with it, you see!—her own daughter! What business can that man have with her?—or she with him? Eldrick & Pascoe are not our solicitors! There's some secret and——"

"Will you answer one or two questions?" said Collingwood quietly. He had never seen Nesta angry before, and he now realized that she had certain possibilities of temper and determination which would be formidable when roused. "First of all, is that maid you speak of, Esther Mawson, reliable?"

"I don't know!" answered Nesta. "My mother has had her two years—she's a Barford woman. Sometimes I think she's sly and cunning. But I've given her such strict orders now that she'll never dare to let any one see my mother again without my consent."

"The other question's this," said Collingwood. "Have you any idea, any suspicion of why Pratt wanted to see your mother?"

"Not unless it was about that stewardship," replied Nesta. "But—how could that frighten her? Besides, all that's over. Normandale is mine!—and if I have a steward, or an estate agent, I shall see to the appointment myself. No!—I do not know why he should have come here! But—there's some mystery. The curious thing is——"

"What?" asked Collingwood, as she paused.

"Why," she said, shaking her head wonderingly, "that I'm absolutely certain that my mother never even knew this man Pratt—I don't I think she even knew his name—until quite recently. I know when she got to know him, too. It was just about the time that you first called here—at the time of Mr. Bartle's death. Our butler told me this morning that Pratt came here late one evening—just about that time!—and asked to see my mother, and was with her for some time in the study. Oh! what is it all about?—and why doesn't she tell me?"

Collingwood stood silently staring out of the window. At the time of Antony Bartle's death? An evening visit?—evidently of a secret nature. And why paid to Mrs. Mallathorpe at that particular time? He suddenly turned to Nesta.

"What do you wish me to do?" he asked.

"Will you speak to Mr. Eldrick?" she said. "Tell him that his clerk must not call upon, or attempt to see, my mother. I will not have it!"

Collingwood went off to Barford, and straight to Eldrick's office. He noticed as he passed through the outer rooms that Pratt was not in his accustomed place—as a rule, it was impossible to get at either Eldrick or Pascoe without first seeing Pratt.

"Hullo!" said Eldrick. "Just got in from town? That's lucky—I've got a big case for you."

"I got in last night," replied Collingwood. "But I went out to Normandale first thing this morning: I've just come back from there. I say, Eldrick, here's an unpleasant matter to tell you of"; and he told the solicitor all that Nesta had just told him, and also of Pratt's visit to Mrs. Mallathorpe about the time of Antony Bartle's death. "Whatever it is," he concluded sternly, "it's got to stop! If you've any influence over your clerk——"

Eldrick made a grimace and waved his hand.

"He's our clerk no longer!" he said. "He left us the week after you went up to town, Collingwood. He was only a weekly servant, and he took advantage of that to give me a week's notice. Now, what game is Master Pratt playing? He's smart, and he's deep, too. He——"

Just then an office-boy announced Mr. Robson, the Mallathorpe family solicitor, a bustling, rather rough-and-ready type of man, who came into Eldrick's room looking not only angry but astonished. He nodded to Collingwood, and flung himself into a chair at the side of Eldrick's desk.

"Look here, Eldrick!" he exclaimed. "What on earth has that clerk of yours, Pratt, got to do with Mrs. Mallathorpe? Do you know what Mrs. Mallathorpe has done? Hang it, she must be out of her senses,—or—or there's something I can't fathom. She's given your clerk, Linford Pratt, a power of attorney to deal with all her affairs and all her property! Oh, it's all right, I tell you! Pratt's been to my office, and exhibited it to me as if—as if he were the Lord Chancellor!"

Eldrick turned to Collingwood, and Collingwood to Eldrick—and then both turned to Robson.

13. THE FIRST TRICK

The Mallathorpe family solicitor shook his head impatiently under those questioning glances.

"It's not a bit of use appealing to me to know what it means!" he exclaimed. "I know no more than what I've told you. That chap walked into my office as bold as brass, half an hour ago, and exhibited to me a power of attorney, all duly drawn up and stamped, executed in his favour by Mrs. Mallathorpe yesterday. And as Mrs. Mallathorpe is, as far as I know, in her senses,—why—there you are!"

"What is it?" asked Eldrick. "A general power? Or a special?"

"General!" answered Robson, with an air of disgust. "Authorizes him to act for her in all business matters. It means, of course, that that fellow now has full control over—why, a tremendous amount of money! The estate, of course, is Miss Mallathorpe's—he can't interfere with that. But Mrs. Mallathorpe shares equally with her daughter as regards the personal property of Harper Mallathorpe—his share in the business, and all that he left, and what's more, Mrs. Mallathorpe is administratrix of the personal property. She's simply placed in Pratt's hands an enormous power! And—for what reason? Who on earth is Pratt—what right, title, age, or qualification, has he to be entrusted with such a big affair? I never knew of such a business in the whole course of my professional experiences!"

"Nor I!" agreed Eldrick. "But there's one thing in which you're mistaken, Robson. You ask what qualification Pratt has for a post of that sort? Pratt's a very smart, clever, managing chap!"

"Oh, of course! He's your clerk!" retorted Robson, a little sneeringly. "Naturally, you've a big idea of his abilities. But——"

"He's not our clerk any longer," said Eldrick. "He left us about a week ago. I heard this morning that he's set up an office in Market Street—in the Atlas Building—and I wondered for what purpose."

"Purpose of fleecing Mrs. Mallathorpe, I should say!" grumbled Robson. "Of course, everything of hers must pass through his hands. What on earth can her daughter have been thinking of to allow——"

"Stop a bit!" interrupted Eldrick. "Collingwood came in to tell me about that—he's just come from Normandale Grange. Miss Mallathorpe complains that Pratt called there yesterday in her absence. That's probably when this power of attorney was signed. But Miss Mallathorpe doesn't know anything of it—she insists that Pratt shall not visit her mother."

Robson stirred impatiently in his chair.

"That's all bosh!" he said. "She can't prevent it. I saw Mrs. Mallathorpe myself three days ago—she's recovering very well, and she's in her right senses, and she's capable of doing business. Her daughter can't prevent her from doing anything she likes! And if she did what she liked yesterday when she signed that document—why, everybody's powerless—except Pratt."

"There's the question of how the document was obtained," remarked Collingwood. "There may have been undue influence."

The two solicitors looked at each other. Then Eldrick rose from his chair. "I'll tell you what I'll do," he said. "It's no affair of mine, but we employed Pratt for years, and he'll confide in me. I'll go and see him, and ask him what it's all about. Wait here a while, you two."

He went out of his office and across into Market Street, where the Atlas Building, a modern range of offices and chambers, towered above the older structures at its foot. In the entrance hall a man was gilding the name of a new tenant on the address board—that name was Pratt's, and Eldrick presently found himself ascending in the lift to Pratt's quarters on the fifth floor. Within five minutes of leaving Collingwood and Robson, he was closeted with Pratt in a well-furnished and appointed little office of two rooms, the inner one of which was almost luxurious in its fittings. And Pratt himself looked extremely well satisfied, and confident—and quite at his ease. He wheeled forward an easy chair for his visitor, and pushed a box of cigarettes towards him.

"Glad to see you, Mr. Eldrick," he said, with a cordial politeness which suggested, however, somehow, that he and the solicitor were no longer master and servant. "How do you like my little place of business?"

"You're making a comfortable nest of it, anyhow, Pratt," answered Eldrick, looking round. "And—what sort of business are you going to do, pray?"

"Agency," replied Pratt, promptly. "It struck me some little time ago that a smart man,—like myself, eh?—could do well here in Barford as an agent in a new sort of fashion—attending to things for people who aren't fitted or inclined to do 'em for themselves—or are rich enough to employ somebody to look after their affairs. Of course, that Normandale stewardship dropped out when young Harper died, and I don't suppose the notion 'll be revived now that his sister's come in. But I've got one good job to go on with—-Mrs. Mallathorpe's given me her affairs to look after."

Eldrick took one of the cigarettes and lighted it—as a sign of his peaceable and amicable intentions.

"Pratt!" he said. "That's just what I've come to see you about. Unofficially, mind—in quite a friendly way. It's like this"; and he went on to tell Pratt of what had just occurred at his own office. "So—there you are," he concluded. "I'm saying nothing, you know, it's no affair of mine—but if these people begin to say that you've used any undue influence——"

"Mr. Collingwood, and Mr. Robson, and Miss Mallathorpe—and anybody," answered Pratt, slowly and firmly, "had better mind what they are saying, Mr. Eldrick. There's such a thing as slander, as you're well aware. I'm not the man to be slandered, or libelled, or to have my character defamed—without fighting for my rights. There has been no undue influence! I went to see Mrs. Mallathorpe yesterday at her own request. The arrangement between me and her is made with her approval and free will. If her daughter found her a bit upset, it's because she'd such a shock at the time of her son's death. I did nothing to frighten her, not I! The fact is, Miss Mallathorpe doesn't know that her mother and I have had a bit of business together of late. And all that Mrs. Mallathorpe has entrusted to me is the power to look after her affairs for her. And why not? You know that I'm a good man of business, a really good hand at commercial accountancy, and well acquainted with the trade of this town. You know too, Mr. Eldrick, that I'm scrupulously honest—I've had many and many a thousand pounds of yours and your partner's through my hands! Who's got anything to say against me? I'm only trying to earn an honest living."

"Well, well!" said Eldrick, who, being an easy-going and kindly-dispositioned man, was somewhat inclined to side with his old clerk. "I suppose Mr. Robson thinks that if Mrs. Mallathorpe wished to put her affairs in anybody's hands, she should have put them in his. He's their family solicitor, you know, Pratt, while you're a young man with no claim on Mrs. Mallathorpe."

Pratt smiled—a queer, knowing smile—and reached out his hand to some papers which lay on his desk.

"You're wrong there, Mr. Eldrick," he said. "But of course, you don't know. I didn't know myself, nor did Mrs. Mallathorpe, until lately. But I have a claim—and a good one—to get a business lift from Mrs. Mallathorpe. I'm a relation."

"What—of the Mallathorpe family?" exclaimed Eldrick, whose legal mind was at once bitten by notion of kinship and succession, and who knew that Harper Mallathorpe was supposed to have no male relatives at all, of any degree. "You don't mean it?"

"No!—but of hers, Mrs. Mallathorpe," answered Pratt. "My mother was her cousin. I found that out by mere chance, and when I'd found it, I worked out the facts from our parish church register. They're all here—fairly copied—Mrs. Mallathorpe has seen them. So I have some claim—even if it's only that of a poor relation."

Eldrick took the sheets of foolscap which Pratt handed to him, and looked them over with interest and curiosity. He was something of an expert in such matters, and had helped to edit a print more than once of the local parish registers. He soon saw from a hasty examination of the various entries of marriages and births that Pratt was quite right in what he said.

"I call it a poor—and a mean—game," remarked Pratt, while his old master was thus occupied, "a very mean game indeed, of well-to-do folk like Mr. Collingwood and Mr. Robson to want to injure me in a matter which is no business of theirs. I shall do my duty by Mrs. Mallathorpe—you yourself know I'm fully competent to do it—and I shall fully earn the percentage that she'll pay me. What right have these people—what right has her daughter—to come between me and my living?"

"Oh, well, well!" said Eldrick, as he handed back the papers and rose. "It's one of those matters that hasn't been understood. You made a mistake, you know, Pratt, when you went to see Mrs. Mallathorpe yesterday in her daughter's absence. You shouldn't have done that."

Pratt pulled open a drawer and, after turning over some loose papers, picked out a letter.

"Do you know Mrs. Mallathorpe's handwriting?" he asked. "Very well—there it is! Isn't that a request from her that I should call on her yesterday afternoon? Very well then!"

Eldrick looked at the letter with some surprise. He had a good memory, and he remembered that Collingwood had told him that Nesta had said that Pratt had gone to Normandale Grange, seen Esther Mawson, and told her that it was absolutely necessary for him to see Mrs. Mallathorpe. And though Eldrick was naturally unsuspicious, an idea flashed across his mind—had Pratt got Mrs. Mallathorpe to write that letter while he was there—yesterday—and brought it away with him?

"I think there's a good deal of misunderstanding," he said. "Mr. Collingwood says that you went there and told her maid that it was absolutely necessary for you to see her mistress—sort of forced yourself in, you see, Pratt."

"Nothing of the sort!" retorted Pratt. He flourished the letter in his hand. "Doesn't it say there, in Mrs. Mallathorpe's own handwriting, that she particularly desires to see me at three o'clock? It does! Then it was absolutely necessary for me to see her. Come, now! And Mr. Collingwood had best attend to his own business. What's he got to do with all this? After Miss Mallathorpe and her money, I should think!—that's about it!"

Eldrick said another soothing word or two, and went back to his own office. He was considerably mystified by certain things, but inclined to be satisfied about others, and in giving an account of what had just taken place he unconsciously seemed to take Pratt's side—much to Robson's disgust, and to Collingwood's astonishment.

"You can't get over this, you know, Robson," said Eldrick. "Pratt went there yesterday by appointment— went at Mrs. Mallathorpe's own express desire, made in her own handwriting. And it's quite certain that what he says about the relationship is true—-I examined the proof myself. It's not unnatural that Mrs. Mallathorpe should desire to do something for her own cousin's son."

"To that extent?" sneered Robson. "Bless me, you talk as if it were no more than presenting him with a twenty pound note, instead of its being what it is—giving him the practical control of many a thousand pounds every year. There'll be more heard of this—yet!"

He went away angrier than when he came, and Eldrick looked at Collingwood and shook his head.

"I don't see what more there is to do," he said. "So far as I can make out, or see, Pratt is within his rights. If Mrs. Mallathorpe liked to entrust her business to him, what is to prevent it? I see nothing at all strange in that. But there is a fact which does seem uncommonly strange to me! It's this—how is it that Mrs. Mallathorpe doesn't consult, hasn't consulted—doesn't inform, hasn't informed—her daughter about all this?"

"That," answered Collingwood, "is precisely what strikes me—and I can't give any explanation. Nor, I believe, can Miss Mallathorpe."

He felt obliged to go back to Normandale, and tell Nesta the result of the afternoon's proceedings. And having seen during his previous visit how angry she could be, he was not surprised to see her become angrier and more determined than ever.

"I will not have Mr. Pratt coming here!" she exclaimed. "He shall not see my mother—under my roof, at any rate. I don't believe she sent for him."

"Mr. Eldrick saw her letter!" interrupted Collingwood quietly.

"Then that man made her write it while he was here!" exclaimed Nesta. "As to the relationship—it may be so. I never heard of it. But I don't care what relation he is to my mother—he is not going to interfere with her affairs!"

"The strange thing," said Collingwood, as pointedly as was consistent with kindness, "is that your mother—just now, at any rate—doesn't seem to be taking you into her confidence."

Nesta looked steadily at him for a moment, without speaking. When she did speak it was with decision.

"Quite so!" she said. "She is keeping something from me! And if she won't tell me things—well, I must find them out for myself."

She would say no more than that, and Collingwood left her. And as he went back to Barford he cursed Linford Pratt soundly for a deep and underhand rogue who was most certainly playing some fine game.

But Pratt himself was quite satisfied—up to that point. He had won his first trick and he had splendid cards still left in his hand. And he was reckoning his chances on them one morning a little later when a ring at his bell summoned him to his office door—whereat stood Nesta Mallathorpe, alone.

14. CARDS ON THE TABLE

Had any third person been present, closely to observe the meeting of these two young people, he would have seen that the one to whom it was unexpected and a surprise was outwardly as calm and self-possessed as if the other had come there to keep an ordinary business appointment.

Nesta Mallathorpe, looking very dignified and almost stately in her mourning, was obviously angry, indignant, and agitated. But Pratt was as cool and as fully at his ease as if he were back in Eldrick's office, receiving the everyday ordinary client. He swept his door open and executed his politest bow—and was clever enough to pretend that he saw nothing of his visitor's agitation. Yet deep within himself he felt more tremors than one, and it needed all his powers of dissimulation to act and speak as if this were the most usual of occurrences.

"Good morning, Miss Mallathorpe!" he said. "You wish to see me? Come into my private office, if you please. I haven't fixed on a clerk yet," he went on, as he led his visitor through the outer room, and to the easy chair by his desk. "I have several applications from promising aspirants, but I have to be careful, you know, Miss Mallathorpe—it's a position of confidence. And now," he concluded, as he closed the door upon Nesta and himself, "how is Mrs. Mallathorpe today? Improving, I hope?"

Nesta made no reply to these remarks, or to the question. And instead of taking the easy chair which Eldrick had found so comfortable, she went to one which stood against the wall opposite Pratt's desk and seated herself in it in as upright a position as the wall behind her.

"I wish to speak to you—plainly!" she said, as Pratt, who now regarded her somewhat doubtfully, realizing that he was in for business of a serious nature, sat down at his desk. "I want to ask you a plain question—and I expect a plain answer. Why are you blackmailing my mother?"

Pratt shook his head—as if he felt more sorrow than anger. He glanced deprecatingly at his visitor.

"I think you'll be sorry—on reflection—that you said that, Miss Mallathorpe," he answered. "You're a little— shall we say—upset? A little—shall we say—angry? If you were calmer, you wouldn't say such things—you wouldn't use such a term as—blackmailing. It's—dear me, I dare say you don't know it!—it's actionable. If I were that sort of man, Miss Mallathorpe, and you said that of me before witnesses—ah! I don't know what mightn't happen. However—I'm not that sort of man. But—don't say it again, if you please!"

"If you don't answer my question—and at once," said Nesta, whose cheeks were pale with angry determination, "I shall say it again in a fashion you won't like—not to you, but to the police!"

Pratt smiled—a quiet, strange smile which made his visitor feel a sudden sense of fear. And again he shook his head, slowly and deprecatingly.

"Oh, no!" he said gently. "That's a bigger mistake than the other, Miss Mallathorpe! The police! Oh, not the police, I think, Miss Mallathorpe. You see—other people than you might go to the police—about something else."

Nesta's anger cooled down under that scarcely veiled threat. The sight of Pratt, of his self-assurance, his comfortable offices, his general atmosphere of almost sleek satisfaction, had roused her temper, already strained to breaking point. But that smile, and the quiet look which accompanied his last words, warned her that anger was mere foolishness, and that she was in the presence of a man who would have to be dealt with calmly if the dealings were to be successful. Yet—she repeated her words, but this time in a different tone.

"I shall certainly go to the police authorities," she said, "unless I get some proper explanation from you. I shall have no option. You are forcing—or have forced—my mother to enter into some strange arrangements with you, and I can't think it is for anything but what I say—blackmail. You've got—or you think you've got—some hold on her. Now what is it? I mean to know, one way or another!"

"Miss Mallathorpe," said Pratt. "You're taking a wrong course—with me. Now who advised you to come here and speak to me like this, as if I were a common criminal? Mr. Collingwood, no doubt? Or perhaps Mr. Robson? Now if either——"

"Neither Mr. Robson nor Mr. Collingwood know anything whatever about my coming here!" retorted Nesta. "No one knows! I am quite competent to manage my own affairs—of this sort. I want to know why my mother has been forced into that arrangement with you—for I am sure you have forced her! If you will not tell me why—then I shall do what I said."

"You'll go to the police authorities?" asked Pratt. "Ah!—but let us consider things a little, Miss Mallathorpe. Now, to start with, who says there has been any forcing? I know one person who won't say so—and that's your mother herself!"

Nesta felt unable to answer that assertion. And Pratt smiled triumphantly and went on.

"She'll tell you—Mrs. Mallathorpe'll tell you—that she's very pleased indeed to have my poor services," he said. "She knows that I shall serve her well. She's glad to do a kind service to a poor relation. And since I am your mother's relation, Miss Mallathorpe, I'm yours, too. I'm some degree of cousin to you. You might think rather better, rather more kindly, of me!"

"Are you going to tell me anything more than that?" asked Nesta steadily. Pratt shrugged his shoulders and waved his hands.

"What more can I tell?" he asked. "The fact is, there's a business arrangement between me and your mother—and you object to it. Well—I'm sorry, but I've my own interests to consider."

"Are you going to tell me what it was that induced my mother to sign that paper you got from her the other day?" asked Nesta.

"Can I say more than that it was—a business arrangement?" pleaded Pratt. "There's nothing unusual in one party in a business arrangement giving a power of attorney to another party. Nothing!"

"Very well!" said Nesta, rising from the straight-backed chair, and looking very rigid herself as she stood up. "You won't tell me anything! So—I am now going to the police. I don't know what they'll do. I don't know what they can do. But—I can tell them what I think and feel about this, at any rate. For as sure as I am that I see you, there's something wrong! And I'll know what it is."

Pratt recognized that she had passed beyond the stage of mere anger to one of calm determination. And as she marched towards the door he called her back—as the result of a second's swift thought on his part.

"Miss Mallathorpe," he said. "Oblige me by sitting down again. I'm not in the least afraid of your going to the police. But my experience is that if one goes to them on errands of this sort, it sets all sorts of things going—scandal, and suspicion, and I don't know what! You don't want any scandal. Sit down, if you please, and let us think for a moment. And I'll see if I can tell you—what you want to know."

Nesta already had a hand on the door. But after looking at him for a second or two, she turned back, and sat down in her old position. And Pratt, still seated at his desk, plunged his hands in his trousers pockets, tilted back his chair, and for five minutes stared with knitted brows at his blotting pad. A queer silence fell on the room. The windows were double-sashed; no sound came up from the busy street below. But on the mantelpiece a cheap Geneva clock ticked and ticked, and Nesta felt at last that if it went on much longer, without the accompaniment of a human voice, she should suddenly snatch it up, and hurl it—anywhere.

Pratt was in the position of the card-player, who, confronted by a certain turn in the course of a game which he himself feels sure he is bound to win, wonders whether he had better not expedite matters by laying his cards on the table, and asking his opponent if he can possibly beat their values and combination. He had carefully reckoned up his own position more than once during the progress of recent events, and the more carefully he calculated it the more he felt convinced that he had nothing to fear. He had had to alter his ground in consequence of the death of Harper Mallathorpe, and he had known that he would have to fight Nesta. But he had not anticipated that hostilities would come so soon, or begin with such evident determination on her part. How would it be, then, at this first stage to make such a demonstration in force that she would recognize his strength?

He looked up at last and saw Nesta regarding him sternly. But Pratt smiled—the quiet smile which made her uneasy.

"Miss Mallathorpe!" he said. "I was thinking of two things just then—a game at cards—and the science of warfare. In both it's a good thing sometimes to let your adversary see what a strong hand you've got. Now, then, a question, if you please—are you and I adversaries?"

"Yes!" answered Nesta unflinchingly. "You're acting like an enemy—you are an enemy!"

"I've hoped that you and I would be friends—good friends," said Pratt, with something like a sigh. "And if I may say so, I've no feeling of enmity towards you. When I speak of us being adversaries, I mean it in—well, let's say

a sort of legal sense. But now I'll show you my hand—
that is, as far as I please. Will you listen quietly to me?"

"I've no choice," replied Nesta bluntly. "And I came
here to know what you've got to say for yourself. Say it!"

Pratt moved his chair a little nearer to his visitor.

"Now," he said, speaking very quietly and
deliberately, "I'll go through what I have to say to you
carefully, point by point. I shall ask you to go back a little
way. It is now some time since I discovered a secret about
your mother, Mrs. Mallathorpe. Ah, you start!—it may be
with indignation, but I assure you I'm telling you, and am
going to tell you, the absolute truth. I say—a secret! No
one knows it but myself—not one living soul! Except, of
course, your mother. I shall not reveal it to you—under
any consideration, or in any circumstances—but I can tell
you this—if that secret were revealed, your mother would
be ruined for life—and you yourself would suffer in more
ways than one."

Nesta looked at him incredulously—and yet she began
to feel he was telling some truth. And Pratt shook his
head at the incredulous expression.

"It's quite so!" he said. "You'll begin to believe it—-
from other things. Now, it was in connection with this
that I paid a visit to Normandale Grange one evening
some months ago. Perhaps you never heard of that? I was
alone with your mother for some time in the study."

"I have heard of it," she answered.

"Very good," said Pratt. "But you haven't heard that
your mother came to see me at my rooms here in
Barford—my lodgings—the very next night! On the same
business, of course. But she did—I know how she came,
too. Secretly—heavily veiled—naturally, she didn't want
anybody to know. Are you beginning to see something in
it, Miss Mallathorpe?"

"Go on with your—story," answered Nesta.

"I go on, then, to the day before your brother's death,"
continued Pratt. "Namely, a certain Friday. Now, if you
please, I'll invite you to listen carefully to certain facts—

which are indisputable, which I can prove, easily. On that Friday, the day before your brother's death, Mrs. Mallathorpe was in the shrubbery at Normandale Grange which is near the north end of the old foot-bridge. She was approached by Hoskins, an old woodman, who has been on the estate a great many years—you know him well enough. Hoskins told Mrs. Mallathorpe that the foot-bridge between the north and south shrubberies, spanning the cut which was made there a long time since so that a nearer road could be made to the stables, was in an extremely dangerous condition—so dangerous, in fact, that in his opinion, it would collapse under even a moderate weight. I impress this fact upon you strongly."

"Well?" said Nesta.

"Hoskins," Pratt went on. "urged upon Mrs. Mallathorpe the necessity of having the bridge closed at once, or barricaded. He pointed out to her from where they stood certain places in the bridge, and in the railing on one side of it, which already sagged in such a fashion, that he, as a man of experience, knew that planks and railings were literally rotten with damp. Now what did Mrs. Mallathorpe do? She said nothing to Hoskins, except that she'd have the thing seen to. But she immediately went to the estate carpenter's shop, and there she procured two short lengths of chain, and two padlocks, and she herself went back to the foot-bridge and secured its wicket gates at both ends. I beg you will bear that in mind, too, Miss Mallathorpe."

"I am bearing everything in mind," said Nesta resolutely. "Don't be afraid that I shall forget one word that you say."

"I hear that sneer in your voice," answered Pratt, as he turned, unlocked a drawer, and drew out some papers. "But I think you will soon learn that the sneer at what I'm telling you is foolish. Mrs. Mallathorpe had a set purpose in locking up those gates—as you will see presently. You will see it from what I am now going to tell you. Oblige me, if you please, by looking at that letter. Do you recognize your mother's handwriting?"

"Yes!" admitted Nesta, with a sudden feeling of apprehension. "That is her writing."

"Very good," said Pratt. "Then before I read it to you, I'll just tell you what this letter is. It formed, when it was written, an invitation from Mrs. Mallathorpe to me—an invitation to walk, innocently, into what she knew— knew, mind you!—to be a death-trap! She meant *me* to fall through the bridge!"

15. PRATT OFFERS A HAND

For a full moment of tense silence Nesta and Pratt looked at each other across the letter which he held in his outstretched hand—looked steadily and with a certain amount of stern inquiry. And it was Nesta's eyes which first gave way—beaten by the certainty in Pratt's. She looked aside; her cheeks flamed; she felt as if something were rising in her throat—to choke her.

"I can't believe that!" she muttered. "You're—mistaken! Oh—utterly mistaken!"

"No mistake!" said Pratt confidently. "I tell you your mother meant me—me!—to meet my death at that bridge. Here's the proof in this letter! I'll tell you, first, when I received it: then I'll read you what's in it, and if you doubt my reading of it, you shall read it yourself—but it won't go out of my hands! And first as to my getting it, for that's important. It reached me, by registered post, mind you, on the Saturday morning on which your brother met his death. It was handed in at Normandale village post-office for registration late on the Friday afternoon. And—by whom do you think?"

"I—don't know!" replied Nesta faintly. This merciless piling up of details was beginning to frighten her—already she felt as if she herself were some criminal, forced to listen from the dock to the opening address of a prosecuting counsel. "How should I know?—how can I think?"

"It was handed in for registration by your mother's maid, Esther Mawson," said Pratt with a dark look. "I've got her evidence, anyway! And that was all part of a plan—just as a certain something that was enclosed was a part of the same plan—a plot. And now I'll read you the letter—and you'll bear it in mind that I got it by first post that Saturday morning. This is what it—what your mother—says:—

"I particularly wish to see you again, at once, about the matter   between us and to have another look at *that document*. Can you   come here, bringing it with you, tomorrow, Saturday afternoon,   by the train which leaves soon after two o'clock? As I am most   anxious that your visit should be private and unknown to any one here, do not come to the house. Take the path across the park to   the shrubberies near the house, so that if you are met people   would think you were taking a near cut to the village. I will   meet you in the shrubbery on the house side of the little   foot-bridge. The gates—'"

Pratt suddenly paused, and before proceeding looked hard at his visitor.

"Now listen to what follows—and bear in mind what your mother knew, and had done, at the time she wrote this letter. This is how the letter goes on——let every word fix itself in your mind, Miss Mallathorpe!"

"'The gates of the foot-bridge are locked, but the enclosed keys   will open them. I will meet you amongst the trees on the further   side. Be sure to come and to bring *that document*—I have   something to say about it on seeing it again.'"

Pratt turned to the drawer from which he had taken the letter and took out two small keys, evidently belonging to patent padlocks. He held them up before Nesta.

"There they are!" he said triumphantly. "Been in my possession ever since—and will remain there. Now—do you wish to read the letter? I've read it to you word for word. You don't? Very good—back it goes in there, with these keys. And now then," he continued, having replaced letter and keys in his drawer, and turned to her again, "now then, you see what a diabolical scheme it was that was in your mother's mind against me. She meant me to meet with the fate which overtook her own son! She meant me to fall through that bridge. Why? She hoped that I should break my neck—as he did! She wanted to silence me—but she also wanted more—she wanted to take from my dead body, or my unconscious body, the certain something which she was so anxious I should bring with me, which she referred to as *that document.* She was willing to risk anything—even to murder!—to get hold of that. And now you know why I went to Normandale Grange that Saturday—you know, now, the real reason. I told a deliberate lie at the inquest, for your mother's sake—for your sake, if you know it. I did not go there to hand in my application for the stewardship—I went in response to the letter I've just read. Is all this clear to you?"

Nesta could only move her head in silent acquiescence. She was already convinced, that whether all this was entirely true or not, there was truth of some degree in what Pratt had told her. And she was thinking of her mother—and of the trap which she certainly appeared to have laid—and of her brother's fate—and for the moment she felt sick and beaten. But Pratt went on in that cold, calculating voice, telling his story point by point.

"Now I come to what happened that Saturday afternoon," he said. "I may as well tell you that in my own interest I have carefully collected certain evidence which never came out at the inquest—which, indeed, has nothing to do with the exact matter of the inquest. Now, that Saturday, your mother and you had lunch together—your brother, as we shall see in a moment, being away—at your lunch time—a quarter to two. About twenty minutes past two your mother left the house. She went out into the gardens. She left the gardens for the shrubberies. And at twenty-five minutes to three, she was seen by one of your gardeners, Featherstone, in what was, of course, hiding, amongst the trees at the end of the north shrubbery. What was she doing there, Miss Mallathorpe? She was waiting!—waiting until a certain hoped-for accident happened—to me. Then she would come out of her hiding-place in the hope of getting that document from my pocket! Do you see how cleverly she'd laid her plans—murderous plans?"

Nesta was making a great effort to be calm. She knew now that she was face to face with some awful mystery which could only be solved by patience and strenuous endeavour. She knew, too, that she must show no sign of fear before this man!

"Will you finish your story, if you please?" she asked.

"In my own way—in my own time," answered Pratt. "I now come to—your mother. On the Friday noon, the late Mr. Harper Mallathorpe went to Barford to visit a friend—young Stemthwaite, at the Hollies. He was to stay the night there, and was not expected home until Saturday evening. He did stay the night, and remained in Barford until noon on Saturday; but he—unexpectedly—returned to the house at half past two. And almost as soon as he'd got in, he picked up a gun and strolled out—into the gardens and the north shrubbery. And, as you know, he went to the foot-bridge. You see, Miss Mallathorpe, your mother, clever as she was, had forgotten one detail—the gates of that footbridge were merely low, four-barred things, and there was nothing to prevent an active young man from climbing them. She forgot another thing, too—that warning had not been given at the house that the bridge was dangerous. And, of course, she'd never, never calculated that your brother would return sooner than he was expected, or that, on his return, he'd go where he did. And so—but I'll spare you any reference to what happened. Only—you know now how it was that Mrs. Mallathorpe was found by her son's body. She'd been waiting about—for me! But—the fate she'd meant for me was dealt out to—him!"

In spite of herself Nesta gave way to a slight cry.

"I can't bear any more of that!" she said. "Have you finished?"

"There's not much more to say—now at any rate," replied Pratt. "And what I have to say shall be to the point. I'm sorry enough to have been obliged to say all that I have said. But, you know, you forced me to it! You threatened me. The real truth, Miss Mallathorpe, is just this—you don't understand me at all. You come here—excuse my plain speech—hectoring and bullying me with talk about the police, and blackmail, and I don't know what! It's I who ought to go to the police! I could have your mother arrested, and put in the dock, on a charge of attempted murder, this very day! I've got all the proofs."

"I suppose you held that out as a threat to her when you forced her to sign that power of attorney?" observed Nesta.

For the first time since her arrival Pratt looked at his visitor in an unfriendly fashion. His expression changed and his face flushed a little.

"You think that, do you?" he said. "Well, you're wrong. I'm not a fool. I held out no such threat. I didn't even tell your mother what I'd found out. I wasn't going to show her my hand all at once—though I've shown you a good deal of it."

"Not all?" she asked quickly.

"Not all," answered Pratt with a meaning glance. "To use more metaphors—I've several cards up my sleeve, Miss Mallathorpe. But you're utterly wrong about the threats. I'll tell you—I don't mind that—how I got the authority you're speaking about. Your mother had promised me that stewardship—for life. I'd have been a good steward. But we recognized that your brother's death had altered things—that you, being, as she said, a self-willed young woman—you see how plain I am—would insist on looking after your own affairs. So she gave me—another post. I'll discharge its duties honestly."

"Yes," said Nesta, "but you've already told me that you'd a hold on my mother before any of these recent events happened, and that you possess some document which she was anxious to get into her hands. So it comes to this—you've a double hold on her, according to your story."

"Just so," agreed Pratt. "You're right, I have—a double hold."

Nesta looked at him silently for a while: Pratt looked at her.

"Very well," she said at last. "How much do you want—to be bought out?"

Pratt laughed.

"I thought that would be the end of it!" he remarked. "Yes—I thought so!"

"Name your price!" said Nesta.

"Miss Mallathorpe!" answered Pratt, bending forward and speaking with a new earnestness. "Just listen to me. It's no good. I'm not to be bought out. Your mother tried that game with me before. She offered me first five, then ten thousand pounds—cash down—for that document, when she came to see me at my rooms. I dare say she'd have gone to twenty thousand—and found the money there and then. But I said no then—and I say no to you! I'm not to be purchased in that way. I've my own ideas, my own plans, my own ambitions, my own—hopes. It's not any use at all for you to dangle your money before me. But—I'll suggest something else—that you can do."

Nesta made no answer. She continued to look steadily at the man who evidently had her mother in his power, and Pratt, who was watching her intently, went on speaking quietly but with some intensity of tone.

"You can do this," he said. "To start with—and it'll go a long way—just try and think better of me. I told you, you don't understand me. Try to! I'm not a bad lot. I've great abilities. I'm a hard worker. Eldrick & Pascoe could tell you that I'm scrupulously honest in money matters. You'll see that I'll look after your mother's affairs in a fashion that'll commend itself to any firm of auditors and accountants who may look into my accounts every year. I'm only taking the salary from her that I was to have had for the stewardship. So—why not leave it at that? Let things be! Perhaps—in time you'll come to see that—I'm to be trusted."

"How can I trust a man who deliberately tells me that he holds a secret and a document over a woman's head?" demanded Nesta. "You've admitted a previous hold on my mother. You say you're in possession of a secret that would ruin her—quite apart from recent events. Is that honest?"

"It was none of my seeking," retorted Pratt. "I gained the knowledge by accident."

"You're giving yourself away," said Nesta. "Or you've some mental twist or defect which prevents you from seeing things straight. It's not how you got your knowledge, but the use you're making of it that's the important thing! You're using it to force my mother to——"

"Excuse me!" interrupted Pratt with a queer smile. "It's you who don't see things straight. I'm using my knowledge to protect—all of you. Let your mind go back to what was said at first—to what I said at first. I said that I'd discovered a secret which, if revealed, would ruin your mother and injure—you! So it would—more than ever, now. So, you see, in keeping it, I'm taking care, not only of her interests, but of—yours!"

Nesta rose. She realized that there was no more to be said—or done. And Pratt rose, too, and looked at her almost appealingly.

"I wish you'd try to see things as I've put them, Miss Mallathorpe," he said. "I don't bear malice against your mother for that scheme she contrived—I'm willing to put it clear out of my head. Why not accept things as they are? I'll keep that secret for ever—no one shall ever know about it. Why not be friends, now—why not shake hands?"

He held out his hand as he spoke. But Nesta drew back.

"No!" she said. "My opinion is just what it was when I came here."

Before Pratt could move she had turned swiftly to the door and let herself out, and in another minute she was amongst the crowds in the street below. For a few minutes she walked in the direction of Robson's offices, but when she had nearly reached them, she turned, and went deliberately to those of Eldrick & Pascoe.

16. A HEADQUARTERS CONFERENCE

By the time she had been admitted to Eldrick's private room, Nesta had regained her composure; she had also had time to think, and her present action was the result of at any rate a part of her thoughts. She was calm and collected enough when she took the chair which the solicitor drew forward.

"I called on you for two reasons, Mr. Eldrick," she said. "First, to thank you for your kindness and thoughtfulness at the time of my brother's death, in sending your clerk to help in making the arrangements."

"Very glad he was of any assistance, Miss Mallathorpe," answered Eldrick. "I thought, of course, that as he had been on the spot, as it were, when the accident happened, he could do a few little things——"

"He was very useful in that way," said Nesta. "And I was very much obliged to him. But the second reason for my call is—I want to speak to you about him."

"Yes?" responded Eldrick. He had already formed some idea as to what was in his visitor's mind, and he was secretly glad of the opportunity of talking to her. "About Pratt, eh? What about him, Miss Mallathorpe?"

"He was with you for some years, I believe?" she asked.

"A good many years," answered Eldrick. "He came to us as office-boy, and was head-clerk when he left us."

"Then you ought to know him—well," she suggested.

"As to that," replied Eldrick, "there are some people in this world whom other people never could know well— that's to say, really well. I know Pratt well enough for what he was—our clerk. Privately, I know little about him. He's clever—he's ability—he's a chap who reads a good deal—he's got ambitions. And I should say he is a bit—subtle."

"Deceitful?" she asked.

"I couldn't say that," replied Eldrick. "It wouldn't be true if I said so. I think he's possibilities of strategy in him. But so far as we're concerned, we found him hardworking, energetic, truthful, dependable and honest, and absolutely to be trusted in money matters. He's had many and many a thousand pounds of ours through his hands."

"I believe you're unaware that my mother, for some reason or other, unknown to me, has put him in charge of her affairs?" asked Nesta.

"Yes—Mr. Collingwood told me so," answered Eldrick. "So, too, did your own solicitor, Mr. Robson—who's very angry about it."

"And you?" she said, putting a direct question. "What do you think? Do please, tell me!"

"It's difficult to say, Miss Mallathorpe," replied Eldrick, with a smile and a shake of the head. "If your mother—who, of course, is quite competent to decide for herself—wishes to have somebody to look after her affairs, I don't see what objection can be taken to her procedure. And if she chooses to put Linford Pratt in that position—why not? As I tell you, I, as his last—and only—employer, am quite convinced of his abilities and probity. I suppose that as your mother's agent, he'll supervise her property, collect money due to her, advise her in investments, and so on. Well, I should say—personally, mind—he's quite competent to do all that, and that he'll do it honestly, I should certainly say so."

"But—why should he do it at all?" asked Nesta.

Eldrick waved his hands.

"Ah!" he exclaimed. "Now you ask me a very different question! But—I understand—in fact, I know—that Pratt turns out to be a relation of yours—distant, but it's there. Perhaps your mother—who, of course, is much better off since your brother's sad death—is desirous of benefiting Pratt—as a relation."

"Do you advise anything?" asked Nesta.

"Well, you know, Miss Mallathorpe," replied Eldrick, smiling. "I'm not your legal adviser. What about Mr. Robson?"

"Mr. Robson is so very angry about all this—with my mother," said Nesta, "that I don't even want to ask his advice. What I really do want is the advice, counsel, of somebody—perhaps more as a friend than as a solicitor."

"Delighted to give you any help I can—either professionally or as a friend," exclaimed Eldrick. "But— let me suggest something. And first of all—is there anything—something—in all this that you haven't told to anybody yet?"

"Yes—much!" she answered. "A great deal!"

"Then," said Eldrick, "let me advise a certain counsel. Two heads are better than one. Let me ask Mr. Collingwood to come here."

He was watching his visitor narrowly as he said this, and he saw a faint rise of colour in her cheeks. But for the moment she did not answer, and Eldrick saw that she was thinking.

"I can get him across from his chambers in a few minutes," he said. "He's sure to be in just now."

"Can I have a few minutes to decide?" asked Nesta.

Eldrick jumped up.

"Of course!" he said. "I'll leave you a while. It so happens I want to see my partner, I'll go up to his room, and return to you presently."

Nesta, left alone, gave herself up to deep thought, and to a careful reckoning of her position. She was longing to confide in some trustworthy person or persons, for Pratt's revelations had plunged her into a maze of perplexity. But her difficulties were many. First of all, she would have to tell all about the terrible charge brought by Pratt against her mother. Then about the second which he professed to—or probably did—hold. What sort of a secret

could it be? And supposing her advisers suggested strong
measures against Pratt—what then, about the danger to
her mother, in a twofold direction?

Would it be better, wiser, if she kept all this to herself
at present, and waited for events to develop? But at the
mere thought of that, she shrank, feeling mentally and
physically afraid—to keep all that knowledge to herself,
to brood over it in secret, to wonder what it all meant,
what lay beneath, what might develop, that was more
than she felt able to bear. And when Eldrick came back
she looked at him and nodded.

"I should like to talk to you and Mr. Collingwood," she
said quietly.

Collingwood came across to Eldrick's office at once.
And to these two Nesta unbosomed herself of every detail
that she could remember of her interview with Pratt—
and as she went on, from one thing to another, she saw
the men's faces grow graver and graver, and realized that
this was a more anxious matter than she had thought.

"That's all," she said in the end. "I don't think I've
forgotten anything. And even now, I don't know if I've
done right to tell you all this. But—I don't think I could
have faced it—alone!"

"My dear Miss Mallathorpe!" said Eldrick earnestly.
"You've done the wisest thing you probably ever did in
your life! Now," he went on, looking at Collingwood, "just
let us all three realize what is to me a more important
fact. Nobody would be more astonished than Pratt to
know that you have taken the wise step you have. You
agree, Collingwood?"

"Yes!" answered Collingwood, after a moment's
reflection. "I think so."

"Miss Mallathorpe doesn't quite see what we mean,"
said Eldrick, turning to Nesta. "We mean that Pratt
firmly believed, when he told you what he did, that for
your mother's sake and your own, you would keep his
communication a dead secret. He firmly believed that you
would never dare to tell anybody what he told you. Most

people—in your position—wouldn't have told. They'd have let the secret eat their lives out. You're a wise and a sensible young woman! And the thing is—we must let Pratt remain under the impression that you are keeping your knowledge to yourself. Let him continue to believe that you'll remain silent under fear. And let us meet his secret policy with a secret strategy of our own!"

Again he glanced at Collingwood, and again Collingwood nodded assent.

"Now," continued Eldrick, "just let us consider matters for a few minutes from the position which has newly arisen. To begin with. Pratt's account of your mother's dealings about the foot-bridge is a very clever and plausible one. I can see quite well that it has caused you great pain; so before I go any further, just let me say this to you—don't you attach one word of importance to it!"

Nesta uttered a heartfelt cry of relief.

"Oh!" she exclaimed. "If you knew how thankful I should be to know that it's all lies—that he was lying! Can I really think that—after what I saw?"

"I won't ask you to think that he's telling lies—just now," answered Eldrick, with a glance at Collingwood, "but I'll ask you to believe that your mother could put a totally different aspect and complexion on all her actions and words in connection with the entire affair. My impression, of course," he went on, with something very like a wink at Collingwood, "is that Mrs. Mallathorpe, when she wrote that letter to Pratt, intended to have the bridge mended first thing next morning, and that something prevented that being done, and that when she was seen about the shrubberies in the afternoon, she was on her way to meet Pratt before he could reach the dangerous point, so that she could warn him. What do you say, Collingwood?"

"I should say," answered Collingwood, regarding the solicitor earnestly, and speaking with great gravity of manner, "that that would make an admirable line of defence to any charge which Pratt was wicked enough to prefer."

"You don't think my mother meant—meant to——" exclaimed Nesta, eagerly turning from one man to the other. "You—don't?"

"There is no evidence worth twopence against your mother!" replied Eldrick soothingly. "Put everything that Pratt has said against her clear out of your mind. Put all recent events out of your mind! Don't interfere with Pratt—just now. The thing to be done about Pratt is this—and it's the only thing. We must find out—exactly, as secretly as possible—what this secret is of which he speaks. What is this hold on Mrs. Mallathorpe? What is this document to which he refers? In other words, we must work back to some point which at present we can't see. At least, I can't see it. But—we may discover it. What do you say, Collingwood?"

"I agree entirely," answered Collingwood. "Let Pratt rest in his fancied security. The thing is, certainly, to go back. But—to what point?"

"That we must consider later," said Eldrick. "Now—for the present, Miss Mallathorpe,—you are, I suppose, going back home?"

"Yes, at once," answered Nesta. "I have my car at the *Crown Hotel*."

"I should just like to know something," continued Eldrick again, looking at Collingwood as if for approval. "That is—Mrs. Mallathorpe's present disposition towards affairs in general and Pratt in particular. Miss Mallathorpe!—just do something which I will now suggest to you. When you reach home, see your mother—she is still, I understand, an invalid, though evidently able to transact business. Just approach her gently and kindly, and tell her that you are a little—should we say uncomfortable?—about certain business arrangements which you hear she has made with Mr. Pratt, and ask her, if she won't talk them over with you, and give you her full confidence. It's now half-past twelve," continued

Eldrick, looking at his watch. "You'll be home before lunch. See your mother early in the afternoon, and then telephone, briefly, the result to me, here, at four o'clock. Then—Mr. Collingwood and I will have a consultation."

He motioned Collingwood to remain where he was, and himself saw Nesta down to the street. When he came back to his room he shook his head at the young barrister.

"Collingwood!" he said. "There's some dreadful business afloat in all this! And it's all the worse because of the fashion in which Pratt talked to that girl. She's evidently a very good memory—she narrated that conversation clearly and fully. Pratt must be very sure of his hand if he showed her his cards in that way—his very confidence in himself shows what a subtle network he's either made or is making. I question if he'd very much care if he knew that we know. But he mustn't know that—yet. We must reply to his mine with a counter-mine!"

"What do you think of Pratt's charge against Mrs. Mallathorpe?" asked Collingwood.

Eldrick made a wry face.

"Looks bad!—very, very bad, Collingwood!" he answered. "Art and scheme of a desperate woman, of course. But—we mustn't let her daughter think we believe it. Let her stick to the suggestion I made—which, as you remarked, would certainly make a very good line of defence, supposing Pratt even did accuse her. But now—what on earth is this document that's been mentioned—this paper of which Pratt has possession? Has Mrs. Mallathorpe at some time committed forgery—or bigamy—or—what is it? One thing's sure, however—we've got to work quietly. We mustn't let Pratt know that we're working. I hope he doesn't know that Miss Mallathorpe came here. Will you come back about four and hear what message she sends me? After that, we could consult."

Collingwood went away to his chambers. He was much occupied just then, and had little time to think of anything but the work in hand. But as he ate his lunch at the club which he had joined on settling in Barford, he tried to get at some notion of the state of things, and once more his mind reverted to the time of his grandfather's death, and his own suspicions about Pratt at that period. Clearly that was a point to which they must hark back— he himself must make more inquiries about the circumstances of Antony Bartle's last hours. For this affair would not have to rest where it was—it was intolerable that Nesta Mallathorpe should in any way be under Pratt's power. He went back to Eldrick at four o'clock with a suggestion or two in his mind. And at the sight of him Eldrick shook his head.

"I've had that telephone message from Normandale," he said, "five minutes ago. Pretty much what I expected— at this juncture, anyway. Mrs. Mallathorpe absolutely declines to talk business with even her daughter at present—and earnestly desires that Mr. Linford Pratt may be left alone."

"Well?" asked Collingwood after a pause. "What now?"

"We must do what we can—secretly, privately, for the daughter's sake," said Eldrick. "I confess I don't quite see a beginning, but——"

Just then the private door opened, and Pascoe, a somewhat lackadaisical-mannered man, who always looked half-asleep, and was in reality remarkably wide-awake, lounged in, nodded to Collingwood, and threw a newspaper in front of his partner.

"I say, Eldrick," he drawled, as he removed a newly-lighted cigar from his lips. "There's an advertisement here which seems to refer to that precious protégé of yours, who left you with such scant ceremony. Same name, anyhow!"

Eldrick snatched up the paper, glanced at it and read a few words aloud.

"INFORMATION WANTED about James Parrawhite, at one time in practice as a solicitor."

17. ADVERTISEMENT

Eldrick looked up at his partner with a sharp, confirmatory glance.

"That's our Parrawhite, of course!" he said. "Who's after him, now?" And he went on to read the rest of the advertisement, murmuring its phraseology half-aloud: "'in practice as a solicitor at Nottingham and who left that town six years ago. If the said James Parrawhite will communicate with the undersigned he will hear something greatly to his advantage. Any person able to give information as to his whereabouts will be suitably rewarded. Apply to Halstead & Byner, 56B, St. Martin's Chambers, London, W.C.' Um!—Pascoe, hand over that Law List."

Collingwood looked on in silence while Eldrick turned over the pages of the big book which his partner took down from a shelf. He wondered at Eldrick's apparent and almost eager interest.

"Halstead & Byner are not solicitors," announced Eldrick presently. "They must be inquiry agents or something of that sort. Anyway, I'll write to them, Pascoe, at once."

"You don't know where the fellow is," said Pascoe. "What's the good?"

"No—but we know where he last was," retorted Eldrick. He turned to Collingwood as the junior partner sauntered out of the room. "Rather odd that Pascoe should draw my attention to that just now," he remarked. "This man Parrawhite was, in a certain sense, mixed up with Pratt—at least, Pratt and I are the only two people who know the secret of Parrawhite's disappearance from these offices. That was just about the time of your grandfather's death."

Collingwood immediately became attentive. His first suspicions of Pratt were formed at the time of which Eldrick spoke, and any reference to events contemporary excited his interest.

"Who was or is—this man you're talking of?" he asked.

"Bad lot—very!" answered Eldrick, shaking his head. "He and I were articled together, at the same time, to the same people: we saw a lot of each other as fellow articled clerks. He afterwards practised in Nottingham, and he held some good appointments. But he'd a perfect mania for gambling—the turf—and he went utterly wrong, and misappropriated clients' money, and in the end he got into prison, and was, of course, struck off the rolls. I never heard anything of him for years, and then one day, some time ago, he turned up here and begged me to give him a job. I did—and I'll do him the credit to say that he earned his money. But—in the end, his natural badness broke out. One afternoon—I'm careless about some things—I left some money lying in this drawer—about forty pounds in notes and gold—and next morning Parrawhite never came to business. We've never seen or heard of him since."

"You mentioned Pratt," said Collingwood.

"Only Pratt and I know—about the money," replied Eldrick. "We kept it secret—I didn't want Pascoe to know I'd been so careless. Pascoe didn't like Parrawhite—and he doesn't know his record. I only told him that Parrawhite was a chap I'd known in better circumstances and wanted to give a hand to."

"You said it was about the time of my grandfather's death?" asked Collingwood.

"It was just about then—between his death and his funeral I should say," answered Eldrick, "The two events are associated in my mind. Anyway, I'd like to know what it is that these people want Parrawhite for. If it's money that's come to him, it'll be of no advantage—it'll only go where all the rest's gone."

Collingwood lost interest in Parrawhite. Parrawhite appeared to have nothing to do with the affairs in which he was interested. He sat down and began to tell Eldrick about his own suspicions of Pratt at the time of Antony Bartle's death; of what Jabey Naylor had told him about the paper taken from the *History of Barford*; of the lad's account of the old man's doings immediately afterwards; and of his own proceedings which had led him to believe for the time being that his suspicions were groundless.

"But now," he went on, "a new idea occurs to me. Suppose that that paper, found by my grandfather in a book which had certainly belonged to the late John Mallathorpe, was something important relating to Mrs. Mallathorpe? Suppose that my grandfather brought it across here to you? Suppose that finding you out, he showed it to Pratt? As my grandfather died suddenly, with nobody but Pratt there, what was there to prevent Pratt from appropriating that paper if he saw that it would give him a hold over Mrs. Mallathorpe? We know now that he has some document in his possession which does give him a hold—may it not be that of which the boy Naylor told me?"

"Might be," agreed Eldrick. "But—my opinion is, taking things all together, that the paper which Antony Bartle found was the one you yourself discovered later— the list of books. No—I'll tell you what I think. I believe that the document which Pratt told Miss Mallathorpe he holds, and to which her mother referred in the letter asking Pratt to meet her, is probably—most probably!— one which he discovered in searching out his relationship to Mrs. Mallathorpe. He's a cute chap—and he may have found some document which—well, I'll tell you what it might be—something which would upset the rights of Harper Mallathorpe to his uncle's estates. No other relatives came forward, or were heard of, or were discoverable when John Mallathorpe was killed in that chimney accident; but there may be some—there may be one in particular. That's my notion!—and I intend, in the first place, to make a personal search of the parish registers from which Pratt got his information. He may have discovered something there which he's keeping to himself."

"You think that is the course to adopt?" asked Collingwood, after a moment's reflection.

"At present—yes," replied Eldrick. "And while I'm making it—I'll do it myself—we'll just go on outwardly—as if nothing had happened. If I meet Pratt—as I shall—I shall not let him see that I know anything. Do you go on in just the usual way. Go out to Normandale Grange now and then—and tell Miss Mallathorpe to think no more of her interview with Pratt until we've something to talk to her about. You talk to her about—something else."

When Collingwood had left him Eldrick laid a telegram form on his plotting pad, and after a brief interval of thought wrote out a message addressed to the people whose advertisement had attracted Pascoe's attention.

"HALSTEAD & BYNER, 56B, St. Martin's Chambers, London, W.C.

"I can give you definite information concerning James Parrawhite   if you will send representative to see me personally.

"CHARLES ELDRICK, Eldrick & Pascoe, Solicitors, Barford."

After Eldrick had sent off a clerk with this message to the nearest telegraph office, he sat thinking for some time. And at the close of his meditations, and after some turning over of a diary which lay on his desk, he picked up pen and paper, and drafted an advertisement of his own.

"TEN POUNDS REWARD will be paid to any person who can give   reliable and useful information as to James Parrawhite, who   until November last was a clerk in the employ of Messrs. Eldrick   & Pascoe, Solicitors, Barford, and who is believed to have left   the town on the evening of November 23.—Apply to Mr. CHARLES ELDRICK, of the above firm."

"Worth risking ten pounds on—anyway," muttered Eldrick. "Whether these London people will cover it or not. Here!" he went on, turning to a clerk who had just entered the room. "Make three copies of this advertisement, and take one to each of the three newspaper offices, and tell 'em to put it in their personal column tonight."

He sat musing for some time after he was left alone again, and when he at last rose, it was with a shake of the head.

"I wonder if Pratt told me the truth that morning?" he said to himself. "Anyway, he's now being proved to be even deeper than I'd ever considered him. Well—other folk than Pratt are possessed of pretty good wits."

Before he left the office that evening Eldrick was handed a telegram from Messrs. Halstead & Byner, of St. Martin's Chambers, informing him that their Mr. Byner would travel to Barford by the first express next morning, and would call upon him at eleven o'clock.

"Then they have some important news for Parrawhite," mused Eldrick, as he put the message in his pocket and went off to his club. "Inquiry agents don't set off on long journeys at a moment's notice for a matter of a trifling agency. But—where is Parrawhite?"

He awaited the arrival of Mr. Byner next morning with considerable curiosity. And soon after eleven there was shown in to him, a smart, well-dressed, alert-looking young man, who, having introduced himself as Mr. Gerald Byner, immediately plunged into business.

"You can tell me something of James Parrawhite, Mr. Eldrick?" he began. "We shall be glad—we've been endeavouring to trace him for some months. It's odd that you didn't see our advertisement before."

"I don't look at that sort of advertisement," replied Eldrick. "I believe it was by mere accident that my partner saw yours yesterday afternoon. But now, a question or two first. What are you—inquiry agents?"

"Just so, sir—inquiry agents—with a touch of private detective business," answered Mr. Gerald Byner with a smile. "We undertake to find people, to watch people, to recover lost property, and so on. In this case we're acting for Messrs. Vickers, Marshall & Hebbleton, Solicitors, of Cannon Street. They want James Parrawhite badly."

"Why?" asked Eldrick.

"Because," replied Byner with a dry laugh, "there's about twenty thousand pounds waiting for him, in their hands."

Eldrick whistled with astonishment.

"Whew!" he said. "Twenty thousand—for Parrawhite! My good sir—if that's so, and if, as you say, you've been advertising——"

"Advertising in several papers," interrupted Byner. "Dailies, weeklies, provincials. Never had one reply, till your wire."

"Then—Parrawhite must be dead!" said Eldrick. "Or—in gaol, under another name. Twenty thousand pounds—waiting for Parrawhite! If Parrawhite was alive, man, or at liberty, he wouldn't let twenty thousand pence wait five minutes! I know him!"

"What can you tell me, Mr. Eldrick?" asked the inquiry agent.

Eldrick told all he knew—concealing nothing. And Byner listened silently and eagerly.

"There's something strikes me at once," he said. "You say that with him disappeared three or four ten-pound notes of yours. Have you the numbers of those notes?"

"I can't say," replied Eldrick, doubtfully. "I haven't, certainly. But—they were paid in to our head-clerk, Pratt, and I think he used to enter such things in a sort of day-ledger. I'll get it."

He went into the clerks' office and presently returned with an oblong, marble-backed book which he began to turn over.

"This may be what you ask about," he said at last. "Here, under date November 23, are some letters and figures which obviously refer to bank-notes. You can copy them if you like."

"Another question, Mr. Eldrick," remarked Byner as he made a note of the entries. "You say some cheque forms were abstracted from a book of yours at the same time. Have you ever heard of any of these cheque forms being made use of?"

"Never!" replied Eldrick.

"No forgery of your name or anything?" suggested the caller.

"No," said Eldrick. "There's been nothing of that sort."

"I can soon ascertain if these bank-notes have reached the Bank of England," said Byner. "That's a simple matter. Now suppose they haven't!"

"Well?" asked Eldrick.

"You know, of course," continued Byner, "that it doesn't take long for a Bank of England note, once issued, to get back to the Bank? You know, too, that it's never issued again. Now if those notes haven't been presented at the Bank—where are they? And if no use has been made of your stolen cheques—where are they?"

"Good!" agreed Eldrick. "I see that you ought to do well in your special line of business. Now—are you going to pursue inquiries for Parrawhite here in Barford, after what I've told you?"

"Certainly!" said Byner. "I came down prepared to stop awhile. It's highly important that this man should be found—highly important," he added smiling, "to other people than Parrawhite himself."

"In what way?" asked Eldrick.

"Why," replied Byner, "if he's dead—as he may be— this money goes to somebody else—a relative. The relative would be very glad to hear he is dead! But— definite news will be welcome, in any case. Oh, yes, now that I've got down here, I shall do my best to trace him. You have the address of the woman he lodged with, you say. I shall go there first, of course. Then I must try to find out what he did with himself in his spare time. But, from all you tell me, it's my impression he's dead—unless, as you say, he's got into prison again—possibly under another name. It seems impossible that he should not have seen our advertisements."

"You never advertised in any Yorkshire newspapers?" asked Eldrick.

"No," said Byner. "Because we'd no knowledge of his having come so far North. We advertised in the Midland papers. But then, all the London papers, daily and weekly, that we used come down to Yorkshire."

"Parrawhite," said Eldrick reflectively, "was a big newspaper reader. He used to go to the Free Library reading-room a great deal. I begin to think he must certainly be dead—or locked up. However, in supplement of your endeavours, I did a little work of my own last night. There you are!" he went on, picking up the local papers and handing them over. "I put that in—we'll see if any response comes. But now a word, Mr. Byner, since you've come to me. You have heard me mention my late clerk—Pratt?"

"Yes," answered Byner.

"Pratt has left us, and is in business as a sort of estate agent in the next street," continued Eldrick. "Now I have particular reasons—most particular reasons!—why Pratt should remain in absolute ignorance of your presence in the town. If you should happen to come across him—as you may, for though there are a quarter of a million of us here, it's a small place, compared with London—don't let him know your business."

"I'm not very likely to do that, Mr. Eldrick," remarked Byner quietly.

"Aye, but you don't take my meaning," said Eldrick eagerly. "I mean this—it's just possible that Pratt may see that advertisement of yours, and that he may write to your firm. In that case, as he's here, and you're here, your partner would send his letter to you. Don't deal with it—

here. Don't—if you should come across Pratt, even let him know your name!"

"When I've a job of this sort," replied Byner, "I don't let anybody know my name—except people like you. When I register at one of your hotels presently, I shall be Mr. Black of London. But—if this Pratt wanted to give any information about Parrawhite, he'd give it to you, surely, now that you've advertised."

"No, he wouldn't!" asserted Eldrick. "Why? Because he's told me all he knows—or says he knows—already!"

The inquiry agent looked keenly at the solicitor for a moment during which they both kept silence. Then Byner smiled.

"You said—'or says he knows,'" he remarked. "Do you think he didn't tell the truth about Parrawhite?"

"I should say—now—it's quite likely he didn't," answered Eldrick. "The truth is, I'm making some inquiry myself about Pratt—and I don't want this to interfere with it. You keep me informed of what you find out, and I'll help you all I can while you're here. It may be——"

A clerk came into the room and looked at his master.

"Mr. George Pickard, of the *Green Man* at Whitcliffe, sir," he said.

"Well?" asked Eldrick.

"Wants to see you about that advertisement in the paper this morning, sir," continued the clerk.

Eldrick looked at Byner and smiled significantly. Then he turned towards the door.

"Bring Mr. Pickard in," he said.

18. THE CONFIDING LANDLORD

The clerk presently ushered in a short, thick-set, round-faced man, apparently of thirty to thirty-five years of age, whose chief personal characteristics lay in a pair of the smallest eyes ever set in a human countenance and a mere apology for a nose. But both nose and eyes combined somehow to communicate an idea of profound inquiry as the round face in which they were placed turned from the solicitor to the man from London, and a podgy forefinger was lifted to a red forehead.

"Servant, gentlemen," said the visitor. "Fine morning for the time of year!"

"Take a chair, Mr. Pickard," replied Eldrick. "Let me see—from the *Green Man*, at Whitcliffe, I believe?"

"Landlord, sir—had that house a many years," answered Pickard, as he took a seat near the wall. "Seven year come next Michaelmas, any road."

"Just so—and you want to see me about the advertisement in this morning's paper?" continued Eldrick. "What about it—now?"

The landlord looked at Eldrick and then at Eldrick's companion. The solicitor understood that look: it meant that what his caller had to say was of a private nature.

"It's all right, Mr. Pickard," he remarked reassuringly. "This gentleman is here on just the same business— whatever you say will be treated as confidential—it'll go no further. You've something to tell about my late clerk, James Parrawhite."

Pickard, who had been nervously fingering a white billycock hat, now put it down on the floor and thrust his hands into the pockets of his trousers as if to keep them safe while he talked.

"It's like this here," he answered. "When I saw that there advertisement in the paper this mornin', says I to my missus, 'I'll away,' I says, 'an' see Lawyer Eldrick about that there, this very day!' 'Cause you see, Mr. Eldrick, there is summat as I can tell about yon man 'at you mention—James Parrawhite. I've said nowt about it to nobody, up to now, 'cause it were private business atween him and me, as it were, but I lost money over it, and of course, ten pound is ten pound, gentlemen."

"Quite so," agreed Eldrick, "And you shall have your ten pounds if you can tell anything useful."

"I don't know owt about it's being useful, sir, nor what use is to be made on it," said Pickard, "but I can tell you a bit o' truth, and you can do what you like wi' what I tell. But," he went on, lowering his voice and glancing at the door by which he had just entered, "there's another name 'at 'll have to be browt in—private, like. Name, as it so happens, o' one o' your clerks—t' head clerk, I'm given to understand—Mr. Pratt."

Eldrick showed no sign of surprise. But he continued to look significantly at Byner as he turned to the landlord.

"Mr. Pratt has left me," he said. "Left me three weeks ago. So you needn't be afraid, Mr. Pickard—say anything you like."

"Oh, I didn't know," remarked Pickard. "It's not oft that I come down in t' town, and we don't hear much Barford news up our way. Well, it's this here, Mr. Eldrick—you know where my place is, of course?"

Eldrick nodded, and turned to Byner.

"I'd better explain to you," he said. "Whitcliffe is an outlying part of the town, well up the hills—a sort of wayside hamlet with a lot of our famous stone quarries in its vicinity. The *Green Man*, of which our friend here is the landlord, is an old-fashioned tavern by the roadside—

where people are rather fond of dropping in on a Sunday,
I fancy, eh, Mr. Pickard?"

"You're right, sir," replied the landlord. "It makes a
nice walk out on a Sunday. And it were on a Sunday, too,
'at I got to know this here James Parrawhite as you want
to know summat about. He began coming to my place of a
Sunday evenin', d'ye see, gentlemen?—he'd walk across t'
valley up there to Whitcliffe and stop an hour or two,
enjoyin' hisself. Well, now, as you're no doubt well aweer,
Mr. Eldrick, he were a reight hand at talkin', were yon
Parrawhite—he'd t' gift o' t' gab reight enough, and
talked well an' all. And of course him an' me, we hed bits
o' conversation at times, 'cause he come to t' house reg'lar
and sometimes o' week-nights an' all. An' he tell'd me 'at
he'd had a deal o' experience i' racin' matters—whether it
were true or not, I couldn't say, but——"

"True enough!" said Eldrick. "He had."

"Well, so he said," continued Pickard, "and he was
allus tellin' me 'at he could make a pile o' brass on t' turf
if he only had capital. An' i' t' end, he persuaded me to
start what he called investin' money with him i' that
way—i' plain language, it meant givin' him brass to put
on horses 'at he said was goin' to win, d'ye understand?"

"Perfectly," replied Eldrick. "You gave him various
amounts which he was to stake for you."

"Just so, sir! And at first," said Pickard, with a shake
of the head, "at first I'd no great reason to grumble. He
cert'ny wor a good hand at spottin' a winner. But as time
went on, I' t' greatest difficulty in gettin' a settlement wi'
him, d'ye see? He wor just as good a hand at makin'
excuses as he wor at pickin' out winners—better, I think!
I nivver knew wheer I was wi' him—he'd pay up, and
then he'd persuade me to go in for another do wi' t' brass
I'd won, and happen we should lose that time, and then of
course we had to hev another investment to get back
what we'd dropped, and so it went on. But t' end wor this
here—last November theer wor about fifty to sixty pound
o' mine i' his hands, and I wanted it. I'd a spirit

merchant's bill to settle, and I wanted t' brass badly for that. I knew Parrawhite had been paid, d'ye see, by t' turf agent, 'at he betted wi', and I plagued him to hand t' brass over to me. He made one excuse and then another— howsumivver, it come to that very day you're talkin' about i' your advertisement, Mr. Eldrick—the twenty-third o' November——"

"Stop a minute, Mr. Pickard," interrupted Eldrick. "Now, how do you know—for a certainty—that this day you're going to talk about was the twenty-third of November?"

The landlord, who had removed his hands from his pockets, and was now twiddling a pair of fat thumbs as he talked, chuckled slyly.

"For a very good reason," he answered. "I had to pay that spirit bill I tell'd about just now on t' twenty-fourth, and that I'm going to tell you happened t' night afore t' twenty-fourth, so of course it were t' twenty-third. D'ye see?"

"I see," asserted Eldrick. "That'll do! And now—what did happen?"

"This here," replied Pickard. "On that night—t' twenty-third November—Parrawhite came into t' *Green Man* at about, happen, half-past eight. He come into t' little private parlour to me, bold as brass—as indeed, he allers wor. 'Ye're a nice un!' I says. 'I've written yer three letters durin' t' last week, and ye've nivver answered one o' 'em!' 'I've come to answer i' person,' he says. 'There's nobbut one answer I want,' says I. 'Wheer's my money?' 'Now then, be quiet a bit,' he says. 'You shall have your money before the evening's over,' he says. 'Or, if not, as soon as t' banks is open tomorrow mornin',' he says. 'Wheer's it coomin' from?' says I. 'Now, never you mind,' he says. 'It's safe!' 'I don't believe a word you're sayin',' says I. 'Ye're havin' me for t' mug!—that's about it.' An' I went on so at him, 'at i' t' end he tell'd me 'at he wor presently goin' to meet Pratt, and 'at he could get t' brass out o' Pratt an' as much more as iwer he liked to ax for.

Well, I don't believe that theer, and I said so. 'What brass has Pratt?' says I. 'Pratt's nowt but a clerk, wi' happen three or four pound a week!' 'That's all you know,' he says. 'Pratt's become a gold mine, and I'm going to dig in it a bit. What's it matter to you,' he says, 'so long as you get your brass?' Well, of course, that wor true enough—all 'at I wanted just then were to handle my brass. And I tell'd him so. 'I'll brek thy neck, Parrawhite,' I says, 'if thou doesn't bring me that theer money eyther to-night or t' first thing tomorrow—so now!' 'Don't talk rot!' he says. 'I've told you!' And he had money wi' him then—'nough to pay for drinks and cigars, any road, and we had a drink or two, and a smoke or two, and then he went out, sayin' he wor goin' to meet Pratt, and he'd be back at my place before closin' time wi' either t' cash or what 'ud be as good. An' I waited—and waited after closin' time, an' all. But I've nivver seen Parrawhite from that day to this—nor heerd tell on him neither!"

Eldrick and Byner looked at each other for a moment. Then the solicitor spoke—quietly and with a significance which the agent understood.

"Do you want to ask Mr. Pickard any questions?" he said.

Byner nodded and turned to the landlord.

"Did Parrawhite tell you where he was going to meet Pratt?" he asked.

"He did," replied Pickard. "Near Pratt's lodgin' place."

"Did—or does—Pratt live near you, then?"

"Closish by—happen ten minutes' walk. There's few o' houses—a sort o' terrace, like, on t' edge o' what they call Whitcliffe Moor. Pratt lodged—lodges now for all I know to t' contrary—i' one o' them."

"Did Parrawhite give you any idea that he was going to the house in which Pratt lodged?"

"No! He were not goin' to t' house. I know he worn't. He tell'd me 'at he'd a good idea what time Pratt 'ud be home, 'cause he knew where he was that evening and he were goin' to meet him just afore Pratt got to his place. I know where he'd meet him."

"Where?" asked Byner. "Tell me exactly. It's important."

"Pratt 'ud come up fro' t' town i' t' tram," answered Pickard. "He'd approach this here terrace I tell'd you about by a narrow lane that runs off t' high road. He'd meet him there, would Parrawhite."

"Did you ever ask any question of Pratt about Parrawhite?"

"No—never! I'd no wish that Pratt should know owt about my dealin's with Parrawhite. When Parrawhite never come back—why, I kep' it all to myself, till now."

"What do you think happened to Parrawhite, Mr. Pickard?" asked Byner.

"Gow, I know what I think!" replied Pickard disgustedly. "I think 'at if he did get any brass out o' Pratt—which is what I know nowt about, and hewn't much belief in—he went straight away fro' t' town— vanished! I do know this—he nivver went back to his lodgin's that neet, 'cause I went theer mysen next day to inquire."

Eldrick pricked up his ears at that. He remembered that he had sent Pratt to make inquiry at Parrawhite's lodgings on the morning whereon the money was missing.

"What time of the day—on the twenty-fourth—was that, Mr. Pickard?" he asked.

"Evenin', sir," replied the landlord. "They'd nivver seen naught of him since he went out the day before. Oh, he did me, did Parrawhite! Of course, I lost mi brass— fifty odd pounds!"

Byner gave Eldrick a glance.

"I think Mr. Pickard has earned the ten pounds you offered," he said.

Eldrick took the hint and pulled out his cheque-book.

"Of course, you're to keep all this private—strictly private, Mr. Pickard," he said as he wrote. "Not a word to a soul!"

"Just as you order, sir," agreed Pickard. "I'll say nowt—to nobody."

"And—perhaps tomorrow—perhaps this afternoon—you'll see me at the *Green Man*," remarked Byner. "I shall just drop in, you know. You needn't know me—if there's anybody about."

"All right, sir—I understand," said Pickard.

"Quiet's the word—what? Very good—much obliged to you, gentlemen."

When the landlord had gone Eldrick motioned Byner to pick up his hat. "Come across the street with me," he said. "I want us to have a consultation with a friend of mine, a barrister, Mr. Collingwood. For this matter is assuming a very queer aspect, and we can't move too warily, nor consider all the features too thoroughly."

Collingwood listened with deep interest to Eldrick's account of the morning's events. And once again he was struck by the fact that all these various happenings in connection with Pratt, and now with Parrawhite, took place at the time of Antony Bartle's death, and he said so.

"True enough!" agreed Eldrick.

"And once more," pointed out Collingwood. "We're hearing of a hold! Pratt claims to have a hold on Mrs. Mallathorpe—now it turns out that Parrawhite boasted of a hold on Pratt. Suppose all these things have a common origin? Suppose the hold which Parrawhite had—or has—on Pratt is part and parcel of the hold which Pratt has on Mrs. Mallathorpe? In that case—or cases—what is the best thing to do?"

"Will you gentlemen allow me to suggest something?" said Byner. "Very well—find Parrawhite! Of all the people concerned in this, Parrawhite, from your account of him, anyway, Mr. Eldrick, is the likeliest person to extract the truth from."

"There's a great deal in that suggestion," said Eldrick. "Do you know what I think?" he went on, turning to Collingwood, "Mr. Byner tells me he means to stay here until he has come across some satisfactory news of

Parrawhite or solved the mystery of his disappearance. Well, now that we've found that there is some ground for believing that Parrawhite was in some fashion mixed up with Pratt about that time, why not place the whole thing in Mr. Byner's hands—let him in any case see what he can do about the Parrawhite-Pratt business of November twenty-third, eh?"

"I take it," answered Collingwood, looking at the inquiry agent, "that Mr. Byner having heard what he has, would do that quite apart from us?"

"Yes," said Byner. "Now that I've heard what Pickard had to say, I certainly shall follow that up."

"I am following out something of my own," said Collingwood, turning to Eldrick. "I shall know more by this time tomorrow. Let us have a conference here—at noon."

They separated on that understanding, and Byner went his own ways. His first proceeding was to visit, one after another, the Barford newspaper offices, and to order the insertion in large type, and immediately, of the Halstead-Byner advertisement for news of Parrawhite. His second was to seek the General Post Office, where he wrote out and dispatched a message to his partner in London. That message was in cypher—translated into English, it read as follows:—

"If person named Pratt sends any communication to us *re* Parrawhite, on no account let him know I am in Barford, but forward whatever he sends to me at once, addressed to H.D. Black, Central Station Hotel."

19. THE EYE-WITNESS

When Collingwood said that he was following out something of his own, he was thinking of an interesting discovery which he had made. It was one which might have no significance in relation to the present perplexities—on the other hand, out of it might come a good deal of illumination. Briefly, it was that on the evening before this consultation with Eldrick & Byner, he had found out that he was living in the house of a man who had actually witnessed the famous catastrophe at Mallathorpe's Mill, whereby John Mallathorpe, his manager, and his cashier, together with some other bystanders, had lost their lives.

On settling down in Barford, Collingwood had spent a couple of weeks in looking about him for comfortable rooms of a sort that appealed to his love of quiet and retirement. He had found them at last in an old house on the outskirts of the town—a fine old stone house, once a farmstead, set in a large garden, and tenanted by a middle-aged couple, who having far more room than they needed for themselves, had no objection to letting part of it to a business gentleman. Collingwood fell in love with this place as soon as he saw it. The rooms were large and full of delightful nooks and corners; the garden was rich in old trees; from it there were fine views of the valley beneath, and the heather-clad hills in the distance; within two miles of the town and easily approached by a convenient tram-route, it was yet quite out in the country.

He was just as much set up by his landlady—a comfortable, middle-aged woman, who fostered true

Yorkshire notions about breakfast, and knew how to cook a good dinner at night. With her Collingwood had soon come to terms, and to his new abode had transferred a quantity of books and pictures from London. He soon became acquainted with the domestic menage. There was the landlady herself, Mrs. Cobcroft, who, having no children of her own, had adopted a niece, now grown up, and a teacher in an adjacent elementary school: there was a strapping, rosy-cheeked servant-maid, whose dialect was too broad for the lodger to understand more than a few words of it; finally there was Mr. Cobcroft, a mild-mannered, quiet man who disappeared early in the morning, and was sometimes seen by Collingwood returning home in the evening.

Lately, with the advancing spring, this unobtrusive individual was seen about the garden at the end of the day: Collingwood had so seen him on the evening before the talk with Eldrick and Byner, busied in setting seeds in the flower-beds. And he had asked Mrs. Cobcroft, just then in his sitting-room, if her husband was fond of gardening.

"It's a nice change for him, sir," answered the landlady. "He's kept pretty close at it all day in the office yonder at Mallathorpe's Mill, and it does him good to get a bit o' fresh air at nights, now that the fine weather's coming on. That was one reason why we took this old place—it's a deal better air here nor what it is in the town."

"So your husband is at Mallathorpe's Mill, eh?" asked Collingwood.

"Been there—in the counting-house—boy and man, over thirty years, sir," replied Mrs. Cobcroft.

"Did he see that terrible affair then—was it two years ago?"

The landlady shook her head and let out a weighty sigh.

"Aye, I should think he did!" she answered. "And a nice shock it gave him, too!—he actually saw that chimney fall—him and another clerk were looking out o' the counting-house window when it gave way."

Collingwood said no more then—except to remark that such a sight must indeed have been trying to the nerves. But for purposes of his own he determined to have a talk with Cobcroft, and the next evening, seeing him in his garden again, he went out to him and got into conversation, and eventually led up to the subject of Mallathorpe's Mill, the new chimney of which could be seen from a corner of the garden.

"Your wife tells me," observed Collingwood, "that you were present when the old chimney fell at the mill yonder?"

Cobcroft, a quiet, unassuming man, usually of few words, looked along the hillside at the new chimney, and nodded his head. A curious, far-away look came into his eyes.

"I was, sir!" he said. "And I hope I may never see aught o' that sort again, as long as ever I live. It was one o' those things a man can never forget!"

"Don't talk about it if you don't want to," remarked Collingwood. "But I've heard so much about that affair that——"

"Oh, I don't mind talking about it," replied Cobcroft. He leaned over the fence of his garden, still gazing at the mill in the distance. "There were others that saw it, of course: lots of 'em. But I was close at hand—our office was filled with the dust in a few seconds."

"It was a sudden affair?" asked Collingwood.

"It was one of those affairs," answered Cobcroft slowly, "that some folk had been expecting for a long time—only nobody had the sense to see that it might happen at some unexpected minute. It was a very old chimney. It looked all right—stood plumb, and all that. But Mr. Mallathorpe—my old master, Mr. John Mallathorpe, I'm talking of—he got an idea from two or three little things, d'ye see, that it wasn't as safe as it ought to be. And he got a couple of these professional steeplejacks to examine it. They made a thorough examination, too—so far as one could tell by what they did. They'd been at the job several days when the accident happened. One of 'em had only just come down when the chimney fell. Mr. Mallathorpe, himself, and his manager, and his cashier, had just stepped out of the counting-house and crossed the yard to hear what this man had got to say when—down it came! Not the slightest warning at the time. It just—collapsed!"

"You saw the actual collapse?" asked Collingwood.

"Aye—didn't I?" exclaimed Cobcroft. "Another man and myself were looking out of the office window, right opposite. It fell in the queerest way—like this," he went on, holding up his garden-rake. "Supposing this shaft was the chimney—standing straight up. As we looked we saw it suddenly bulge out, on all sides—it was a square chimney, same size all the way up till you got to the cornice at the top—bulge out, d'ye see, just about half-way up—simultaneous, like. Then—down it came with a roar that they heard over half the town! O' course, there were some two or three thousands of tons of stuff in that chimney—and when the dust was cleared a bit there it was in one great heap, right across the yard. And it was a good job," concluded Cobcroft, reflectively, "that it fell straight—collapsed in itself, as you might say—for if it had fallen slanting either way, it 'ud ha' smashed right through some of the sheds, and there'd ha' been a terrible loss of life."

"Mr. John Mallathorpe was killed on the spot, I believe?" suggested Collingwood.

"Aye—and Gaukrodger, and Marshall, and the steeplejack that had just come down, and another or two," said Cobcroft. "They'd no chance—they were standing in a group at the very foot, talking. They were all killed there and then—instantaneous. Some others were struck and injured—one or two died. Yes, sir,—I'm not very like to forget that!"

"A terrible experience!" agreed Collingwood. "It would naturally fix itself on your memory."

"Aye—my memory's very keen about it," said Cobcroft. "I remember every detail of that morning. And," he continued, showing a desire to become reminiscent, "there was something happened that morning, before the accident, that I've oft thought over and has oft puzzled me. I've never said aught to anybody about it, because we Yorkshiremen we're not given to talking about affairs that don't concern us, and after all, it was none o' mine! But you're a law gentleman, and I dare say you get things told to you in confidence now and then, and, of course, this is between you and me. I'll not deny that I have oft thought that I would like to tell it to a lawyer of some sort, and find out how it struck him."

"Anything that you like to tell me, Mr. Cobcroft, I shall treat as a matter of confidence—until you tell me it's no longer a secret," answered Collingwood.

"Why," continued Cobcroft, "it isn't what you rightly would call a secret—though I don't think anybody knows aught about it but myself! It was just this—and it may be there's naught in it but a mere fancy o' mine. That morning, before the accident happened, I was in and out of the private office a good deal—carrying in and out letters, and account books, and so on. Mr. John Mallathorpe's private office, ye'll understand, sir, opened out of our counting-house—as it does still—the present manager, Mr. Horsfall, has it, just as it was. Well, now, on one occasion, when I went in there, to take a ledger back to the safe, Mr. Mallathorpe had his manager and cashier, Gaukrodger and Marshall in with him. Mr. Mallathorpe, he always used a stand-up desk to write at—never wrote sitting down, though he had a big desk in the middle of the room that he used to sit at to look over accounts or talk to people. Now when I went in, he and Gaukrodger and Marshall were all at this stand-up desk—in the window-place—and they were signing some papers. At least Gaukrodger had just signed a paper, and

Marshall was taking the pen from him. 'Sign there, Marshall,' says Mr. Mallathorpe. And then he went on, 'Now we'll sign this other—it's well to have these things in duplicate, in case one gets lost.' And then—well, then, I went out, and—why, that was all."

"You've some idea in your mind about that," said Collingwood, who had watched Cobcroft closely as he talked. "What is it?"

Cobcroft smiled—and looked round as if to ascertain that they were alone. "Why!" he answered in a low voice. "I'll tell you what I did wonder—some time afterwards. I dare say you're aware—it was all in the papers—that Mr. John Mallathorpe died intestate?"

"Yes," asserted Collingwood. "I know that."

"I've oft wondered," continued Cobcroft, "if that could ha' been his will that they were signing! But then I reflected a bit on matters. And there were two or three things that made me say naught at all—not a word. First of all, I considered it a very unlikely thing that a rich man like Mr. John Mallathorpe would make a will for himself. Second—I remembered that very soon after I'd been in his private office Marshall came out into the counting-house and gave the office lad a lot of letters and documents to take to the post—some of 'em big envelopes—and I thought that what I'd seen signed was some agreement or other that was in one of them. And third—and most important—no will was ever found in any of Mr. John Mallathorpe's drawers or safes or anywhere, though they turned things upside down at the office, and, I heard, at his house as well. Of course, you see, sir, supposing that to have been a will—why, the only two men who could possibly have proved it was were dead and gone! They were killed with him. And of course, the young people, the nephew and niece, they came in for everything—so there was an end of it. But—I've oft wondered what those papers were. One thing is certain, anyway!" concluded Cobcroft, with a grim laugh, "when those three signed 'em, they were picking up their pens for the last time!"

"How long was it—after you saw the signing of those papers—that the accident occurred?" asked Collingwood.

"It 'ud be twelve or fifteen minutes, as near as I can recollect," replied Cobcroft. "A few minutes after I'd left the private office, Gaukrodger came out of it, alone, and stood at the door leading into the yard, looking up at the chimney. The steeple-jack was just coming down, and his mate was waiting for him at the bottom. Gaukrodger turned back to the private office and called Mr. Mallathorpe out. All three of 'em, Mallathorpe, Gaukrodger, Marshall, went out and walked across the yard to the chimney foot. They stood there talking a bit—and then—down it came!"

Collingwood thought matters over. Supposing that the document which Cobcroft spoke of as being in process of execution before him were indeed duplicate copies of a will. What could have been done with them, in the few minutes which elapsed between the signing and the catastrophe to the chimney? It was scarcely likely that John Mallathorpe would have sent them away by post. If they had been deposited in his own pocket, they would have been found when his clothing was removed and examined. If they were in the private office when the three men left it——

"You're sure the drawers, safe and so on in Mr. Mallathorpe's room were thoroughly searched—after his death?" he asked.

"I should think they were!" answered Cobcroft laconically. "I helped at that, myself. There wasn't as much as an old invoice that was not well fingered and turned over. No!—I came to the conclusion that what I'd seen signed was some contract or something—sent off there and then by the lad to post."

Collingwood made no further remark and asked no more questions. But he thought long and seriously that night, and he came to certain conclusions. First: what

Cobcroft had seen signed was John Mallathorpe's will. Second: John Mallathorpe had made it himself and had taken the unusual course of making a duplicate copy. Third: John Mallathorpe had probably slipped the copy into the *History of Barford* which was in his private office when he went out to speak to the steeple-jack. Fourth: that copy had come into Linford Pratt's hands through Antony Bartle.

And now arose two big questions. What were the terms of that will? And—where was the duplicate copy? He was still putting these to himself when noon of the next day came and brought Eldrick and Byner for the promised serious consultation.

20. THE *GREEN MAN*

Byner, in taking his firm's advertisement for Parrawhite to the three Barford newspaper offices, had done so with a special design—he wanted Pratt to see that a serious wish to discover Parrawhite was alive in more quarters than one. He knew that Pratt was almost certain to see Eldrick's advertisement in his own name; now he wanted Pratt to see another advertisement of the same nature in another name. Already he had some suspicion that Pratt had not told Eldrick the truth about Parrawhite, and that nothing would suit him so well as that Parrawhite should never be heard of or mentioned again: now he wished Pratt to learn that Parrawhite was much wanted, and was likely to be much mentioned—wherefore the supplementary advertisements with Halstead & Byner's name attached. It was extremely unlikely that Pratt could fail to see those advertisements.

There were three newspapers in Barford: one a morning journal of large circulation throughout the county; the other two, evening journals, which usually appeared in three or four editions. As Byner stipulated for large type, and a prominent position, in the personal column of each, it was scarcely within the bounds of probability that a townsman like Pratt would miss seeing the advertisement. Most likely he would see it in all three newspapers. And if he had also seen Eldrick's similar advertisement, he would begin to think, and then——

"Why, then," mused Byner, ruminating on his design, "then we will see what he will do!"

Meanwhile, there was something he himself wanted to do, and on the morning following his arrival in the

town, he set out to do it. Byner had been much struck by
Pickard's account of his dealings with James Parrawhite
on the evening which appeared to be the very last
wherein Parrawhite was ever seen. He had watched the
landlord of the *Green Man* closely as he told his story,
and had set him down for an honest, if somewhat sly and
lumpish soul, who was telling a plain tale to the best of
his ability. Byner believed all the details of that story—he
even believed that when Parrawhite told Pickard that he
would find him fifty pounds that evening, or early next
day, he meant to keep his word. In the circumstances—as
far as Byner could reckon them up from what he had
gathered—it would not have paid Parrawhite to do
otherwise. Byner put the situation to himself in this
fashion—Pratt had got hold of some secret which was
being, or could be made to be, highly profitable to him.
Parrawhite had discovered this, and was in a position to
blackmail Pratt. Therefore Parrawhite would not wish to
leave Pratt's neighbourhood—so long as there was money
to be got out of Pratt, Parrawhite would stick to him like
a leech. But if Parrawhite was to abide peaceably in
Barford, he must pay Pickard that little matter of
between fifty and sixty pounds. Accordingly, in Byner's
opinion, Parrawhite had every honest intention of
returning to the *Green Man* on the evening of the twenty-
third of November after having seen Pratt. And, in
Byner's further—and very seriously considered—opinion,
the whole problem for solution—possibly involving the
solution of other and more important problems—was this:
Did Parrawhite meet Pratt that night, and if he did what
took place between them which prevented Parrawhite
from returning to Pickard?

It was in an endeavour to get at some first stage of a
solution of this problem that Byner, having breakfasted
at the *Central Hotel* on his second day in the town, went
out immediately afterwards, asked his way to Whitcliffe,
and was directed to an electric tram which started from
the Town Hall Square, and after running through a

district of tall warehouses and squat weaving-sheds, began a long and steady climb to the heights along the town. When he left it, he found himself in a district eminently characteristic of that part of the country. The tram set him down at a cross-roads on a high ridge of land. Beneath him lay Barford, its towers and spires and the gables of its tall buildings showing amongst the smoke of its many chimneys. All about him lay open ground, broken by the numerous stone quarries of which Eldrick had spoken, and at a little distance along one of the four roads at the intersection of which he stood, he saw a few houses and cottages, one of which, taller and bigger than the rest, was distinguished by a pole, planted in front of its stone porch and bearing a swinging sign whereon was rudely painted the figure of a man in Lincoln green. Byner walked on to this, entered a flagged hall, and found himself confronting Pickard, who at sight of him, motioned him into a little parlour behind the bar.

"Mornin', mister," said he. "You'll be all right in here—there's nobody about just now, and if my missis or any o' t' servant lasses sees yer, they'll tak' yer for a brewer's traveller, or summat o' that sort. Come to hev a look round, like—what?"

"I want to have a look at the place where you told us Parrawhite was to meet Pratt that night," replied Byner. "I thought you would perhaps be kind enough to show me where it is."

"I will, an' all—wi' pleasure," said the landlord, "but ye mun hev a drop o' summat first—try a glass o' our ale," he went on, with true Yorkshire hospitality. "I hev some bitter beer i' my cellar such as I'll lay owt ye couldn't get t' likes on down yonder i' Barford—no, nor i' London neyther!—I'll just draw a jug."

Byner submitted to this evidence of friendliness, and Pickard, after disappearing into a dark archway and down some deeply worn stone steps, came back with a foaming jug, the sight of which seemed to give him great delight. He gazed admiringly at the liquor which he

presently poured into two tumblers, and drew his visitor's
attention to its colour.

"Reight stuff that, mister—what?" he said. "I nobbut
tapped that barril two days since, and I'd been keepin' it
twelve month, so you've come in for it at what they call t'
opportune moment. I say!" he went on, after pledging
Byner and smacking his lips over the ale. "I heard
summat last night 'at might be useful to you and Lawyer
Eldrick—about this here Parrawhite affair."

"Oh!" said Byner, at once interested. "What now?"

"You'll ha' noticed, as you come along t' road just now,
'at there's a deal o' stone quarries i' this neighbourhood?"
replied Pickard. "Well, now, of course, some o' t' quarry
men comes in here. Last night theer wor sev'ral on 'em i'
t' bar theer, talkin', and one on 'em wor readin' t' evenin'
newspaper—t' *Barford Dispatch*. An' he read out that
theer advertisement about Parrawhite—wi' your address
i' London at t' foot on it. Well, theer wor nowt said, except
summat about advertisin' for disappeared folk, but later
on, one o' t' men, a young man, come to me, private like. 'I
say, Pickard,' he says, 'between you an' me, worrn't t'
name o' that man 'at used to come in here on a Sunday
sometimes, Parrawhite? It runs a' my mind,' he says, "at
I've heerd you call him by that name.' 'Well, an' what if it
wor?' I says. 'Nay, nowt much,' he says, 'but I see fro' t'
Dispatch 'at he's wanted, and I could tell a bit about him,'
he says. 'What could ye tell?' says I—just like that theer.
'Why,' he says, 'this much—one night t' last back-end——
'"

"Stop a bit, Mr. Pickard," interrupted Byner. "What
does that mean—that term 'back-end'?"

"Why, it means t' end o' t' year!" answered the
landlord. "What some folks call autumn, d'ye understand?
'One night t' last back-end,' says this young fellow, 'I wor
hengin' about on t' quiet at t' end o' Stubbs' Lane,' he
says: 'T' truth wor,' he says, 'I wor waitin' for a word wi' a
young woman 'at lives i' that terrace at t' top o' Stubbs'
Lane—she wor goin' to come out and meet me for half an

hour or so. An,' he says, 'I see'd that theer feller 'at I think I've heerd you call Parrawhite, come out o' Stubbs' Lane wi' that lawyer chap 'at lives i' t' Terrace—Pratt. I know Pratt,' he says, "cause them 'at he works for—Eldricks—once did a bit o' law business for me.' 'Where did you see 'em go to, then?' says I. 'I see'd 'em cross t' road into t' owd quarry ground,' he says. 'I see'd 'em plain enough, tho' they didn't see me—I wor keepin' snug agen 't wall—it wor a moonlit night, that,' he says. 'Well,' I says, 'an' what now?' 'Why,' he says, 'd'yer think I could get owt o' this reward for tellin that theer?' So I thowt pretty sharp then, d'ye see, mister. 'I'll tell yer what, mi lad,' I says. 'Say nowt to nobody—keep your tongue still—and I'll tell ye tomorrow night what ye can do—I shall see a man 'at's on that job 'tween now and then,' I says. So theer it is," concluded Pickard, looking hard at Byner. "D'yer think this chap's evidence 'ud be i' your line?"

"Decidedly I do!" replied Byner. "Where is he to be found?"

"I couldn't say wheer he lives," answered the landlord. "But it'll be somewhere close about; anyway, he'll be in here tonight. Bill Thomson t' feller's name is—decent young feller enough."

"I must contrive to see him, certainly," said Byner. "Well, now, can you show me this Stubbs' Lane and the neighbourhood?"

"Just step along t' road a bit and I'll join you in a few o' minutes," assented Pickard. "We'd best not be seen leavin t' house together, or our folk'll think it's a put-up job. Walk forrard a piece."

Byner strolled along the road a little way, and leaned over a wall until Mr. Pickard, wearing his white billycock hat and accompanied by a fine fox-terrier, lounged up with his thumbs in the armholes of his waistcoat. Together they went a little further along.

"Now then!" said the landlord, crossing the road towards the entrance of a narrow lane which ran between two high stone walls. "This here is Stubbs' Lane—so called, I believe, 'cause an owd gentleman named similar used to hev a house here 'at's been pulled down. Ye see, it runs up fro' this high-road towards yon terrace o' houses. Folks hereabouts calls that terrace t' World's End, 'cause they're t' last houses afore ye get on to t' open moorlands. Now, that night 'at Parrawhite wor aimin' to meet Pratt, it wor i' this very lane. Pratt, when he left t' tram-car, t' other side o' my place, 'ud come up t' road, and up this lane. And it wor at t' top o' t' lane 'at Bill Thomson see'd Pratt and Parrawhite cross into what Bill called t' owd quarry ground."

"Can we go into that?" asked Byner.

"Nowt easier!" said Pickard. "It's a sort of open space where t' childer goes and plays about: they hev'n't worked no stone theer for many a long year—all t' stone's exhausted, like."

He led Byner along the lane to its further end, pointed out the place where Thomson said he had seen Pratt and Parrawhite, and indicated the terrace of houses in which Pratt lived. Then he crossed towards the old quarries.

"Don't know what they should want to come in here for—unless it wor to talk very confidential," said Pickard. "But lor bless yer!—it 'ud be quiet enough anywheer about this neighbourhood at that time o' neet. However, this is wheer Bill Thomson says he see'd 'em come."

He led the way amongst the disused quarries, and Byner, following, climbed on a mound, now grown over with grass and weed, and looked about him. To his town eyes the place was something novel. He had never seen the like of it before. Gradually he began to understand it. The stone had been torn out of the earth, sometimes in square pits, sometimes in semi-circular ones, until the various veins and strata had become exhausted. Then, when men went away, Nature had stepped in to assert her rights. All over the despoiled region she had spread a new clothing of green. Turf had grown on the flooring of the quarries; ivy and bramble had covered the deep scars; bushes had sprung up; trees were already springing. And in one of the worn-out excavations some man had planted a kitchen-garden in orderly and formal rows and plots.

"Dangerous place that there!" said Pickard suddenly. "If I'd known o' that, I shouldn't ha' let my young 'uns come to play about here. They might be tummlin' in and drownin' theirsens! I mun tell my missis to keep 'em away!"

Byner turned—to find the landlord pointing at the old shaft which had gradually become filled with water. In the morning sunlight its surface glittered like a plane of burnished metal, but when the two men went nearer and gazed at it from its edge, the water was black and unfathomable to the eye.

"Goodish thirty feet o' water in that there!" surmised Pickard. "It's none safe for childer to play about—theer's nowt to protect 'em. Next time I see Mestur Shepherd I shall mak' it my business to tell him so; he owt either to drain that watter off or put a fence around it."

"Is Mr. Shepherd the property-owner?" asked Byner.

"Aye!—it's all his, this land," answered Pickard. He pointed to a low-roofed house set amidst elms and chestnuts, some distance off across the moor. "Lives theer, does Mestur Shepherd—varry well-to-do man, he is."

"How could that water be drained off?" asked Byner with assumed carelessness.

"Easy enough!" replied Pickard. "Cut through yon ledge, and let it run into t' far quarry there. A couple o' men 'ud do that job in a day."

Byner made no further remark. He and Pickard strolled back to the *Green Man* together. And declining the landlord's invitation to step inside and take another glass, but promising to see him again very soon, the inquiry agent walked on to the tram-car and rode down to Barford to keep his appointment with Eldrick and Collingwood at the barrister's chambers.

21. THE DIRECT CHARGE

While Byner was pursuing his investigations in the neighbourhood of the *Green Man*, Collingwood was out at Normandale Grange, discussing certain matters with Nesta Mallathorpe. He had not only thought long and deeply over his conversation with Cobcroft the previous evening, but had begun to think about the crucial point of the clerk's story as soon as he spoke in the morning, and the result of his meditations was that he rose early, intercepted Cobcroft before he started for Mallathorpe's Mill and asked his permission to re-tell the story to Miss Mallathorpe. Cobcroft raised no objection, and when Collingwood had been to his chambers and seen his letters, he chartered a car and rode out to Normandale where he told Nesta of what he had learned and of his own conclusions. And Nesta, having listened carefully to all he had to tell, put a direct question to him.

"You think this document which Pratt told me he holds is my late uncle's will?" she said. "What do you suppose its terms to be?"

"Frankly—these, or something like these," replied Collingwood. "And I get at my conclusions in this way. Your uncle died intestate—consequently, everything in the shape of real estate came to your brother and everything in personal property to your brother and yourself. Now, supposing that the document which Pratt boasts of holding is the will, one fact is very certain—the property, real or personal, is not disposed of in the way in which it became disposed of because of John Mallathorpe's intestacy. He probably disposed of it in quite another fashion. Why do I think that? Because the probability is that Pratt said to your mother, 'I have got John Mallathorpe's will! It doesn't leave his property to your son and daughter. Therefore, I have all of you at my mercy. Make it worth my while, or I will bring the will forward.' Do you see that situation?"

"Then," replied Nesta, after a moment's reflection, "you do think that my mother was very anxious to get that document—a will—from Pratt?"

Collingwood knew what she was thinking of—her mind was still uneasy about Pratt's account of the affair of the foot-bridge. But—the matter had to be faced.

"I think your mother would naturally be very anxious to secure such a document," he said. "You must remember that according to Pratt's story to you, she tried to buy it from him—just as you did yourself, though you, of course, had no idea of what it was you wanted to buy."

"What I wanted to buy," she answered readily, "was necessity from further interference! But—is there no way of compelling Pratt to give up that document—whatever it is? Can't he be made to give it up?"

"A way is may be being made, just now—through another affair," replied Collingwood. "At present matters are vague. One couldn't go to Pratt and demand something at which one is, after all, only guessing. Your mother, of course, would deny that she knows what it is that Pratt holds. But—there is the possibility of the duplicate to which Cobcroft referred. Now, I want to put the question straight to you—supposing that duplicate will can be found—and supposing—to put it plainly—-its terms dispossess you of all your considerable property—what then?"

"Do you want the exact truth?" she asked. "Well, then, I should just welcome anything that cleared up all this mystery! What is it at present, this situation, but intolerable? I know that my mother is in Pratt's power, and likely to remain so as long as ever this goes on—probably for life. She will not give me her confidence. What is more, I am certain that she is giving it to Esther

Mawson—who is most likely hand-in-glove with Pratt. Esther Mawson is always with her. I am almost sure that she communicates with Pratt through Esther Mawson. It is all what I say—intolerable! I had rather lose every penny that has come into my hands than have this go on."

"Answer me a plain question," said Collingwood. "Is your mother fond of money, position—all that sort of thing?"

"She is fond of power!" replied Nesta. "It pleased her greatly when we came into all this wealth to know that she was the virtual administrator. Even if she could only do it by collusion with Pratt, she would make a fight for all that she—and I—hold. It's useless to deny that. Don't forget," she added, looking appealingly at Collingwood, "don't forget that she has known what it was to be poor—and if one does come into money—I suppose one doesn't want to lose it again."

"Oh, it's natural enough!" agreed Collingwood. "But—if things are as I think, Pratt would be an incubus, a mill-stone, for ever. Anyway, I came out to tell you what I've learned, and what I have an idea may be the truth, and above all, to get your definite opinion. You want the Pratt influence out of the way—at any cost?"

"At any cost!" she affirmed. "Even if I have to go back to earning my own living! Whatever pleasure in life could there be for me, knowing that at the back of all this there is that—what?"

"Pratt!" answered Collingwood. "Pratt! He's the shadow—with his deep schemes. However, as I said—there may be—developing at this moment—another way of getting at Pratt. Gentlemen like Pratt, born schemers, invariably forget one very important factor in life—the unexpected! Even the cleverest and most subtle schemer may have his delicate machinery broken to pieces by a chance bit of mere dust getting into it at an unexpected turn of the wheels. And to turn to plainer language—I'm going back to Barford now to hear what another man has to say concerning certain of Pratt's recent movements."

Eldrick was already waiting when Collingwood reached his chambers: Byner came there a few moments later. Within half an hour the barrister had told his story of Cobcroft, and the inquiry agent his of his visit to the *Green Man* and the quarries. And the solicitor listened quietly and attentively to both, and in the end turned to Collingwood.

"I'll withdraw my opinion about the nature of the document which Pratt got hold of," he said. "What he's got is what you think—John Mallathorpe's will!"

"If I may venture an opinion," remarked Byner, "that's dead certain!"

"And now," continued Eldrick, "we're faced with a nice situation! Don't either of you forget this fact. Not out of willingness on her part, but because she's got to do it, Mrs. Mallathorpe and Pratt are partners in that affair. He's got the will—but she knows its contents. She'll pay any price to Pratt to keep them from ever becoming known or operative. But, as I say, don't you forget something!"

"What?" asked Collingwood.

Eldrick tapped the edge of the table, emphasizing his words as he spoke them.

"They can destroy that will whenever they like!" he said. "And once destroyed, nothing can absolutely prove that it ever existed!"

"The duplicate?" suggested Collingwood.

"Nothing to give us the faintest idea as to its existence!" said Eldrick.

"We might advertise," said Collingwood.

"Lots of advertising was done when John Mallathorpe died," replied the solicitor. "No!—if any person had had it in possession, it would have turned up then. It may be—probably is—possibly must be—somewhere—and may yet come to light. But—there's another way of getting at Pratt. Through this Parrawhite affair. Pratt most likely had not the least notion that he would ever hear of Parrawhite again. He is going to hear of Parrawhite again! I am convinced now that Parrawhite knew something about this, and that Pratt squared him and got him away. Aren't you?" he asked, turning to Byner.

But Byner smiled quietly and shook his head.

"No!" he answered. "I am not, Mr. Eldrick."

"You're not?" exclaimed Eldrick, surprised and wondering that anybody could fail to agree with him. "Why not, then?"

"Because," replied Byner. "I am certain that Pratt murdered Parrawhite on the night of November twenty-third last. That's why. He didn't square him. He didn't get him away. He killed him!"

The effect of this straightforward pronouncement of opinion on the two men who heard it was strikingly different. Collingwood's face at once became cold and inscrutable; his lips fixed themselves sternly; his eyes looked hard into a problematic future. But Eldrick flushed as if a direct accusation had been levelled at himself, and he turned on the inquiry agent almost impatiently.

"Murder!" he exclaimed. "Oh, come! I—really, that's rather a stiff order! I dare say Pratt's been up to all sorts of trickery, and even deviltry—but murder is quite another thing. You're pretty ready to accuse him!"

Byner moved his head in Collingwood's direction— and Eldrick turned and looked anxiously at Collingwood, who, finding the eyes of both men on him, opened his hitherto tight-shut lips.

"I think it quite likely!" he said.

Byner laughed softly and looked at the solicitor.

"Just listen to me a minute or two, Mr. Eldrick," he said. "I'll sum up my own ideas on this matter, got from the various details that have been supplied to me since I came to Barford. Just consider my points one by one. Let's take them separately—and see how they fit in.

"1. Mr. Bartle is seen by his shop-boy to take a certain paper from a book which came from the late John

Mallathorpe's office at Mallathorpe Mill. He puts that paper in his pocket.

"2. Immediately afterwards Mr. Bartle goes to your office. Nobody is there but Pratt—as far as Pratt knows.

"3. Bartle dies suddenly—after telling Pratt that the paper is John Mallathorpe's will. Pratt steals the will. And the probability is that Parrawhite, unknown to Pratt, was in that office, and saw him steal it. Why is that probable? Because—

"4. Next night Parrawhite, who is being pressed for money by Pickard, tells Pickard that he can get it out of Pratt, over whom he has a hold. What hold? We can imagine what hold. Anyway—

"5. Parrawhite leaves Pickard to meet Pratt. He did meet Pratt—in Stubbs' Lane. He was seen to go with Pratt into the disused quarry. And there, in my opinion, Pratt killed him—and disposed of his body.

"6. What does Pratt do next? He goes to your office first thing next morning, and removes certain moneys which you say you carelessly left in your desk the night before, and tears out certain cheque forms from your book. When Parrawhite never turns up that morning, you—and Pratt—conclude that he's the thief, and that he's run away.

"7. If you want some proof of the correctness of this last suggestion, you'll find it in the fact that no use has ever been made of those blank cheques, and that—in all probability—the stolen bank-notes have never reached the Bank of England. On that last point I'm making inquiry—but my feeling is that Pratt destroyed both cheques and bank-notes when he stole them.

"8. This man Parrawhite out of the way, Pratt has a clear field. He's got the will. He's already acquainted Mrs. Mallathorpe with that fact, and with the terms of the will—whatever they may be. We may be sure, however, that they are of such a nature as to make her willing to agree to his demands upon her—and, accidentally, to go to any lengths—upon which we needn't touch, at present—towards getting possession of the will from him.

"9. And the present situation—from Pratt's standpoint of yesterday—is this. He's so sure of his own safety that he doesn't mind revealing to the daughter that the mother's in his power. Why? Because Pratt, like most men of his sort, cannot believe that self-interest isn't paramount with everybody—it's beyond him to conceive it possible that Miss Mallathorpe would do anything that might lose her several thousands a year. He argued—'So long as I hold that will, nobody and nothing can make me give it up nor divulge its contents. But I can bind one person who benefits by it—Miss Mallathorpe, and for the mother's sake I can keep the daughter quiet!' Well—he hasn't kept the daughter quiet! She—spoke!

"10. And last—in all such schemes as Pratt's, the schemer invariably forgets something. Pratt forgot that there might arise what actually has arisen—inquiry for Parrawhite. The search for Parrawhite is afoot—and if you want to get at Pratt, it will have to be through what I firmly believe to be a fact—his murder of Parrawhite and his disposal of Parrawhite's body.

"That's all, Mr. Eldrick," concluded Byner who had spoken with much emphasis throughout. "It all seems very clear to me, and," he added, with a glance at Collingwood, "I think Mr. Collingwood is inclined to agree with most of what I've said."

"Pretty nearly all—if not all," assented Collingwood. "I think you've put into clear language precisely what I feel. I don't believe there's a shadow of doubt that Pratt killed Parrawhite! And we can—and must—get at him in that way. What do you suggest?" he continued, turning to Byner. "You have some idea, of course?"

"First of all," answered Byner, "we mustn't arouse any suspicion on Pratt's part. Let us work behind the screen. But I have an idea as to how he disposed of Parrawhite, and I'm going to follow it up this very day—my first duty, you know, is towards the people who want Parrawhite, or proof of his death. I propose to——"

Just then Collingwood's clerk came in with a telegram.

"Sent on from the *Central Hotel*, sir," he answered. "They said Mr. Black would be found here."

"That's mine," said the inquiry agent. "I left word at the hotel that they were to send to your chambers if any wire came for me. Allow me." He opened the telegram, looked it over, and waiting until the clerk had gone, turned to his companions. "Here's a message from my partner, Mr. Halstead," he continued. "Listen to what he wires:

"'Wire just received from Murgatroyd, shipping agent, Peel Row,   Barford. He says Parrawhite left that town for America on   November 24th last and offers further information. Let me know   what to reply!'"

Byner laid the message before Eldrick and Collingwood without further comment.

22. THE CAT'SPAW

On the evening of the day whereon Nesta Mallathorpe had paid him the visit which had resulted in so much plain speech on both sides, Pratt employed his leisure in a calm review of the situation. He was by no means dissatisfied, it seemed to him that everything was going very well for his purposes. He was not at all sorry that Nesta had been to see him—far from it. He regretted nothing that he had said to her. In his desperate opinion, his own position was much stronger when she left him than it was when he opened his office door to her. She now knew, said Pratt, with what a strong and resourceful man she had to deal: she would respect him, and have a better idea of him, now that she was aware of his impregnable position.

Herein Pratt's innate vanity and his ignorance showed themselves. He had little knowledge of modern young women, and few ideas about them; and such ideas as he possessed were usually mistaken ones. But one was that it is always necessary to keep a firm hand on women—let them see and feel your power, said Pratt. He had been secretly delighted to acquaint Nesta Mallathorpe with his power, to drive it into her that he had the whip hand of her mother, and through her mother, of Nesta herself. He had seen that Nesta was much upset and alarmed by what he told her. And though she certainly seemed to recover her spirits at the end of the interview, and even refused to shake hands with him, he cherished the notion that in the war of words he had come off a decided victor. He did not believe that Nesta would utter to any other soul one word of what had passed between them: she would be too much afraid of calling down his vengeance on her mother. What he did believe was that as time went by, and all progressed smoothly, Nesta would come to face and accept facts: she would find him honest and hardworking in his dealings with Mrs. Mallathorpe (as he fully intended to be, from purely personal and selfish motives) and she herself would begin to tolerate and then to trust him, and eventually—well, who knew what might or might not happen? What said the great Talleyrand?—WITH TIME AND PATIENCE, THE MULBERRY LEAF IS TURNED INTO SATIN.

But Pratt's self-complacency received a shock next morning. If he had been a reader of London newspapers, it would have received a shock the day before. Pratt, however, was essentially parochial in his newspaper tastes—he never read anything but the Barford papers. And when he picked up the Barford morning journal and saw Eldrick's advertisement for Parrawhite in a prominent place, he literally started from sheer surprise—not unmingled with alarm. It was as if he were the occupant of a strong position, only fortified, who suddenly finds a shell dropped into his outworks from a totally unexpected quarter.

Parrawhite! Advertised for by Eldrick! Why? For what reason? For what purpose? With what idea? Parrawhite!—of all men in the world—Parrawhite, of whom he had never wanted to hear again! And what on earth could Eldrick want with him, or with news of him? It would be—or might be—an uncommonly awkward thing for him, Pratt, if a really exhaustive search were made for Parrawhite. For nobody knew better than himself that one little thing leads to another, and—but he forbore to follow out what might have been his train of thought. Once he was tempted to make an excuse for going round to Eldrick & Pascoe's with the idea of fishing for information—but he refrained. Let things develop—that was a safer plan. Still, he was anxious and disturbed all day. Then, towards the end of the afternoon, he bought one of the Barford evening papers—and saw, in staring letters, the advertisement which Byner had caused to be inserted only a few hours previously. And at that, Pratt became afraid.

Parrawhite wanted!—news of Parrawhite wanted!—and in two separate quarters. Wanted by Eldrick—wanted by some London people! What in the name of the devil did it mean? At any rate, he must see to himself. One thing was certain—no search for Parrawhite must be permitted in Barford.

That evening, instead of going home to dinner, Pratt remained in town, and dined at a quiet restaurant. When he dined, he thought, and planned, and schemed—and after treating himself very well in the matter of food and drink, he lighted a cigar, returned to his new offices, opened a safe which he had just set up, and took from a drawer in it a hundred pounds in bank-notes. With these in his pocket-book he went off to a quiet part of the town—the part in which James Parrawhite had lodged during his stay in Barford.

Pratt turned into a somewhat mean and shabby street—a street of small, poor-class shops. He went forward amongst them until he came to one which, if anything, was meaner and shabbier than the others and bore over its window the name Reuben Murgatroyd—Watchmaker and Jeweller. There were few signs of jewellery in Reuben Murgatroyd's window—some cheap clocks, some foreign-made watches of the five-shilling and seven-and-six variety, a selection of flashy rings and chains were spread on the shelves, equally cheap and flashy bangles, bracelets, and brooches lay in dust-covered trays on the sloping bench beneath them. At these things Pratt cast no more than a contemptuous glance. But he looked with interest at the upper part of the window, in which were displayed numerous gaily-coloured handbills and small posters relating to shipping—chiefly in the way of assisted passages to various parts of the globe. These set out that you could get an assisted passage to Canada for so much; to

Australia for not much more—and if the bills and posters themselves did not tell you all you wanted to know, certain big letters at the foot of each invited you to apply for further information to Mr. R. Murgatroyd, agent, within. And Pratt pushed open the shop-door and walked inside.

An untidily dressed, careworn, anxious-looking man came forward from a parlour at the rear of his shop. At sight of Pratt—who in the course of business had once served him with a writ—his pale face flushed, and then whitened, and Pratt hastened to assure him of his peaceful errand.

"All right, Mr. Murgatroyd," he said. "Nothing to be alarmed about—I'm out of that line, now—no papers of that sort tonight. I've a bit of business I can put in your hands—profitable business. Look here!—have you got a quarter of an hour to spare?"

Murgatroyd, who looked greatly relieved to find that his visitor had neither writ nor summons for him, glanced at his parlour door.

"I was just going to put the shutters up, and sit down to a bite of supper, Mr. Pratt," he answered. "Will you come in, sir?"

"No—you come out with me," said Pratt. "Come round to the *Coach and Horses*, and have a drink and we can talk. You'll have a better appetite for your supper when you come back," he added, with a wink. "I've a profitable job for you."

"Glad to hear it, sir," replied Murgatroyd. "I can do with aught of that sort, I assure you!" He went into the parlour, said a word or two to some person within, and came out again. "Not much business doing at present, Mr. Pratt," he said, as he and his visitor turned into the street. "Gets slacker than ever."

"Then you'll do with a slice of good luck," remarked Pratt. "It just happens that I can put a bit in your way."

He led Murgatroyd to the end of the street, where stood a corner tavern, into a side-door of which Pratt turned as if he were well acquainted with the geography of the place. Walking down a narrow passage he conducted his companion into a small parlour, at that moment untenanted, pointed him to a seat in the corner, and rang the bell. Five minutes later, having provided Murgatroyd with rum and water and a cigar, he turned on him with a direct question.

"Look here!" he said in a low voice. "Would a hundred pounds be any use to you?"

Murgatroyd's cheeks flushed.

"It 'ud be a fortune!" he answered with fervour. "A hundred pound! Lor' bless you, Mr. Pratt, it's many a year since I saw a hundred pound—of my own—all in one lump!"

Pratt pulled out his roll of bank-notes, fluttered it in his companion's face, laid it on the table, and set an ashtray on it.

"There's a hundred pounds there!" he said, "It's yours to pick up—if you'll do a little job for me. Easy job, too!—you'll never earn a hundred pounds so easy in your life!"

Murgatroyd pricked up his ears. According to his ideas, money easily come by was seldom honestly earned. He stirred uncomfortably in his seat.

"So long as it's a straight job," he muttered. "I don't want——"

"Straight enough—as straight as it's easy," answered Pratt. "It may seem a bit mysterious, but there's reasons for that. I give you my word it's all right—all a mere bit of diplomacy—and that nobody'll ever know you're in it—that is, beyond a certain stage—and that there's no danger to you."

"What is it?" asked Murgatroyd, still uneasy and doubtful.

Pratt pulled the evening paper out of his pocket and showed Murgatroyd the advertisement signed Halstead & Byner.

"You see that?" he said. "Information wanted about Parrawhite. Do you remember Parrawhite? He once served you with some papers in that affair in which we were against you."

"I remember him," answered Murgatroyd. "I've seen him in here now and again. So he's wanted, is he? I didn't know he'd left the town."

"Left last November," said Pratt. "And—there are folks—influential folks, as you can guess, seeing that they can throw a hundred pounds away!—who don't want any inquiries made for him in Barford. They don't mind— those folks—how many inquiries and searches are made for him anywhere else, but—not here!"

"Well?" asked Murgatroyd anxiously.

"This is it," replied Pratt. "You do a bit now and then as agent for some of these shipping lines. You book passages for emigrants—and for other people, going to New Zealand or Canada or Timbuctoo—never mind where. Now then—couldn't you remember—I'm sure you could—that you booked a passage for Parrawhite to America last November? Come! It's an easy matter to remember is that—for a hundred pounds."

Murgatroyd's thin fingers trembled a little as he picked up his glass. "What do you want me to do— exactly?" he asked.

"This!" said Pratt. "I want you, tomorrow morning, early, to send a telegram to these people, Halstead & Byner, St. Martin's Chambers, London, just saying that James Parrawhite left Barford for America on November 24th last, and that you can give further information if necessary."

"And what if it is necessary?" inquired Murgatroyd.

"Then—in answer to any letter or telegram of inquiry—you'll just say that you knew Parrawhite by sight as a clerk at Eldrick & Pascoe's in this town, that on November 23rd he told you that he was going to emigrate to America, that next day you booked him his passage, for which he paid you whatever it was, and that he thereupon set off for Liverpool. See?"

"It's all lies, you know," muttered Murgatroyd.

"Nobody can find 'em out, anyway," replied Pratt. "That's the one important thing to consider. You're safe! And if you're cursed with a conscience and it's tender—well, that'll make a good plaister for it!"

He pointed to the little wad of bank-notes—and the man sitting at his side followed the pointing finger with hungry eyes. Murgatroyd wanted money badly. His business, always poor, was becoming worse: his shipping agency rarely produced any result: his rent was in arrears: he owed money to his neighbour-tradesmen: he had a wife and young children. To such a man, a hundred pounds meant relief, comfort, the lifting of pressure.

"You're sure there's naught wrong in it, Mr. Pratt," he asked abruptly and assiduously. "It 'ud be a bad job for my family if anything happened to me, you know."

"There's naught that will happen," answered Pratt confidently. "Who on earth can contradict you? Who knows what people you sell passages to—but yourself?"

"There's the folks themselves," replied Murgatroyd. "Suppose Parrawhite turns up?"

"He won't!" exclaimed Pratt.

"You know where he is?" suggested Murgatroyd.

"Not exactly," said Pratt, "But—he's left this country for another—further off than America. That's certain! And—the folks I referred to don't want any inquiry about him here."

"If I am asked questions—later—am I to say he booked in his own name?" inquired Murgatroyd.

"No—name of Parsons," responded Pratt. "Here, I'll write down for you exactly what I want you to say in the telegram to Halstead & Byner, and I'll make a few memoranda for you—to post you up in case they write for further information."

"I haven't said that I'll do it," remarked Murgatroyd. "I don't like the looks of it. It's all a pack of lies."

Pratt paid no heed to this moral reflection. He found some loose paper in his pocket and scribbled on it for a while. Then, as if accidentally, he moved the ash-tray, and the bank-notes beneath it, all new, gave forth a crisp, rustling sound.

"Here you are!" said Pratt, pushing notes and memoranda towards his companion. "Take the brass, man!—you don't get a job like that every day."

And Murgatroyd put the money in his pocket, and presently went home, persuading himself that everything would be all right.

23. SMOOTH FACE AND ANXIOUS BRAIN

Byner watched Eldrick and Collingwood inquisitively as they bent over Halstead's telegram. He was not surprised when Collingwood merely nodded in silence— nor when Eldrick turned excitedly in his own direction.

"There!—what did I tell you?" he exclaimed. "There's been no murder! The man left the town. Probably, Pratt helped him off. Couldn't have better proof than that wire!"

"What do you take that wire to prove, then, Mr. Eldrick?" asked Byner.

"Take it to prove!" answered Eldrick. "Why, that Parrawhite booked a passage to America with this man Murgatroyd, last November. Clear enough, that!"

"What do you take it to prove, Mr. Collingwood?" continued the inquiry agent, as he turned to the barrister with a smile.

"Before I take it for anything," replied Collingwood, "I want to know who Murgatroyd is."

Byner looked at Eldrick and laughed.

"Precisely!" he said. "Who is Murgatroyd? Perhaps Mr. Eldrick knows."

"I do just know that he's a man who carries on a small watch and clock business in a poorish part of the town, and that he has some sort of a shipping agency," answered Eldrick. "But—do you mean to imply that whatever message it is that he's sent to your partner in London this morning has not been sent in good faith?"

"I don't imply anything," answered Byner. "All I say is—before I attach any value to his message I, like Collingwood, want to know something about the sender.

He may have been put up to sending it. He may be in collusion with somebody. Now, Mr. Eldrick, you can come in here—strongly! I don't want to be seen in this affair—yet. Will you go and see Murgatroyd? Tell him his wire to Halstead & Byner in London has been communicated to you here. Ask him for further particulars—and then drop in on me at my hotel and tell me what you've learnt. I'll be found in the smoking-room there any time after two-thirty onward."

Eldrick's intense curiosity in what was rapidly becoming a fascinating mystery to him, led him to accept this embassy. And a little before three o'clock he walked into the smoking-room at the *Central Hotel* and discovered Byner in a comfortable corner.

"I've seen Murgatroyd," he whispered, as he took an adjacent chair. "Decent honest enough man—very poor, I should say. He tells a plain enough story. Parrawhite, whom he knew as one of our clerks, told him, last November 23rd——"

"He was exact about dates, then, was he?" interrupted Byner.

"He mentioned them readily enough," replied the solicitor. "But to go on—Parrawhite mentioned to him, November 23rd last, that he wanted to go to America at once, Murgatroyd told him about bookings. Parrawhite called very early next morning, paid for his passage under the name of Parsons, and went off—en route for Liverpool, of course. So—there you are!"

"That's all Murgatroyd could tell?" inquired Byner.

"That's all he knows," answered Eldrick.

"You say Murgatroyd knew Parrawhite as one of your clerks?" asked Byner after a moment's thought.

"We had some process in hand against this man last autumn," replied Eldrick. "I dare say Parrawhite served him with papers."

"Would he—Murgatroyd—be likely to know Pratt?" continued Byner.

"He might—in the same connection," admitted Eldrick.

Byner smoked in silence for a while.

"Do you know what I think, Mr. Eldrick?" he said at last. "I think Pratt put up Murgatroyd to sending that telegram to us in London this morning."

"You do!" exclaimed Eldrick.

"Surely! And now," continued the inquiry agent, "if you will, you can do more—much more—without appearing to do anything. Pratt's office is only a few minutes away. Can you drop in there, making some excuse, and while there, mention, more or less casually, that Parrawhite, or information about him, is wanted; that you and a certain Halstead & Byner are advertising for him; that you've just seen Murgatroyd in respect of a communication which he wired to Halstead's this morning, and that—most important of all—a fortune of twenty thousand pounds is awaiting Parrawhite! Don't forget the last bit of news."

"Why that particularly?" asked Eldrick.

"Because," answered Byner solemnly, "I want Pratt to know that the search for Parrawhite is going to be a thorough one!"

Eldrick went off on his second mission, promising to return in due course. Within a few minutes he was in Pratt's office, talking over some unimportant matter of business which he had invented as he went along. It was not until he was on the point of departure that he referred to the real reason of his visit.

"Did you notice that Parrawhite is being advertised for?" he asked, suddenly turning on his old clerk.

Pratt was ready for this—had been ready ever since Eldrick walked in. He affected a fine surprise.

"Parrawhite!" he exclaimed. "Why—who's advertising for him?"

"Don't you see the newspapers?" asked Eldrick, pointing to some which lay about the room. "It's in there—there's an advertisement of mine, and one of Halstead & Byner's, of London."

Pratt picked up a Barford paper and looked at the advertisements with a clever affectation of having never seen them before.

"I haven't had much time for newspaper reading this last day or two," he remarked. "Advertisements for him—from two quarters!"

"Acting together—acting together, you know!" replied Eldrick. "It's those people who really want him—Halstead & Byner, inquiry agents, working for a firm of City solicitors. I'm only local agent—as it were."

"Had any response, Mr. Eldrick?" asked Pratt, throwing aside the paper. "Any one come forward?"

"Yes," answered Eldrick, watching Pratt narrowly without seeming to do so. "This morning, a man named Murgatroyd, in Peel Row, who does a bit of shipping agency, wired to Halstead & Byner to say that he booked Parrawhite to New York last November. Of course, they at once communicated with me, and I've just been to see Murgatroyd. He's that man—watchmaker—we had some proceedings against last year."

"Oh, that man!" said Pratt. "Thought the name was familiar. I remember him. And what does he say?"

"Just about as much as—and little more than—he said in his wire to London," replied Eldrick. "Booked Parrawhite to America November 24th last, and believes he left for Liverpool there and then."

"Ah!" remarked Pratt, "That explains it, then?"

"Explains—what?" asked Eldrick.

Pratt gave his old employer a look—confidential and significant.

"Explains why he took that money out of your desk," he said. "You remember—forty odd pounds. He'd use some of that for his passage-money. America eh? Now—I suppose he's vanished for good, then—it's not very likely he'll ever be heard of from across there."

Eldrick laughed—meaningly, of set purpose.

"We don't know that he's gone there," he observed. "He mightn't get beyond Liverpool, you know. Anyhow, we're going to make a very good search for him here in Barford, first. We've nothing but Murgatroyd's word for his having set out for Liverpool."

"What's he wanted for?" asked Pratt as unconcernedly as possible. "Been up to something?"

"No," answered Eldrick, as he turned on his heel. "A relation has left him twenty thousand pounds. That's what he's wanted for—and why he must be found—or his death proved."

He gave Pratt another quick glance and went off—to return to the hotel and Byner, to whom he at once gave a faithful account of what had just taken place.

"And he didn't turn a hair," he remarked. "Cool as a cucumber, all through! If your theory is correct, Pratt's a cleverer hand than I ever took him for—and I've always said he was clever."

"Didn't show anything when you mentioned Murgatroyd?" asked Byner.

"Not a shred of a thing!" replied Eldrick.

"Nor when you spoke of the twenty thousand pounds?"

"No more than what you might call polite and interested surprise!"

Byner laughed, threw away the end of a cigar, and rose out of his lounging posture.

"Now, Mr. Eldrick," he said, leaning close to the solicitor, "between ourselves, do you know what I'm going to do—next—which means at once?"

"No," replied Eldrick.

"The police!" whispered Byner. "That's my next move. Just now! Within a few minutes. So—will you give me a couple of notes—one to the principal man here—chief constable, or police superintendent, or whatever he is; and another to the best detective there is here—in your opinion. They'll save me a lot of trouble."

"Of course—if you wish it," answered Eldrick. "But you don't mean to say you're going to have Pratt arrested—on what you know up to now?"

"Not at all!" replied Byner. "Much too soon! All I want is—detective help of the strictly professional kind. No—we'll give Mr. Pratt a little more rope yet—for another four-and-twenty-hours, say. But—it'll come! Now, who is the best local detective—a quiet, steady fellow who knows how to do his work unobtrusively?"

"Prydale's the man!" said Eldrick "Detective-Sergeant Prydale—I've had reason to employ him, more than once. I'll give you a note to him, and one to Superintendent Waterson."

He went over to a writing-table and scribbled a few lines on half-sheets of notepaper which he enclosed in envelopes and handed to Byner.

"I don't know what line you're taking," he said, "nor where it's going to end—exactly. But I do know this—Pratt never turned a hair when I let out all that to him."

But if Eldrick went away from his old clerk's fine new offices thinking that Pratt was quite unperturbed and unmoved by the news he had just acquired, he was utterly mistaken. Pratt was very much perturbed, deeply moved, not a little frightened. He had so schooled himself to keep a straight and ever blank expression of countenance in any sudden change of events that he had shown nothing to Eldrick—but he was none the less upset by the solicitor's last announcement. Twenty thousand pounds was lying to be picked up by Parrawhite—or by Parrawhite's next-of-kin! What an unhappy turn of fortune! For the next-of-kin would never rest until either Parrawhite came to light, or it was satisfactorily established that he was dead—and if search begun to be made in Barford, where might not that search end? Unmoved?—cool?—if Eldrick had turned back, he would have found that Pratt had suddenly given way to a fit of nerves.

But that soon passed, and Pratt began to think. He left his office early, and betook himself to his favourite gymnasium. Exercise did him good—he thought a lot while he was exercising. And once more, instead of going home to dinner, he dined in town, and he sat late over his dinner in a snug corner of the restaurant, and he thought and planned and schemed—and after twilight had fallen on Barford, he went out and made his way to Peel Row. He must see Murgatroyd again—at once.

Half-way along Peel Row, Pratt stopped, suddenly—and with sudden fear. Out of a side street emerged a man, a quiet ordinary-looking man whom he knew very well indeed—Detective-Sergeant Prydale. He was accompanied by a smart-looking, much younger man, whom Pratt remembered to have seen in Beck Street that afternoon—a stranger to him and to Barford. And as he watched, these two covered the narrow roadway, and walked into Murgatroyd's shop.

24. THE BETTER HALF

Under the warming influence of two glasses of rum and water, and lulled by Pratt's assurance that all would be well, Murgatroyd had carried home his hundred pounds with pretty much the same feeling which permeates a man who, having been within measurable distance of drowning, suddenly finds a substantial piece of timber drifting his way, and takes a firm grip on it. After all, a hundred pounds was a hundred pounds. He would be able to pay his rent, and his rates, and give something to the grocer and the butcher and the baker and the milkman; the children should have some much-needed new clothes and boots—when all this was done, there would be a nice balance left over. And it was Pratt's affair, when all was said and done, and if any trouble arose, why, Pratt would have to settle it. So he ate his supper with the better appetite which Pratt had prophesied, and he slept more satisfactorily than usual, and next morning he went to the nearest telegraph office and sent off the stipulated telegram to Halstead & Byner in London, and hoped that there was the end of the matter as far as he was concerned. And then, shortly after noon, in walked Mr. Eldrick, one of the tribe which Murgatroyd dreaded, having had various dealings with solicitors, in the way of writs and summonses, and began to ask questions.

Murgatroyd emerged from that ordeal very satisfactorily. Eldrick's questions were few, elementary, and easily answered. There were no signs of suspicion about him, and Murgatroyd breathed more freely when he was gone. It seemed to him that the solicitor's visit would certainly wind things up—for him. Eldrick asked all that could be asked, as far as he could see, and he had replied: now, he would probably be bothered no more. His spirits had assumed quite a cheerful tone by evening—but they received a rude shock when, summoned from his little workshop to the front premises, he found himself confronting one man whom he certainly knew to be a detective, and another who might be one. Do what he would he could not conceal some agitation, and Detective-Sergeant Prydale, a shrewdly observant man, noticed it—and affected not to.

"Evening, Mr. Murgatroyd," he said cheerily. "We've come to see if you can give us a bit of information. You've had Mr. Eldrick, the lawyer, here today on the same business. You know—this affair of an old clerk of his—Parrawhite?"

"I told Mr. Eldrick all I know," muttered Murgatroyd.

"Very likely," replied Prydale, "but there's a few questions this gentleman and myself would like to ask. Can we come in?"

Murgatroyd fetched his wife to mind the shop, and took the callers into the parlour which she had unwillingly vacated. He knew Prydale by sight and reputation; about Byner he wondered. Finally he set him down as a detective from London—and was all the more afraid of him.

"What do you want to know?" he asked, when the three men were alone. "I don't think there's anything that I didn't tell Mr. Eldrick."

"Oh, there's a great deal that Mr. Eldrick didn't ask," said Prydale. "Mr. Eldrick sort of just skirted round things, like. We want to know a bit more. This Parrawhite's got to be found, d'ye see, Mr. Murgatroyd, and as you seem to be the last man who had aught to do with him in Barford, why, naturally, we come to you. Now, to start with, you say he came to you about getting a passage to America? Just so—now, when would that be?"

"Day before he did get it," answered Murgatroyd, rapidly thinking over the memoranda which Pratt had jotted down for his benefit.

"That," said Prydale, "would be on the 23rd?"

"Yes," replied Murgatroyd, "23rd November, of course."

"What time, now, on the 23rd?" asked the detective.

"Time?" said Murgatroyd. "Oh—in the evening."

"Bit vague," remarked Prydale. "What time in the evening?"

"As near as I can recollect," replied Murgatroyd, "it 'ud be just about half-past eight. I was thinking of closing."

"Ah!" said Prydale, with a glance at Byner, who had already told him of Parrawhite's presence at the *Green Man* on the other side of the town, a good two miles away, at the hour which Murgatroyd mentioned. "Ah!—he was here in your shop at half-past eight on the evening of November 23rd last? Asking about a ticket to America?"

"New York," muttered Murgatroyd.

"And he came next morning and bought one?" asked the detective.

"I told Mr. Eldrick that," said Murgatroyd, a little sullenly.

"How much did it cost?" inquired Byner.

"Eight pound ten," replied Murgatroyd. "Usual price."

"What did he pay for it in?" continued Prydale.

"He gave me a ten-pound note and I gave him thirty shillings change," answered Murgatroyd.

"Just so," assented Prydale. "Now what line might that be by?"

Murgatroyd was becoming uneasy under all these questions, and his uneasiness was deepened by the way in which both his visitors watched him. He was a man who would have been a bad witness in any case—nervous, ill at ease, suspicious, inclined to boggle—and in this instance he was being forced to invent answers.

"It was—oh, the Royal Atlantic!" he answered at last. "I've an agency for them."

"So I noticed from the bills and placards in your window," observed the detective. "And of course you issue these tickets on their paper—I've seen 'em before. You fill up particulars on a form and a counterfoil, don't you? And you send a copy of those particulars to the Royal Atlantic offices at Liverpool?"

Murgatroyd nodded silently—this was much more than he bargained for, and he did not know how much further it was going. And Prydale gave him a sudden searching look.

"Can you show us the counterfoil in this instance?" he asked.

Murgatroyd flushed. But he managed to get out a fairly quick reply. "No, I can't," he answered, "I sent that book back at the end of the year."

"Oh, well—they'll have it at Liverpool," observed Prydale. "We can get at it there. Of course, they'll have your record of the entire transaction. He'd be down on their passenger list—under the name of Parsons, I think, Mr. Murgatroyd?"

"He gave me that name," said Murgatroyd.

Prydale gave Byner a look and both rose.

"I think that's about all," said the detective. "Of course, our next inquiry will be at Liverpool—-at the Royal Atlantic. Thank you, Mr. Murgatroyd—much obliged."

Before the watchmaker could collect himself sufficiently to say or ask more, Prydale and his companion had walked out of the shop and gone away. And then Murgatroyd realized that he was in for—but he did not know what he was in for. What he did know was that if Prydale went or sent over to Liverpool the whole thing would burst like a bubble. For the Royal Atlantic people would tell the detectives at once that no passenger named Parsons had sailed under their auspices on

November 24th last, and that he, Murgatroyd, had been telling a pack of lies.

Mrs. Murgatroyd, a sharp-featured woman whose wits had been sharpened by a ten years' daily acquaintance with poverty, came out of the shop into the parlour and looked searchingly at her husband.

"What did them fellows want?" she demanded. "I knew one of 'em—Prydale, the detective. Now what's up, Reuben? More trouble?"

Murgatroyd hesitated a moment. Then he told his wife the whole story concealing nothing.

"If they go to the Royal Atlantic, it'll all come out," he groaned. "I couldn't make any excuse or explanation— anyhow! What's to be done?"

"You should ha' had naught to do wi' that Pratt!" exclaimed Mrs. Murgatroyd. "A scoundrelly fellow, to come and tempt poor folk to do his dirty work! Where's the money?"

"Locked up!" answered Murgatroyd. "I haven't touched a penny of it. I thought I'd wait a bit and see if aught happened. But he assured me it was all right, and you know as well as I do that a hundred pound doesn't come our way every day. We want money!"

"Not at that price!" said his wife. "You can pay too much for money, my lad! I wish you'd told me what that Pratt was after—he should have heard a bit o' my tongue! If I'd only known——"

Just then the shop door opened, and Pratt walked in. He at once saw Murgatroyd and his wife standing between shop and parlour, and realized at a glance that his secret in this instance was his no longer.

"Well?" he said, walking up to the watchmaker. "You've had Prydale here—and you'd Eldrick this morning. Of course, you knew what to say to both?"

"I wish we'd never had you here last night, young man!" exclaimed Mrs. Murgatroyd fiercely. "What right have you to come here, making trouble for folk that's got plenty already? But at any rate, ours was honest trouble.

Yours is like to land my husband in dishonesty—if it hasn't done so already! And if my husband had only spoken to me——"

"Just let your husband speak a bit now," interrupted Pratt, almost insolently. "It's you that's making all the trouble or noise, anyhow! There's naught to fuss about, missis. What's upset you, Murgatroyd?"

"They're going to the Royal Atlantic people," muttered the watchmaker. "Of course, it'll all come out, then. They know that I never booked any Parsons—nor anybody else for that matter—last November. You should ha' thought o' that!"

Pratt realized that the man was right. He had never thought of that—never anticipated that inquiry would go beyond Murgatroyd. But his keen wits at once set to work.

"What's the system?" he asked quickly. "Tell me— what's done when you book anybody like that? Come on!—explain, quick!"

Murgatroyd turned to a drawer and pulled out a book and some papers. "It's simple enough," he said. "I've this book of forms, d'ye see? I fill up this form—sort of ticket or pass for the passenger, and hand it to him—it's a receipt as well, to him. Then I enter the same particulars on that counterfoil. Then I fill up one of these papers, giving just the same particulars, and post it at once to the Company with the passage money, less my commission. When one of these books is finished, I return the counterfoils to Liverpool—they check 'em. Prydale's up to all that. He asked to see the counterfoil in this case. I had to say I hadn't got it—I'd sent it to the Company. Of course, he'll find out that I didn't."

"Lies!" said Mrs. Murgatroyd, vindictively. "And they didn't start wi' us neither!"

"Who was that other man with Prydale?" asked Pratt.

"London detective, I should say," answered the watchmaker. "And judging by the way he watched me, a sharp 'un, too!"

"What impression did you get—altogether?" demanded Pratt.

"Why!—that they're going to sift this affair—whatever it is—right down to the bottom!" exclaimed Murgatroyd. "They're either going to find Parrawhite or get to know what became of him. That's my impression. And what am I going to do, now! This'll lose me what bit of business I've done with yon shipping firm."

"Nothing of the sort!" answered Pratt scornfully. "Don't be a fool! You're all right. You listen to me. You write—straight off—to the Royal Atlantic. Tell 'em you had some inquiry made about a man named Parsons, who booked a passage with you for New York last November. Say that on looking up your books you found that you unaccountably forgot to send them the forms for him and his passage money. Make out a form for that date, and crumple it up—as if it had been left lying in a drawer. Enclose the money in it—here, I'll give you ten pounds to cover it," he went on, drawing a bank-note from his purse. "Get it off at once—you've time now—plenty—to catch the night-mail at the General. And then, d'ye see, you're all right. It's only a case then—as far as you're concerned—of forgetfulness. What's that?—we all forget something in business, now and then. They'll overlook that—when they get the money."

"Aye, but you're forgetting something now!" remarked Murgatroyd. "You're forgetting this—no such passenger ever went! They'll know that by their passenger lists."

"What the devil has that to do with it?" snarled Pratt impatiently. "What the devil do we care whether any such passenger went or not? All that you're concerned about is to prove that you issued a ticket to Parrawhite, under the name of Parsons. What's it matter to you where Parrawhite, *alias* Parsons, went, when he'd once left your shop? You naturally thought he'd go straight to the Lancashire and Yorkshire Station, on his way to Liverpool and New York! But, for aught you know, he may have fallen down a drain pipe in the next street!

Don't you see, man? There's nothing, there's nobody, not all the detectives in London and Barford, can prove that you didn't issue a ticket to Parrawhite on that date? It isn't up to you to prove that you did!—it's up to them to prove that you didn't! And—they can't. It's impossible. You get that letter off—at once—to Liverpool, with that money inside it, and you're as safe as houses—and your hundred pounds as well. Get it done! And if those chaps come asking any more questions, tell 'em you're not going to answer a single one! Mind you!—do what I tell you, and you're safe!"

With that Pratt walked out of the shop and went off towards the centre of the town, inwardly raging and disturbed. It was very evident that these people meant to find Parrawhite, alive or dead; evident, too, that they had called in the aid of the Barford police. And in spite of all his assurances to the watchmaker and his suggestion for the next move, Pratt was far from easy about the whole matter. He would have been easier if he had known who Prydale's companion was—probably he was, as Murgatroyd had suggested, a London detective who might have been making inquiries in the town for some time and knew much more than he, Pratt, could surmise. That was the devil of the whole thing!—in Pratt's opinion. Adept himself in working underground, he feared people who adopted the same tactics. What was this stranger chap after? What did he know? What was he doing? Had he let Eldrick know anything? Was there a web of detectives already being spun around himself? Was that silly, unfortunate affair with Parrawhite being slowly brought to light—to wreck him on the very beginning of what he meant to be a brilliant career? He cursed Parrawhite again and again as he left Peel Row behind him.

The events of the day had made Pratt cautious as well as anxious. He decided to keep away from his lodgings that night, and when he reached the centre of the town he took a room at a quiet hotel. He was up early next morning; he had breakfasted by eight o'clock; by half-past eight he was at his office. And in his letter-box he found one letter—a thickish package which had not come by post, but had been dropped in by hand, and was merely addressed to Mr. Pratt.

Pratt tore that package open with a conviction of imminent disaster. He pulled out a sheet of cheap note-paper—and a wad of bank-notes. His face worked curiously as he read a few lines, scrawled in illiterate, female handwriting.

"MR PRATT,—My husband and me don't want any more to do with   either you or your money which it is enclosed. Been honest up to   now though poor, and intending to remain so our purpose is to   make a clean breast of everything to the police first thing   tomorrow morning for which you have nobody but yourself to blame for wickedness in tempting poor people to do wrong.

"Yours, MRS. MURGATROYD."

25. DRY SHERRY

Pratt wasted no time in cursing Mrs. Murgatroyd. There would be plenty of opportunity for such relief to his feelings later on. Just then he had other matters to occupy him—fully. He tore the indignant letter to shreds; he hastily thrust the bank-notes into one pocket and drew his keys from another. Within five minutes he had taken from his safe a sealed packet, which he placed in an inside pocket of his coat, and had left his office—for the last time, as he knew very well. That part of the game was up—and it was necessary to be smart in entering on another phase of it.

Since Eldrick's visit of the previous day, Pratt had been prepared for all eventuality. He had made ready for flight. And he was not going empty-handed. He had a considerable amount of Mrs. Mallathorpe's money in his possession; by obtaining her signature to one or two documents he could easily obtain much more in London, at an hour's notice. Those documents were all ready, and in the sealed packet which he had just taken from the safe; in it, too, were some other documents—John Mallathorpe's will; the letter which Mrs. Mallathorpe had written to him on the evening previous to her son's fatal accident; and the power of attorney which Pratt had obtained from her at his first interview after that occurrence. All was ready—and now there was nothing to do but to get to Normandale Grange, see Mrs. Mallathorpe, and—vanish. He had planned it all out, carefully, when he perceived the first danger signals, and knew that his other plans and schemes were doomed to failure. Half an hour at Normandale Grange—a journey to London—a couple of hours in the City—and then the next train to the Continent, on his way to regions much

further off. Here, things had turned out badly,
unexpectedly badly—but he would carry away
considerable, easily transported wealth, to a new career
in a new country.

Pratt began his flight in methodical fashion. He
locked up his office, and left the building by a back
entrance which took him into a network of courts and
alleys at the rear of the business part of Barford. He
made his way in and out of these places until he reached
a bicycle-dealer's shop in an obscure street, whereat he
had left a machine of his own on the previous evening
under the excuse of having it thoroughly cleaned and
oiled. It was all ready for him on his arrival, and he
presently mounted it and rode away through the
outskirts of the town, carefully choosing the less
frequented streets and roads. He rode on until he was
clear of Barford: until, in fact, he was some miles from it,
and had reached a village which was certainly not on the
way to Normandale. And then, at the post-office he
dismounted, and going inside, wrote out and dispatched a
telegram. It was a brief message containing but three
words—"One as usual"—and it was addressed Esther
Mawson, The Grange, Normandale. This done, he
remounted his bicycle, rode out of the village, and turned
across country in quite a different direction. It was not
yet ten o'clock—he had three hours to spare before the
time came for keeping the appointment which he had just
made.

At an early stage of his operations, Pratt had found
that even the cleverest of schemers cannot work unaided.
It had been absolutely necessary to have some tool close
at hand to Normandale Grange and its inhabitants; to
have some person there upon whom he could depend for
news. He had found that person, that tool, in Esther
Mawson, who, as Mrs. Mallathorpe's maid, had
opportunities which he at once recognized as being likely
to be of the greatest value to him. The circumstances of
Harper Mallathorpe's death had thrown Pratt and the

maid together, and he had quickly discovered that she was to be bought, and would do anything for money. He had soon come to an understanding with her; soon bargained with her, and made her a willing accomplice in certain of his schemes, without letting her know their full meaning and extent: all, indeed, that she had learned from Pratt was that he had some considerable hold on her mistress.

But it is dangerous work to play with edged tools, and if Pratt had only known it, he was running great risks in using Esther Mawson as a semi-accomplice. Esther Mawson was in constant touch with her mistress, and Mrs. Mallathorpe, afraid of her daughter, and not greatly in sympathy with her, badly needed a confidante. Little by little the mistress began to confide in the maid, and before long Esther Mawson knew the secret—and thenceforward she played a double game. Pratt found her useful in arranging meetings with Mrs. Mallathorpe unknown to Nesta, and he believed her to be devoted to him. But the truth was that Esther Mawson had only one object of devotion—herself—and she was waiting and watching for an opportunity to benefit that object—at Pratt's expense.

Pratt knew nothing of this as he slowly made his way to Normandale that morning. Having plenty of time he went by devious and lonely roads and by-lanes. Eventually he came to the boundary of Normandale Park at a point far away from the Grange. There he dismounted, hid his bicycle in a coppice wherein he had often left it before, and went on towards the house through the woods and plantations. He knew every yard of the ground he traversed, and was skilled in taking cover if he saw any sign of woodman or gamekeeper. And in the end, just as one o'clock chimed from the clock over the stables, he came to a quiet spot in the shrubberies behind the Grange, and found Esther Mawson waiting for him in an old summer-house in which they had met on previous and similar occasions.

Esther Mawson immediately realized that something unusual was in the air. Clever as Pratt was at concealing his feelings, she was cleverer in seeing small signs, and she saw that this was no ordinary visit.

"Anything wrong?" she asked at once.

"Bit of bother—nothing much—it'll blow over," answered Pratt, who knew that a certain amount of candour was necessary in dealing with this woman. "But—I shall have to be away for a bit—week or two, perhaps."

"You want to see her?" inquired Esther.

"Of course! I've some papers for her to sign," replied Pratt. "How do things stand? Coast clear?"

"Miss Mallathorpe's going into Barford after lunch," answered Esther. "She'll be driving in about half-past two. I can manage it then. How long shall you want to be with her?"

"Oh, a quarter of an hour'll do," said Pratt. "Ten minutes, if it comes to that."

"And after that?" asked Esther.

"Then I want to get a train at Scaleby," replied Pratt, mentioning a railway junction which lay ten miles across country in another direction. "So make it as soon after two-thirty as you can."

"You can see her as soon as Miss Mallathorpe's gone," said Esther. "You'd better come into the house—I've got the key of the turret door, and all's clear—the servants are all at dinner."

"I could do with something myself," observed Pratt, who, in his anxiety, had only made a light breakfast that morning. "Can it be managed?"

"I'll manage it," she answered. "Come on—now."

Behind the summer-house in which they had met a narrow path led through the shrubberies to an old part of the Grange which was never used, and was, in fact, partly ruinous. Esther Mawson led the way along this until she and Pratt came to a turret in the grey walls, in the lower story of which a massive oaken door, heavily clamped with iron, gave entrance to a winding stair, locked it from inside when she and Pratt had entered, and preceded her companion up the stair, and across one or two empty and dust-covered chambers to a small room in which a few pieces of ancient furniture were slowly dropping to decay. Pratt had taken refuge in this room before, and he sat down in one of the old chairs and mopped his forehead.

"I want something to drink, above everything," he remarked. "What can you get?"

"Nothing but wine," answered Esther Mawson. "As much as you like of that, because I've a stock that's kept up in Mrs. Mallathorpe's room. I couldn't get any ale without going to the butler. I can get wine and sandwiches without anybody knowing."

"That'll do," said Pratt. "What sort of wine?"

"Port, sherry, claret," she replied. "Whichever you like."

"Sherry, then," answered Pratt. "Bring a bottle if you can get it—I want a good drink."

The woman went away—through the disused part of the old house into the modern portion. She went straight to a certain store closet and took from it a bottle of old dry sherry which had been brought there from a bin in the cellars—it was part of a quantity of fine wine laid down by John Mallathorpe, years before, and its original owner would have been disgusted to think that it should ever be used for the mere purpose of quenching thirst. But Esther Mawson had another purpose in view, with respect to that bottle. Carrying it to her own sitting-room, she carefully cut off the thick mass of sealing-wax at its neck, drew the cork, and poured a little of the wine away. And that done, she unlocked a small box which stood on a corner of her dressing table, and took from it a glass phial, half full of a colourless liquid. With steady hands and sure fingers, she dropped some of that liquid into the wine, carefully counting the drops. Then she restored the phial to its hiding-place and re-locked the box—after which, taking up a spoon which lay on her table, she poured out a little of the sherry and smelled and tasted it. No smell—other than that which ought to be there; no taste—other than was proper. Pratt would suspect nothing even if he drunk the whole bottle.

Esther Mawson had anticipated Pratt's desires in the way of refreshment, and she now went to a cupboard and took from it a plate of sandwiches, carefully swathed in a napkin. Carrying these in one hand, and the bottle of sherry and a glass in the other, she stole quietly back to the disused part of the house, and set her provender before its expectant consumer. Pratt poured out a glassful of the sherry, and drank it eagerly.

"Good stuff that!" he remarked, smacking his lips. "Some of old John Mallathorpe's—no doubt."

"It was here when we came, anyhow," replied Esther. "Well—I shall have to go. You'll be all right until I come back."

"What time do you think it'll be?" asked Pratt. "Make it as soon as the coast's clear—I want to be off."

"As soon as ever she's gone," agreed Esther. "I heard her order the carriage for half-past two."

"And no fear of anybody else being about?" asked Pratt. "That butler man, for instance? Or servants?"

"I'll see to it," replied Esther reassuringly. "I'll lock this door and take the key until I come back—make yourself comfortable."

She locked Pratt in the old room and went off, and the willing prisoner ate his sandwiches and drank his sherry, and looked out of a mullioned window on the wide stretches of park and coppice and the breezy moorlands beyond. He indulged in some reflections—not wholly devoid of sentiment. He had cherished dreams of becoming the virtual owner of Normandale. Always confident in his own powers, he had believed that with time and patience he could have persuaded Nesta Mallathorpe to marry him—why not? Now—all owing to that cursed and unfortunate contretemps with Parrawhite, that seemed utterly impossible—all he could do now was to save himself—and to take as much as he could get. More than once that morning, as he made his way across country, he had remembered Parrawhite's advice to take cash and be done with it—perhaps, he reflected, it might have been better. Still—when he presently began his final retreat, he would carry away with him a lot of the Mallathorpe money.

But before long Pratt indulged in no more reflections—sentiment or practical. He had eaten all his sandwiches; he had drunk three-quarters of the bottle of sherry. And suddenly he felt unusually drowsy, and he laid his head back in his big chair, and fell soundly asleep.

26. THE TELEPHONE MESSAGE

If Pratt had only known what was going on in the old quarries at Whitcliffe, about the very time that he was riding slowly out to Barford on his bicycle, he would not only have accelerated his pace, but would have taken good care to have chosen another route: he would also have made haste to exchange bicycle for railway train as quickly as possible, and to have got himself far away before anybody could begin looking for him in his usual haunts, or at places wherein there was a possibility of his being found. But Pratt knew nothing of what Byner had done. He was conscious of Byner's visit to the *Green Man*. He did not know what Pickard had been told by Bill Thomson. He was unaware of anything which Pickard had told to Byner. If he had known that Byner, guided by Pickard, had been to the old quarries, had fixed his inquiring eye on the shaft which was filled to its brim with water, and had got certain ideas from the mere sight of it, Pratt would have hastened to put hundreds of miles between himself and Barford as quickly as possible. But all that Pratt knew was that there was a possibility of suspicion—which might materialize eventually, but not immediately.

On the previous evening, Pratt—had he but known it—made a great mistake. Instead of going into Murgatroyd's shop after he had watched Byner and Prydale away from it—he should have followed those two astute and crafty persons, and have ascertained something of their movements. Had he done so, he would certainly not have troubled to return to Peel Row, nor to remain in Barford an hour longer than was absolutely necessary. For Pratt was sharp-witted enough when it came to a question of putting one and two together, and if he had tracked Prydale and the unknown man who was with him to a certain house whereto they repaired as soon as they quitted Murgatroyd's shop, he would have drawn an inference from the mere fact of their visit which would have thrown him into a cold sweat of fear. But Pratt, after all, was only one man, one brain, one body, and could not be in two places, nor go in two ways, at the same time. He took his own way—ignorant of his destruction.

Byner also took a way of his own. As soon as he and Prydale left Murgatroyd's shop, they chartered the first cab they met with, and ordered its driver to go to Whitcliffe Moor.

"It's the quickest thing to do—if my theory's correct," observed Byner, as they drove along, "Of course, it is all theory—mere theory! But I've grounds for it. The place— the time—mere lonely situation—that scrap iron lying about, which would be so useful in weighting a dead body!—I tell you, I shall be surprised if we don't find Parrawhite at the bottom of that water!"

"I shouldn't wonder," agreed Prydale. "One thing's very certain, as we shall prove before we're through with it—Pratt's put that poor devil Murgatroyd up to this passage-to-America business. And a bit clumsily, too— fancy Murgatroyd being no better posted up than to tell me that Parrawhite called on him at a certain hour that night!"

"But you've got to remember that Pratt didn't know of Parrawhite's affairs with Pickard, nor that he was at the *Green Man* at that hour," rejoined Byner. "My belief is that Pratt thinks himself safe—that he fancies he's provided for all contingencies. If things turn out as I think they will, I believe we shall find Pratt calmly seated at his desk tomorrow morning."

"Well—if things do turn out as you expect, we'll lose no time in seeking him there!" observed Prydale dryly. "We'd better arrange to get the job done first thing."

"This Mr. Shepherd'll make no objection, I suppose?" asked Byner.

"Objection! Lor' bless you—he'll love it!" exclaimed Prydale. "It'll be a bit of welcome diversion to a man like him that's naught to do. He'll object none, not he!"

Shepherd, a retired quarry-owner, who lived in a picturesque old stone house in the middle of Whitcliffe Moor, with nothing to occupy his attention but the growing of roses and vegetables, and an occasional glance at the local newspapers, listened to Prydale's request with gradually rising curiosity. Byner had at once seen that this call was welcome to this bluff and hearty Yorkshireman, who, without any question as to their business, had immediately welcomed them to his hearth and pressed liquor and cigars on them: he sized up Shepherd as a man to whom any sort of break in the placid course of retired life was a delightful event.

"A dead man i' that old shaft i' one o' my worked out quarries!" he exclaimed. "Ye don't mean to say so! An' how long d'yer think he might ha' been there, now, Prydale?"

"Some months, Mr. Shepherd," replied the detective.

"Why, then it's high time he were taken out," said Shepherd. "When might you be thinkin' o' doin' t' job, like?"

"As soon as possible," said Prydale. "Tomorrow morning, early, if that's convenient to you."

"I'll tell you what I'll do," observed the retired quarry-owner. "You leave t' job to me. I'll get two or three men first thing tomorrow morning, and we'll do it reight. You be up there by half-past eight o'clock, and we'll soon satisfy you as to whether there's owt i' t' shape of a dead man or not i' t' pit. You hev' grounds for believin' 'at theer is——what?"

"Strong grounds!" replied the detective, "and equally strong ones for believing the man came there by foul play, too."

"Say no more!" said Shepherd. "T' mystery shall be cleared up. Deary me! An' to think 'at I've walked past yon theer pit many a dozen times within this last few o' months, and nivver dreamed 'at theer wor owt in it but watter! Howivver, gentlemen, ye can put yer minds at ease—we'll investigate the circumstances, as the sayin' goes, before noon tomorrow."

"One other matter," remarked Prydale. "We want things kept quiet. We don't want all the folk of the neighbourhood round about, you know."

"Leave it to me," answered Shepherd. "There'll be me, and these men, and yourselves—and a pair of grapplin' irons. We'll do it quiet and comfortable—and we'll do it reight."

"Odd character!" remarked Byner, when he and Prydale went away.

"Useful man—for a job of that sort," said the detective laconically. "Now then—are we going to let anybody else know what we're after—Mr. Eldrick or Mr. Collingwood, for instance? Do you want them, or either of them, to be present?"

"No!" answered Byner, after a moment's reflection. "Let us see what results. We can let them know, soon enough, if we've anything to tell. But—what about Pratt?"

"Keeping an eye on him—you mean?" said Prydale. "You said just now that in your opinion we should find him at his desk."

"Just so—but that's no reason why he shouldn't be looked after tomorrow morning," answered Byner.

"All right—I'll put a man on to shadow him, from the time he leaves his lodgings until—until we want him," said the detective. "That is—if we do want him."

"It will be one of the biggest surprises I ever had in my life if we don't!" asserted Byner. "I never felt more certain of anything than I do of finding Parrawhite's body in that pit!"

It was this certainty which made Byner appear extraordinarily cool and collected, when next day, about noon, he walked into Eldrick's private room, where Collingwood was at that moment asking the solicitor what was being done. The certainty was now established, and it seemed to Byner that it would have been a queer thing if he had not always had it. He closed the door and gave the two men an informing glance.

"Parrawhite's body has been found," he said quietly.

Eldrick started in his chair, and Collingwood looked a sharp inquiry.

"Little doubt about his having been murdered, just as I conjectured," continued Byner. "And his murderer had pretty cleverly weighted his body with scrap iron, before dropping it into a pit full of water, where it might have remained for a long time undiscovered. However—that's settled!"

Eldrick got out the first question.

"Pratt?"

"Prydale's after him," answered Byner. "I expect we shall hear something in a few minutes—if he's in town. But I confess I'm a bit doubtful and anxious now, on that score. Because, when Prydale and I got down from Whitcliffe half an hour ago—where the body's now lying, at the *Green Man*, awaiting the inquest—we found Murgatroyd hanging about the police station. He'd come to make a clean breast of it—about Pratt. And it unfortunately turns out that Pratt saw Prydale and me go to Murgatroyd's shop last night, and afterwards went in there himself, and of course pumped Murgatroyd dry as to why we'd been."

"Why unfortunately?" asked Collingwood.

"Because that would warn Pratt that something was afoot," said Byner. "And—he may have disappeared during the night. He——"

But just then Prydale came in, shaking his head.

"I'm afraid he's off!" he announced. "I'd a man watching for him outside his lodgings from an early hour this morning, but he never came out, and finally my man made an excuse and asked for him there, and then he heard that he'd never been home last night. And his office is closed."

"What steps are you taking?" asked Byner.

"I've got men all over the place already," replied Prydale. "But—if he got off in the night, as I'm afraid he did, we shan't find him in Barford. It's a most unlucky thing that he saw us go to Murgatroyd's last evening! That, of course, would set him off: he'd know things were reaching a crisis."

Eldrick and Collingwood had arranged to lunch together that day, and they presently went off, asking the detective to keep them informed of events. But up to half-past three o 'clock they heard no more—then, as they were returning along the street Byner came running up to them.

"Prydale's just had a telephone message from the butler at Normandale!" he exclaimed. "Pratt is there!—and something extraordinary is going on: the butler wants the police. We're off at once—there's Prydale in a motor, waiting for me. Will you follow?"

He darted away again, and Eldrick looking round for a car, suddenly recognized the Mallathorpe livery.

"Great Scott!" he said. "There's Miss Mallathorpe—just driving in. Better tell her!"

A moment later, he and Collingwood had joined Nesta in her carriage, and the horses' heads were turned in the direction towards which Byner and Prydale were already hastening.

27. RESTORED TO ENERGY

Esther Mawson, leaving Pratt to enjoy his sherry and sandwiches at his leisure, went away through the house, out into the gardens, and across the shrubbery to the stables. The coachman and grooms were at dinner—with the exception of one man who lived in a cottage at the entrance to the stable-yard. This was the very man she wanted to see, and she found him in the saddle-room, and beckoned him to its door.

"Mrs. Mallathorpe wants me to go over to Scaleby on an errand for her this afternoon," she said. "Can you have the dog-cart ready, at the South Garden gate at three o'clock sharp? And—without saying anything to the coachman? It's a private errand."

Of late this particular groom had received several commissions of this sort, and being a sharp fellow he had observed that they were generally given to him when Miss Mallathorpe was out.

"All right," he answered. "The young missis is going out in the carriage at half-past two. South Garden gate— three sharp. Anybody but you?"

"Only me," replied Esther. "Don't say anything to anybody about where we're going. Get the dog-cart ready after the carriage has gone."

The groom nodded in comprehension, and Esther went back to the house and to her own room. She ought at that time of day to have been eating her dinner with the rest of the upper servants, but she had work to do which was of much more importance than the consumption of food and drink. There was going to be a flight that afternoon—but it would not be Pratt who would undertake it. Esther Mawson had carefully calculated all her chances as soon as Pratt told her that he was going to be away for a while. She knew that Pratt would not have left Barford for any indefinite period unless something had gone seriously wrong. But she knew more—by inference and intuition. If Pratt was going away—rather, since he was going away, he would have on his person things of value—documents, money. She meant to gain possession of everything that he had; she meant to have a brief interview with Mrs. Mallathorpe; then she meant to drive to Scaleby—and to leave that part of the country just as thoroughly and completely as Pratt had meant to leave it. And now in her own room she was completing her preparations. There was little to do. She knew that if her venture came off successfully, she could easily afford to leave her personal possessions behind her, and that she would be all the more free and unrestricted in her movements if she departed without as much as a change of clothes and linen. And so by two o'clock she had arrayed herself in a neat and unobtrusive tailor-made travelling costume, had put on an equally neat and plain hat, had rolled her umbrella, and laid it, her gloves, and a cloak where they could be readily picked up, and had attached to her slim waist a hand-bag—by means of a steel chain which she secured by a small padlock as soon as she had arranged it to her satisfaction. She was not the sort of woman to leave a hand-bag lying about in a railway carriage at any time, but in this particular instance she was not going to run any risk of even a moment's forgetfulness.

Everything was in readiness by twenty minutes past two, and she took up her position in a window from which she could see the front door of the house. At half-past two the carriage and its two fine bay horses came round from the stables; a minute or two later Nesta Mallathorpe emerged from the hall; yet another minute and the carriage was whirling down the park in the direction of Barford. And then Esther moved from the window, picked up the umbrella, the cloak, the gloves, and went off in the direction of the room wherein she had left Pratt.

No one ever went near those old rooms except on some special errand or business, and there was a dead silence all around her as she turned the key in the lock and slipped inside the door—to lock it again as soon as she had entered. There was an equally deep silence within the room—and for a moment she glanced a little fearfully at the recumbent figure in the old, deep-backed chair. Pratt had stretched himself fully in his easy quarters—his legs lay extended across the moth-eaten hearth-rug; his head and shoulders were thrown far back against the faded tapestry, and he was so still that he might have been supposed to be dead. But Esther Mawson had tried the effect of that particular drug on a good many people, and she knew that the victim in this instance was merely plunged in a sleep from which nothing whatever could wake him yet awhile. And after one searching glance at him, and one lifting of an eyelid by a practised finger, she went rapidly and thoroughly through Pratt's pockets, and within a few minutes of entering the room had cleared them of everything they contained. The sealed packet which he had taken from his safe that morning; the bank-notes which Mrs. Murgatroyd had returned in her indignant letter; another roll of notes, of considerable value, in a note-case; a purse containing notes and gold to a large amount—all those she laid one by one on a dust-covered table. And finally—and as calmly as if she were sorting linen—she swept bank-notes, gold, and purse into her steel-chained bag, and tore open the sealed envelope.

There were five documents in that envelope—Esther examined each with meticulous care. The first was an authority to Linford Pratt to sell certain shares standing in the name of Ann Mallathorpe. The second was a similar document relating to other shares: each was complete, save for Ann Mallathorpe's signature. The third document was the power of attorney which Ann Mallathorpe had given to Linford Pratt: the fourth, the letter which she had written to him on the evening before

the fatal accident to Harper. And the fifth was John
Mallathorpe's will.

At last she held in her hand the half-sheet of foolscap
paper of which Mrs. Mallathorpe, driven to distraction,
and knowing that she would get no sympathy from her
own daughter, had told her. She was a woman of a quick
and an understanding mind, and she had read the will
through and grasped its significance as swiftly as her
eyes ran over it. And those eyes turned to the unconscious
Pratt with a flash of contempt—she, at any rate, would
not follow his foolish example, and play for too high a
stake—no, she would make hay while the sun shone its
hottest! She was of the Parrawhite persuasion—better,
far better one good bird in the hand than a score of
possible birds in the bush.

She presently restored the five documents to the stout
envelope, picked up her other belongings, and without so
much as a glance at Pratt, left the room. She turned the
key in the door and took it away with her. And now she
went straight to a certain sitting-room which Mrs.
Mallathorpe had tenanted by day ever since her illness.
The final and most important stage of Esther's venture
was at hand.

Mrs. Mallathorpe sat at an open window, wearily
gazing out on the park. Ever since her son's death she
had remained in a more or less torpid condition, rarely
talking to any person except Esther Mawson: it had been
manifest from the first that her daughter's presence
distressed and irritated her, and by the doctor's advice
Nesta had gone to her as little as possible, while taking
every care to guard her and see to her comfort. All day
long she sat brooding—and only Esther Mawson, now for
some time in her full confidence, knew that her brooding
was rapidly developing into a monomania. Mrs.
Mallathorpe, indeed, had but one thought in her mind—
the eventual circumventing of Pratt, and the destruction
of John Mallathorpe's will.

She turned slowly as the maid came in and carefully closed the door behind her, and her voice was irritable and querulous as she at once began to complain.

"You've never been near me for two hours!" she said. "Your dinner time was over long since! I might have been wanting all sorts of things for aught you cared!"

"I've had something else to do—for you!" retorted Esther, coming close to her mistress. "Listen, now!—I've got it!"

Mrs. Mallathorpe's attitude and manner suddenly changed. She caught sight of the packet of papers in the woman's hand, and at once sprang to her feet, white and trembling. Instinctively she held out her own hands and moved a little nearer to the maid. And Esther quickly put the table between them, and shook her head.

"No—no!" she exclaimed. "No handling of anything—yet! You keep your hands off! You were ready enough to bargain with Pratt—now you'll have to bargain with me. But I'm not such a fool as he was—I'll take cash down, and be done with it."

Mrs. Mallathorpe rested her trembling hands on the table and bent forward across it.

"Is it—is it—really—the will?" she whispered hoarsely.

Instead of replying in words, Esther, taking care to keep at a safe distance behind the table, and with the door only a yard or two in her rear, drew out the documents one by one and held them up.

"The will!" she said. "Your letter to Pratt. The power of attorney. Two papers that he brought for you to sign. That's the lot! And now, as I said, we'll bargain."

"Where is—he?" asked Mrs. Mallathorpe. "How—how did you get them? Does he know—did he give them up?"

"If you want to know, he's safe and sound asleep in one of the rooms in the old part of the house," answered Esther. "I drugged him. There's something afoot—something gone wrong with his schemes—at Barford, and he came here on his way—elsewhere. And so—I took the chance. Now then—what are you going to give me?"

Mrs. Mallathorpe, whose nervous agitation was becoming more and more marked, wrung her hands.

"I've nothing to give!" she cried. "You know very well he's had the management of everything—I don't know how things are——"

"Stuff!" exclaimed Esther. "I know better than that. You've a lot of ready money in that desk there—you know you drew a lot out of the bank some time ago, and it's there now. You kept it for a contingency—the contingency's here. And—you've your rings—the diamond and ruby rings—I know what they're worth! Come on, now—I mean to have the whole lot, so it's no use hesitating."

Mrs. Mallathorpe looked at the maid's bold and resolute eyes—and then at the papers. And she glanced from eyes and papers to a bright fire which burned in the grate close by.

"You'll give everything up?" she asked nervously.

"Put those bank-notes that you've got in your desk, and those rings that are in your jewel-case, on the table between us," answered Esther, "and I'll hand over these papers on the instant! I'm not going to be such a fool as to keep them—not I! Come on, now!—isn't this the chance you've wanted?"

Mrs. Mallathorpe drew a small bunch of keys from her gown, and went over to the desk which Esther had pointed to. Within a minute she was back again at the table, a roll of bank notes in one hand, half a dozen magnificent rings in the other. She put both hands halfway across and unclasped them. And Esther Mawson, with a light laugh, threw the papers over the table, and hastily swept their price into her handbag.

Mrs. Mallathorpe's nerves suddenly became steady. With a deep sigh she caught up the various documents and looked them quickly and thoroughly over. Then she tore them into fragments and flung the fragments in the fire—and as they blazed up, she turned and looked at Esther Mawson in a way which made Esther shrink a little. But she was already at the door—and she opened it and walked out and down the stair.

She was half-way across the hall beneath, where the butler and one of the footmen were idly talking, when a sharp cry from above made her then look up. Mrs. Mallathorpe, suddenly restored to life and energy, was leaning over the balustrade.

"Stop that woman, you men!" she said. "Seize her! Fasten her up!—lock the door wherever you put her! She's stolen my rings, and a lot of money out of my desk! And telephone instantly to Barford, and tell them to send the police here—at once!"

28. THE WOMAN IN BLACK

Nesta Mallathorpe, who had just arrived in Barford when Eldrick caught sight of her, was seriously startled as he and Collingwood came running up to her carriage. The solicitor entered it without ceremony or explanation, and turning to the coachman bade him drive back to Normandale as fast as he could make his horses go. Meanwhile Collingwood turned to Nesta. "Don't be alarmed!" he said. "Something is happening at the Grange—your mother has just telephoned to the police here to go there at once—there they are—in front of us, in that car!"

"Did my mother say if she was in danger?" demanded Nesta.

"She can't be!" exclaimed Eldrick, turning from the coachman, as the horses were whipped round and the carriage moved off. "She evidently gave orders for the message. No—Pratt's there! And—but of course, you don't know—the police want Pratt. They've been searching for him since noon. He's wanted for murder!"

"Don't frighten Miss Mallathorpe," said Collingwood. "The murder has nothing to do with present events," he went on reassuringly. "It's something that happened some time ago. Don't be afraid about your mother—there are plenty of people round her, you know."

"I can't help feeling anxious if Pratt is there," she answered. "How did he come to be there? It's not an hour since I left home. This is all some of Esther Mawson's work! And we shall have to wait nearly an hour before we know what is going on!—it's all uphill work to Normandale, and the horses can't do it in the time."

"Eldrick!" said Collingwood, as the carriage came abreast of the Central Station and a long line of motorcars. "Stop the coachman! Let's get one of those cars—we shall get to Normandale twice as quickly. The main thing is to relieve Miss Mallathorpe of anxiety. Now!" he went on, as they hastily left the carriage and transferred themselves to a car quickly scented by Eldrick as the most promising of the lot. "Tell the driver to go as fast as he can—the other car's not very far in front—tell him to catch it up."

Eldrick leaned over and gave his orders.

"I've told him not only to catch him up, but to get in front of 'em," he said, settling down again in his seat. "This is a better car than theirs, and we shall be there first. Now, Miss Mallathorpe, don't you bother—this is probably going to be the clearing-up point of everything. One feels certain, at any rate—Pratt has reached the end of his tether!"

"If I seem to bother," replied Nesta, "it's because I know that he and Esther Mawson are at Normandale— working mischief."

"We shall be there in half an hour," said Collingwood, as their own car ran past that in which the detectives and Byner were seated. "They can't do much mischief in that time."

None of the three spoke again until the car pulled up suddenly at the gates of Normandale Park. The lodge-keeper, an old man, coming out to open them, approached the door of the car on seeing Nesta within.

"There's a young woman just gone up to the house that wants to see you very particular, miss," he said. "I tell'd her that you'd gone to Barford, but she said she'd come a long way, and she'd wait till you come back. She's going across the park there—crossin' yon path."

He pointed over the level sward to the slight figure of a woman in black, who was obviously taking a near cut up to the Grange. Nesta looked wonderingly across the park as the car cleared the gate and went on up the drive.

"Who can she be?" she said musingly. "A woman from a long way—to see me?"

"She'll get to the house soon after we reach it," said Eldrick. "Let's attend to this more pressing business first. We should know what's afoot here in a minute or two."

But it was somewhat difficult to make out or to discover what really was afoot. The car stopped at the hall door: the second car came close behind it; Nesta, Collingwood, Eldrick, Byner, and the detectives poured into the hall—encountered a much mystified-looking butler, a couple of footmen, and the groom whose services Esther Mawson had requisitioned, and who, weary of waiting for her, had come up to the house.

"What's all this?" asked Eldrick, taking the situation into his own hands. "What's the matter? Why did you send for the police?"

"Mrs. Mallathorpe's orders, sir," answered the butler, with an apologetic glance at his young mistress. "Really, sir, I don't know—exactly—what is the matter! We are all so confused! What happened was, that not very long after Miss Mallathorpe had left for town in the carriage, Esther Mawson, the maid, came downstairs from Mrs. Mallathorpe's room, and was crossing the lower part of the hall, when Mrs. Mallathorpe suddenly appeared up there and called to me and James to stop her and lock her up, as she'd stolen money and jewels! We were to lock her up and telephone for the police, sir, and to add that Mr. Pratt was here."

"Well?" demanded Eldrick.

"We did lock her up, sir! She's in my pantry," continued the butler, ruefully. "We've got her in there because there are bars to the windows—she can't get out of that. A terrible time we had, too, sir—she fought us like—like a maniac, protesting all the time that Mrs. Mallathorpe had given her what she had on her. Of course, sir, we don't know what she may have on her—we simply obeyed Mrs. Mallathorpe."

"Where is Mrs. Mallathorpe?" asked Collingwood. "Is she safe?"

"Oh, quite safe, sir!" replied the butler. "She returned to her room after giving those orders. Mrs. Mallathorpe appeared to be—quite calm, sir."

Prydale pushed himself forward—unceremoniously and insistently.

"Keep that woman locked up!" he said. "First of all—where's Pratt?"

"Mrs. Mallathorpe said he would be found in a room in the old part of the house," answered the butler, shaking his head as if he were thoroughly mystified. "She said you would find him fast asleep—Mawson had drugged him!"

Prydale looked at Byner and at his fellow-detectives. Then he turned to the butler.

"Come on!" he said brusquely. "Take us there at once!" He glanced at Eldrick. "I'm beginning to see through it, Mr. Eldrick!" he whispered. "This maid's caught Pratt for us. Let's hope he's still——"

But before he could say more, and just as the butler opened a door which led into a corridor at the rear of the hall, a sharp crack which was unmistakably that of a revolver, rang through the house, waking equally sharp echoes in the silent room. And at that, Nesta hurried up the stairway to her mother's apartment, and the men, after a hurried glance at each other, ran along the corridor after the butler and the footmen.

Pratt came out of his stupor much sooner than Esther Mawson had reckoned on. According to her previous experiments with the particular drug which she had administered to him, he ought to have remained in a profound and an undisturbed slumber until at least five o'clock. But he woke at four—woke suddenly, sharply, only conscious at first of a terrible pain in his head, which kept him groaning and moaning in his chair for a minute or two before he fairly realized where he was and what had happened. As the pain became milder and gave way to a dull throbbing and a general sense of discomfort, he looked round out of aching eyes and saw the bottle of sherry. And so dull were his wits that his only thought at first was that the wine had been far stronger than he had known, and that he had drunk far too much of it, and that it had sent him to sleep—and just then his wandering glance fell on some papers which Esther Mawson had taken from one of his pockets and thrown aside as of no value.

He leapt to his feet, trembling and sweating. His hands, shaking as if smitten with a sudden palsy, went to his pockets—he tore off his coat and turned his pockets out, as if touch and feeling were not to be believed, and his eyes must see that there was really nothing there. Then he snatched up the papers on the floor and found nothing but letters, and odd scraps of unimportant memoranda. He stamped his feet on those things, and began to swear and curse, and finally to sob and whine. The shock of his discovery had driven all his stupefaction away by that time, and he knew what had happened. And his whining and sobbing was not that of despair, but the far worse and fiercer sobbing and whining of rage and terrible anger. If the woman who had tricked him had been there he would have torn her limb from limb, and have glutted himself with revenge. But—he was alone.

And presently, after moving around his prison more like a wild beast than a human being, his senses having deserted him for a while, he regained some composure, and glanced about him for means of escape. He went to the door and tried it. But the old, substantial oak stood firm and fast—nothing but a crow-bar would break that door. And so he turned to the mullioned window, set in a deep recess.

He knew that it was thirty or forty feet above the level of the ground—but there was much thick ivy growing on the walls of Normandale Grange, and it might be possible to climb down by its aid. With a great effort he forced open one of the dirt-encrusted sashes and looked out— and in the same instant he drew in his head with a harsh groan. The window commanded a full view of the hall door—and he had seen Prydale, and two other detectives, and the stranger from London whom he believed to be a detective, hurrying from their motorcar into the house.

There was but one thing for it, now. Esther Mawson had robbed him of everything that was on him in the way of papers and money. But in his hip-pocket she had left a revolver which Pratt had carried, always loaded, for some time. And now, without the least hesitation, he drew it out and sent one of its bullets through his brain.

*   *   *   *   *

Eldrick and Collingwood, returning to the hall from the room in which they and the detectives had found Pratt's dead body, stood a little later in earnest conversation with Prydale, who had just come there from an interview with Esther Mawson. Nesta Mallathorpe suddenly called to them from the stairs, at the same time beckoning them to go up to her.

"Will you come with me and speak to my mother?" she said. "She knows you are here, and she wants to say something about what has happened—something about that document which Pratt said he possessed."

Eldrick and Collingwood exchanged glances without speaking. They followed Nesta into her mother's sitting-room. And instead of the semi-invalid whom they had expected to find there, they saw a woman who had evidently regained not only her vivacity and her spirits but her sense of authority and her inclination to exercise it.

"I am sorry that you gentlemen should have been drawn into all this wretched business!" she exclaimed, as she pointed the two men to chairs. "Everything must seem very strange, and indeed have seemed so for some time. But I have been the victim of as bad a scoundrel as ever lived—I'm not going to be so hypocritical as to pretend that I'm sorry he's dead—I'm not! I only wish he'd met his proper fate—on the scaffold. I don't know what you may have heard, or gathered—my daughter herself, from what she tells me, has only the vaguest notions—but I wanted to tell you, Mr. Eldrick, and you, Mr. Collingwood—seeing that you're one a solicitor and the other a barrister, that Pratt invented a most abominable plot against me, which, of course, hasn't a word of truth in it, yet was so clever that——"

Eldrick suddenly raised his hand.

"Mrs. Mallathorpe!" he said quietly. "I think you had better let me speak before you go any further. Perhaps we—Mr. Collingwood and I—know more than you think. Don't trifle, Mrs. Mallathorpe, for your own and your daughter's sake! Tell the truth—and answer a plain question, which I assure you, is asked in your own interest. What have you done with John Mallathorpe's will?"

Collingwood, anxious for Nesta, was watching her closely, and now he saw her turn a startled and inquiring look on her mother, who, in her turn, dashed a surprised glance at Eldrick. But if Mrs. Mallathorpe was surprised, she was also indignant, or she simulated indignation, and she replied to the solicitor's question with a sharp retort.

"What do you mean?—John Mallathorpe's will!" she exclaimed. "What do I know of John Mallathorpe's will? There never was——"

"Mrs. Mallathorpe!" interrupted Eldrick. "Don't! I'm speaking in your interest, I tell you! There was a will! It was made on the morning of John Mallathorpe's death. It was found by Mr. Collingwood's late grandfather, Antony Bartle: when he died suddenly in my office, it fell into Pratt's hands. That is the document which Pratt held over you—and not an hour ago, Esther Mawson took it from Pratt, and she gave it to you. Again I ask you—what have you done with it?"

Mrs. Mallathorpe hesitated a moment. Then she suddenly faced Eldrick with a defiant look. "Let them— let everybody—do what they like!" she exclaimed. "It's

burnt! I threw it in that fire as soon as I got it! And now—
—"

Nesta interrupted her mother.

"Does any one know the terms of that will?" she asked, looking at Eldrick. "Tell me!—if you know. Hush!" she went on, as Mrs. Mallathorpe tried to speak again. "I will know!"

"Yes!" answered Eldrick. "Esther Mawson knows them. She read the will carefully. She told Prydale just now what they were. With the exception of three legacies of ten thousand pounds each to your mother, your brother, and yourself, John Mallathorpe left everything he possessed to the town of Barford for an educational trust."

"Then," asked Nesta quietly, as she made a peremptory sign to her mother to be silent, "we—never had any right to be here—at all?"

"I'm afraid not," replied Eldrick.

"Then of course we shall go," said Nesta. "That's certain! Do you hear that, mother? That's my decision. It's final!"

"You can do what you like," retorted Mrs. Mallathorpe sullenly. "I am not going to be frightened by anything that Esther Mawson says. Nor by what you say!" she continued, turning on Eldrick. "All that has got to be proved. Who can prove it? What can prove it? Do you think I am going to give up my rights without fighting for them? I shall swear that every word of Esther Mawson's is a lie! No one can bring forward a will that doesn't exist. And what concern is it of yours, Mr. Eldrick? What right have you?"

"You are quite right, Mrs. Mallathorpe," said Eldrick. "It is no concern of mine. And so——"

He turned to the door—and as he turned the door opened, to admit the old butler who looked apologetically but earnestly at Nesta as he stepped forward.

"A Mrs. Gaukrodger wishes to see you on very particular business," he murmured. "She's been waiting some little time—something, she says, about some papers she has just found—belonging to the late Mr. John Mallathorpe."

Collingwood, who was standing close to Nesta, caught all the butler said.

"Gaukrodger!" he exclaimed, with a quick glance at Eldrick. "That was the name of the manager—a witness. See the woman at once," he whispered to Nesta.

"Bring Mrs. Gaukrodger in, Dickenson," said Nesta. "Stay—I'll come with you, and bring her in myself."

She returned a moment later with a slightly built, rather careworn woman dressed in deep mourning—the woman in black whom they had seen crossing the park—who looked nervously round her as she entered.

"What is it you have for me, Mrs. Gaukrodger?" asked Nesta. "Papers belonging to the late Mr. John Mallathorpe? How—where did you get them?"

Mrs. Gaukrodger drew a large envelope from under her cloak. "This, miss," she answered. "One paper—I only found it this morning. In this way," she went on, addressing herself to Nesta. "When my husband was killed, along with Mr. John Mallathorpe, they, of course, brought home the clothes he was wearing. There were a lot of papers in the pockets of the coat—two pockets full of them. And I hadn't heart or courage to look at them at that time, miss!—I couldn't, and I locked them up in a box. I never looked at them until this very day—but this morning I happened to open that box, and I saw them, and I thought I'd see what they were. And this was one—you see, it's in a plain envelope—it was sealed, but there's no writing on it. I cut the envelope open, and drew the paper out, and I saw at once it was Mr. John Mallathorpe's will—so I came straight to you with it."

She handed the envelope over to Nesta, who at once gave it to Eldrick. The solicitor hastily drew out the enclosure, glanced it over, and turned sharply to Collingwood with a muttered exclamation.

"Good gracious!" he said. "That man Cobcroft was right! There *was* a duplicate! And here it is!"

Mrs. Mallathorpe had come nearer. The sight of the half sheet of foolscap in Eldrick's hands seemed to fascinate her. And the expression of her face as she came close to his side was so curious that the solicitor involuntarily folded up the will and hastily put it behind his back—he had not only seen that expression but had caught sight of Mrs. Mallathorpe's twitching fingers.

"Is—that—that—another will?" she whispered. "John Mallathorpe's?"

"Precisely the same—another copy—duly signed and witnessed!" answered Eldrick firmly. "What you foolishly did was done for nothing. And—it's the most fortunate thing in the world, Mrs. Mallathorpe, that this has turned up!—most fortunate for you!"

Mrs. Mallathorpe steadied herself on the edge of the table and looked at him fixedly. "Everything'll have to be given up?" she asked.

"The terms of this will will be carried out," answered Eldrick.

"Will—will they make me give up—what we've— saved?" she whispered.

"Mother!" said Nesta appealingly. "Don't! Come away somewhere and let me talk to you—come!"

But Mrs. Mallathorpe shook off her daughter's hand and turned again to Eldrick.

"Will they?" she demanded. "Answer!"

"I don't think you'll find the trustees at all hard when it comes to a question of account," answered Eldrick. "They'll probably take matters over from now and ignore anything that's happened during the past two years."

Again Nesta tried to lead her mother away, and again Mrs. Mallathorpe pushed the appealing hand from her. All her attention was fixed on Eldrick. "And—and will the police give me—now—what they found on that woman?" she whispered.

"I have no doubt they will," replied Eldrick. "It's—yours."

Mrs. Mallathorpe drew a sigh of relief. She looked at the solicitor steadily for a moment—then without another word she turned and went away—to find Prydale.

Eldrick turned to Nesta.

"Don't forget," he said in a low voice, "it's a terrible blow to her, and she's been thinking of your interests! Leave her alone for a while—she'll get used to the altered circumstances. I'm sorry for her—and for you!"

But Nesta made a sign of dissent.

"There's no need to be sorry for me, Mr. Eldrick," she answered. "It's a greater relief than you can realize." She turned from him and went over to Mrs. Gaukrodger who had watched this scene without fully comprehending it. "Come with me," she said. "You look very tired and you must have some tea and rest awhile—come now."

Eldrick and Collingwood, left alone, looked at each, other in silence for a moment. Then the solicitor shook his head expressively.

"Well, that's over!" he exclaimed. "I must go back and hand this will over to the two trustees. But you, Collingwood—stay here a bit—if ever that girl needs company and help, it's now!"

"I'm stopping," said Collingwood.

He remained for a time where Eldrick left him; at last he went down to the hall and out into the gardens. And presently Nesta came to him there, and as if with a mutual understanding they walked away into the nearer stretches of the park. Normandale had never looked more beautiful than it did that afternoon, and in the midst of a silence which up to then neither of them had cared to break, Collingwood suddenly turned to the girl who had just lost it.

"Are you sure that you won't miss all this—greatly?" he asked. "Just think!"

"I'd rather lose more than this, however fond I'd got of it, than go through what I've gone through lately," she answered frankly. "Do you know what I want to do?"

"No—I think not," he said. "What?"

"If it's possible—to forget all about this," she replied. "And—if that's also possible—to help my mother to forget, too. Don't think too hardly of her—I don't suppose any of us know how much all this place—and the money—meant to her."

"I've got no hard thoughts about her," said Collingwood. "I'm sorry for her. But—is it too soon to talk about the future?"

Nesta looked at him in a way which showed him that she only half comprehended the question. But there was sufficient comprehension in her eyes to warrant him in taking her hands in his.

"You know why I didn't go to India?" he said, bending his face to hers.

"I—guessed!" she answered shyly.

Then Collingwood, at this suddenly arrived supreme moment, became curiously bereft of speech. And after a period of silence, during which, being in the shadow of a grove of beech-trees which kindly concealed them from the rest of the world, they held each other's hands, all that he could find to say was one word.

"Well?"

Nesta laughed.

"Well—what?" she whispered.

Collingwood suddenly laughed too and put his arm round her.

"It's no good!" he said. "I've often thought of what I'd to say to you—and now I've forgotten all. Shall I say it all at once!"

"Wouldn't it be best?" she murmured with another laugh.

"Then—you're going to marry me?" he asked.

"Am I to answer—all at once?" she said.

"One word will do!" he exclaimed, drawing her to him.

"Ah!" she whispered as she lifted her face to his. "I couldn't say it all in one word. But—we've lots of time before us!"

THE END

Resurrected Press Mysteries by J. S. Fletcher

The Orange-Yellow Diamond

When an elderly pawnbroker is murdered in the London parish of Paddington, a young, down on his luck writer is accused of the crime. But then it's found the pawnbroker had had in his possession an extraordinary South African diamond worth over eighty-thousand pounds — a diamond that's now missing. It falls to Melky Rubenstein to unravel the mystery and prove the young man's innocence.

The Middle Temple Murder

When an elderly man's body is found on the steps of chambers in the Midde Temple, one of the Inns of Court, it falls to newspaperman Frank Spargo and Detective-Sergeant Rathbury to solve the crime. The murdered man, for indeed it was murder, was found with no money or identification on his person except for a piece of paper with the name and address of a young barrister. Who is the victim? Why was he killed? Who is the murderer?

Scarhaven Keep

Bassett Oliver, the famed actor, has gone missing. When Oliver fails to show for a rehearsal, aspiring playwright Richard Copplestone finds himself sent to the small village of Scarhaven on the northern coast of England to track down the actors movements. What he finds is mystery. Find the answers as Copplestone unravels the mystery of Scarhaven Keep.

Visit www.resurrectedpress.com

Resurrected Press Mysteries by Fergus Hume

The Green Mummy

Professor Braddock hoped to compare the burial practices of the Egyptians with those of the ancient Peruvians with his latest acquisition, the mummy of the last Inca, Caxas. But on arrival, the packing case proved to hold not the mummy, but the body of his assistant Sidney Bolton. It falls to Archie Hope to discover the murderer if he is to marry the professors step-daughter, Lucy Kendal. Who killed Bolton and where is the mummy? Was it the sea captain Hervey? The mysterious Don Pedro? Cockatoo the Polynesian servant? The professor, himself? And what has become of the emeralds? These are the questions that Hope must answer amongst the secrets of the past in The Green Mummy.

The Mystery of a Hansom Cab

"Truth is said to be stranger than fiction, and certainly the extraordinary murder which took place in Melbourne Friday morning goes a long way towards verifying that saying." Thus opens The Mystery of a Hansom Cab, the best selling mystery of the nineteenth century. When a man is found dead in a hansom cab one of Melbourne's leading citizens is accused of the murder. He pleads his innocence, yet refuses to give an alibi. It falls to a determined lawyer and an intrepid detective to find the truth, revealing long kept secrets along the way. Fergus Hume's first and perhaps most famous mystery... The Mystery Of A Hansom Cab.

Visit www.resurrectedpress.com

Resurrected Press Mysteries from the Dr. John Thorndyke Series

Dr. John Thorndyke - Lecturer on Medical Jurisprudence and Forensic Medicine. Before Bones, before CSI, before Quincy, M.E – there was Dr. John Thorndyke solving the most baffling cases of Edwardian London using the latest tools of medical science. Read about his cases in:

The Eye of Osiris
John Bellingham, noted Egyptologist has vanished not once but twice in the same day. Now Dr, Thorndyke must unravel the tangled claims on his estate, solve the riddle of the missing man and find the "Eye of Osiris".

The Mystery of 31 New Inn
When Dr. Jervis is whisked away in a coach with no windows to an unknown location to treat a man in a coma from undivulged causes it is Dr. Thorndyke who must come up with the solution.

The Red Thumb Mark
The first of Dr. Thorndyke's cases finds him trying to prove the innocence of a young man accused of being a diamond thief despite the fact that his finger print was found at the scene of the crime.

John Thorndyke's Cases
More cases of medical mysteries as told by his trusted assistant Jervis, M.D. Eight stories of crime and deduction in Edwardian London.

Visit www.resurrectedpress.com

Resurrected Press Mysteries by John R. Watson & Arthur J. Rees

The Hampstead Mystery

High Court Justice Sir Horace Fewbanks found shot dead in his Hampstead home, a butler with a criminal past, a scorned lover and a hint of scandal. These are the elements of the Hampstead Mystery that Detective Inspector Chippenfield of Scotland Yard must unravel with the assistance of the ambitious Detective Rolfe. But will he be able to sort out the tangled threads of this case and arrest the culprit before he is upstaged by the celebrated gentleman detective Crewe. Follow the details of this amazing case at it plays out across Hampstead, London and Scotland until it reaches a stunning conclusion in the courts of the Old Bailey.

The Mystery of the Downs

When Harry Marsland was caught in a sudden down pour he sought shelter at Cliff Farm. Met at the door by a young woman clearly expecting someone else he is only too glad to get inside to wait out the storm. When they hear a noise upstairs in the deserted house they investigate only to discover the body of the farm's owner, Frank Lumsden, dead of a gunshot wound. Who then, killed Lumsden, and why? Who was the woman expecting and did she have any roll in the murder? These are the questions that private detective Crewe must answer in The Mystery of the Downs.

Visit www.resurrectedpress.com

Other Resurrected Press Mysteries

Mysteries on a Train

Before the Orient Express there was:

The Rome Express by Arthur Griffiths
A man is found dead in his first class sleeping compartment on the express from Rome to Paris. Who was his murderer? The Countess? The English General? His brother the clergy man? The maid who has disappeared? Is the French justice system up to solving the crime? Read about it in The Rome Express.

The Passenger from Calais by Arthur Griffiths
Colonel Basil Annesley finds he is the only passenger on the train from Calais to Lucerne. That is until a mysterious woman shows up at the last minute to book a compartment. Who is after her? What is her secret? Is she a criminal or a victim? Read about it in The Passenger from Calais

Visit us at www.resurrectedpress.com

About Resurrected Press

A division of Intrepid Ink, LLC, Resurrected Press is dedicated to bringing high quality, vintage books back into publication. See our entire catalogue and find out more at www.ResurrectedPress.com.

About Intrepid Ink, LLC

Intrepid Ink, LLC provides full publishing services to authors of fiction and non-fiction books, eBooks and websites. From editing to formatting, from publishing to marketing, Intrepid Ink gets your creative works into the hands of the people who want to read them. Find out more at www.IntrepidInk.com.